Anne...
Enjoy the s

JS Crane

The Jersey Devil

Written by
J.J. Crane

The Jersey Devil

Copyright © 2015 by J.J. Crane.

# CHAPTER 1

Gil Denten shot up out of his bed. "What the hell was that?"

His eyes darted around the dark room. He looked over at his wife Linda, who remained asleep, the covers pulled high above her shoulders, her face sunk deep into a pillow.

"Did I have a bad dream?" he whispered.

He listened but heard nothing. Another moment passed. He then thought he heard scuffling going on outside. He listened again. Yes, something was happening outside. He came out from under the covers, put his slippers on and stood up.

"What's the matter?" Linda asked, still half-asleep. She always stirred when Gil got out of bed for anything.

"Shhhh, I'm trying to listen," he said. "I thought I heard something out by the barn."

Again, the soft scuffling sound caught his attention, then, faint noises of animals in panic. He darted from the bedroom and down the nightlight lit stairs. He looked out the kitchen window towards the barn. He couldn't see anything unusual, just the dark shape of the structure. Adrenaline rushed through his body as he went to grab his rifle out of a thin closet most would mistake as a pantry. The cold of the steel barrel gave him notice that his palms were moist. He proceeded to the back porch door, opened it and slowly stepped out.

"I'll bet it's a friggin wild dog in my stock," he mumbled tucking the butt of his rifle into his armpit. Stepping off the porch, he glanced over to his recently tilled field. A light fog settled in on the barren landscape.

Gil felt himself holding the rifle tight. He had held his Browning X-Bolt hundreds of times in the past but couldn't remember the last time he felt this nervous with it.

*'What the hell was that noise?'* he kept thinking as he approached the barn. No sound came from within and a quiet barn full of animals was never a good sign. He paused and looked at his hands clenching the rifle. *'Stop it'* he yelled to himself, lightening his grip. He tried to soften his steps. *'I know I heard something'* he kept telling himself. He raised his weapon as he came closer to the barn. *'I should at least hear a cow, a horse, one of the chickens.'* The loudest noise he could hear was his own deep breathing.

Gil stopped, surveyed the area again. Nothing seemed out of place. Tiny drops of sweat now ran down his face. One dripped into his eye and began to burn. After clearing the sweat, he looked at the door – *'all right now, let's see.'* He put his hand on the latch securing the barn doors. He unlocked it and pulled them open with a forceful tug. He peered into blackness. All was well for a split second, enough to settle his soul. Then the blackness took form and rushed straight towards him. He stumbled backwards in shock, pulling the trigger to his rifle. A single shot rang out. Gil didn't know which way it fired as he fell to the ground. The large dark figure went flying by him. He couldn't make out its form. It was a blur. Then he heard a screech. It was a terrible sound; a penetrating shrill that cut into his spine causing him to cower into a fetal like position. Lying on the ground, he turned and watched as the figure bounded quickly through the fog-covered field, disappearing into the night. Another screech wailed but this time more distant.

Gil sat up. He shook his head to clear it, re-gripped his rifle and stood up. The wide-open barn doors in the dim moon light shaped a haunting entrance, featureless silhouettes of darkness contrasting each other. With caution, he proceeded into the barn. Nestling the rifle back into his armpit, he took his free hand and searched for the light switch. The click brought an instant reaction to his presence as the animals stomped and shuffled into the corner of their stalls seeking protection. He could see nothing out of place from where he stood. Gil surveyed the barn more, not wanting to miss an iota of detail before continuing. Then he smelled something. He took another, deeper sniff. Something was wrong. His eyes darted around from stable to stable. He sniffed again; a foul rank, yet strangely fresh. His hand fell away from the switch and, with measured steps, he walked deeper into the barn.

As before, he felt his hand grip the rifle too tight. Taking a few steps, he could sense how spooked the animals had become. None of them showed themselves as they normally would when he entered the barn. Instead, they hid themselves in the shadows of their stalls. Gil peered into the first stable, Missy, his horse looked petrified, her eyes wide, body pressed into the back corner. He whispered everything was okay but could clearly see the horse was not comforted. When he peered into Molly's stable, the cow looked as if it wanted to push its way through the wall. He walked closer to the edges of the stables. Gil looked into the third one. His mouth dropped as he felt the acids in his stomach start to rush up into his throat. He lowered his rifle as his knees buckled, yet his eyes never strayed from the sight before him.

"What is it? What do you see?" his wife asked, frightening Gil. She had gotten up after hearing the gunshot to make sure everything was okay.

"Stay back," he said, the words barely escaping his mouth. Gazing back into the pen, he noticed lots of hay strewn about as if a small tornado had landed. The smell now punched him square in the face, the aroma closing his throat as he choked back vomit. Five goats lay disemboweled. Large pools of coagulating blood began to seep into the hard dirt floor.

Examining more closely he saw legs ripped clean off several of the animals, leaving only the head and their torn open bodies. One goat resembled nothing more than a shredded bloody body of fur.

"Gil, what happened? Are you okay?" Linda asked, her voice coming closer to him.

"Stay back, you don't want to see this," he said holding his hand up.

She came closer anyway. "What happened..." she stopped, frozen in place. Her muscles twitched as her body went limp. After several rapid breaths, she dropped to her knees.

"My Lord," she paused looking at the slaughter, "What could have done this?"

Gil shook his head without giving an answer.

"I heard a gunshot," she said.

"Yes," he replied in stunned disbelief.

"At what? Why? Did you see something? You must've," she said searching for any answer.

"I don't know... something," he said trying to make sense of the scene. "Something flew out."

"Flew?" she asked. She didn't doubt his word but couldn't comprehend it either.

"I don't know." He turned to her. His face was blank. "It flew out into the field."

"Like a hawk, an owl?" She knew of nothing that could do this kind of destruction.

"I don't... no... definitely not those," he mumbled. "It was hideous, did you hear it?"

"I thought I heard something but then I heard the gun shot and I came running out to see what happened."

"It was terrible. It screamed."

"Did you see it?"

"I... it was dark... I saw a blur... it surprised me," Gil said trying to make sense of it all. "I opened the doors and then it knocked me over."

"We have to call the police," she said standing up. She gathered her composure until she once again glanced at the decimated animals. "Oh my God" she gasped. "What on earth could do this?"

He grabbed her hand and gave it a reassuring grip. "Let's call the police."

# CHAPTER 2

Hunter Matthews was not a sound sleeper. In fact, he considered a good night's sleep as awakening only once or twice, tossing and turning for ten to fifteen minutes, while cursing minimally. Generally, he woke up three, four or even five times during the night cursing profusely. He could not ever remember sleeping an entire night without waking, let alone something as foreign as eight hours of straight rest.

The landline phone Hunter had next to his bed rang like a jackhammer into his brain. He grabbed it, choking the handset as if he wanted to crush it into dust.

"What?" he barked.

"Detective Matthews?" the timid voice responded.

"Yes," he replied smoldering.

"Officer Jenkins at dispatch, there's a situation that needs your attention."

"It can't wait til morning?"

"Well, it's almost morning now" the officer said with a hint of nervousness.

Hunter turned over and saw the clock read five after five. "Almost morning my ass."

"There's been a peculiar disturbance on a farm off route five thirty nine."

Sitting up on the bed, Hunter began to shake off the last remnants of sleep. "Peculiar how?"

"Some mutilation of farm animals."

Hunter didn't see the urgency. He ran his fingers through his dark hair as he looked around his bedroom for something to wear. "Mutilation of farm stock, justifies waking me in the middle of the night?"

"Sir, it's said to be peculiar, that is all I know. You were requested to investigate as soon as possible."

"Of course I was, that figures." He paused, taking a deep breath. "Yeah sure, I'll be there as soon as I can. Where was it again?"

The county roads of the Pine Barrens at night are dark, desolate places. Some might say otherworldly, twisted pitch pines boarding its shoulders, branches reaching into the sky looking like the broken or disfigured arms of ancient giants. Tall cedars and oaks rise up intermixed as if standing guard over their misshapen counterparts.

Tucked away south of New York City, east of Philadelphia and bordering Atlantic City, consuming roughly one third of the state of New Jersey, this 1.1 million acre region of forest stands in stark contrast to the congested, metropolises that surround it. At night, drivers can go on for miles in the dark before encountering any man made light. One quickly wants to get beyond its bounds, as if the forest is telepathically whispering its displeasure of the trespassers presence.

Hunter Matthews drummed his fingers on the steering wheel as he sped along the empty road. He looked at his bloodshot blue eyes in the rear view mirror and knew rubbing them wouldn't help in trying to wake up. He glanced around, a wall of black to either side, the jagged fringes of treetops only visible because of the stars beyond them. It all created a gloomy landscape. Thoughts of getting lost out here always mesmerized him. Intersections and turns appeared out of nowhere. Street signs are almost nonexistent. It was so easy to find one's self miles off course driving along in the darkness.

"Peculiar" he whispered, half in disgust for having to get up so early. *What could be so peculiar about a mutilation that it needs immediate attention,* he thought. He could imagine the farmer talking about seeing a UFO hover over his barn only to find out that an empty bottle of Jack Daniels turned up under some hay next to a bloody blade.

Then the other side of his brain broke in and reminded him that it was his overly cynical and negative attitude that kept him from continually getting better cases. Taking a deeper breath, he realized he just needed to let go of the negativity and just deal with the situation as best he could.

"Stupid self-help CDs," he mumbled as he glanced at the CD case on his front seat where a middle-aged man with his arms open and a wide tooth filled grin smiled at him.

The dark blue hue of pre-dawn light began to emerge over the skies to the east as Hunter pulled into the driveway of the Denten farm. He saw two other police cars parked near the two story colonial styled house. His initial scan of the surroundings revealed nothing out of the ordinary.

Stepping out of the car, a brisk chill filled the morning air along with the scent of moist hay and farm animals. *Why is the air always different in open spaces,* he thought? *I didn't feel this chill when I left my place.*

He had not taken more than a couple steps towards the house when he saw an officer approach.

"Detective Hunter Matthews?" the police officer asked looking to identify Hunter through the flashing lights of the patrol car.

"Yep," Hunter answered raising his hand to shield his eyes. "How about turning those lights off now, I think everyone knows we're here."

"Sorry, I just arrived on the scene a few minutes ago," the young officer said. "What you want to see is inside the barn sir."

Hunter looked past the officer, hardly paying attention to a word he said. "Your name?" he asked only half caring as he continued to check out the area.

"Officer Tinneson, rookie sir, just started a couple weeks ago," he answered with energy.

"I guess it's that time of year," Hunter said. Depending on the police department, rookies tended to start all at once.

"Yes sir. This way," the patrolman said, leading Hunter towards the barn.

He nodded and followed noticing the pep of the young officer's steps while he took relaxed strides. Standing at six foot two, he was easily four inches taller than the rookie patrolman.

"Nice morning," Officer Tinneson said, trying to break the ice.

Hunter smiled a smug 'yeah-right' grin. He grimaced to himself for the knee jerk response, knowing it was wrong.

"I'm more a late evening guy," Hunter said trying a friendlier approach. "The morning isn't always agreeable with me. If I come off as an ass of sorts... well...it's because I can."

The rookie looked back, "I'm just the opposite. I love a brisk morning."

Hunter shot him another 'I don't give a crap smile.' As they came closer to the barn, Hunter recognized the police officer checking out the scene.

"Hunter Matthews," said the voice with all the sarcasm he could muster. "Well well, isn't it just grand to see you out here on this fine fine early morning."

"Jack Powell," Hunter shot back with an equal amount of joyful vinegar in his voice. "How are ya?"

Hunter respected Jack Powell, one of the few officers he trusted. They didn't always get along, but Hunter valued his talents as an even-tempered, quick thinking cop.

"As you've no doubt heard, this situation is a peculiar one," Powell said.

"Yes, the word peculiar has come up quite a bit over the last hour."

"It's a good word once you hear the story and see the scene."

Powell filled him in about how the mysterious assailant knocked the farmer over and disappeared into the fog. Powell also informed Hunter about the farmer discharging a round and the gory details of the carnage in the barn. Hunter listened with curious intent, especially at the use of the word 'flying'. He glanced at the field. The fog had dissipated and did not hold the ominous allure reported.

"Well Scully… let's take a peek at our little X-File adventure," Hunter said.

"Right this way Monger," Powell shot back.

"It's Mulder," Hunter said. "I know the show's been off the air for a while but if you're going to play the TV detective show reference game properly… it's Mulder."

"This is Gil Denten the owner of the farm. Mr. Denten, this is Detective Hunter Matthews," said Officer Powell standing at the entrance of the barn. Hunter shook the farmers hand and instantly felt the strong grip of a man who had long worked the land, his calloused fingers and palms scrapping against his own desk soft skin.

"The animals are still spooked. Not like before but still they're off kilter," Gil said.

Hunter nearly said, *We'll make sure they get proper counseling* but refrained. Instead, he kept a respectful face.

"I understand you were rushed by the assailant," Hunter said.

"You could say that I guess," Gil replied.

Hunter chose his words right. He didn't want to say fly. That would only reinforce the farmer's version. He wanted to see if Gil was waxing poetic with his story.

"Let's check out the scene," Hunter said.

With the barn doors open, the smell of dead flesh had diminished and much of the blood had soaked into the ground. Regardless of those diminishing qualities, it didn't take away from the shock of the carnage that still lay before them.

"Oh Jesus," Hunter gasped. He usually maintained his composure but seeing body parts scattered all over as if a grenade went off, wasn't exactly what he envisioned when he heard the term animal mutilations.

"These were goats?" he asked, trying to identify the various parts. He took a deep breath and stepped into the ten by fifteen foot space. He leaned down by one of the many limbs to get a closer look. He noticed a bone protruding from a clump of flesh and thought it looked like an upper leg. Another section of a body appeared as though a fast moving shredder sliced it. He moved over to another body. The neck, head and three legs were missing. He traced the opening with his finger. "This looks like the clean cut of a blade." He pointed to where the flesh was smooth along the edge.

"What do you think?" Powell asked.

Hunter stood up. He looked around at all the tiny parts. "Well," he paused, "Peculiar *is* a good word."

## CHAPTER 3

"After the assailant rushed you, the perpetrator fled into the field?" Hunter asked the farmer as they walked out of the barn.

"Yes, but…" Gil said before Hunter interrupted him.

"What kind of crops do you grow here?" Hunter asked not looking at Gil, just the field.

"Mostly corn… some tomatoes. If I have a good crop, I do very well for myself," Gil said with a bit of pride.

"Did you do well last year?" Hunter asked.

"I've done better but it wasn't bad."

"Good to hear," Hunter said looking directly at him. "It was foggy this past evening?" he asked already knowing it was.

"Yep, a strange rolling fog. More like a cloud passing than fog if ya get my meaning." Gil said while motioning his hands to demonstrate how the fog just limped along.

Hunter watched and nodded, not particularly seeing the imagery. "Now you said the perpetrator ran out into the field and disappeared, is that right?"

"Well it did disappear into the fog yes, but it didn't run. It more hopped and flew."

Hunter tensed his lips against his teeth. "Hopped?"

"Yes. It went by me and I saw it bounce once off the ground, and out into the field. Then it landed, leaped again and there were these wings and it disappeared in the fog." Gil said with frankness and a pinch of bewilderment.

"Really? Wings and hopping?" Hunter replied, trying not to sound condescending. He could tell the farmer believed what he thought he saw. Gil's eye contact was strong, his voice assured, his composure confident.

"Alright, let's say 'it' did fly. Did you get a good look at it?" Hunter asked.

"No. It was dark. I saw a blur. It moved fast."

"You fired a shot at it?"

"I fired a shot but not at it, not intentionally. It scared the hell out of me when it burst through the door. I fell over and accidentally pulled the trigger."

Hunter nodded. "Can we walk into the field?"

"Sure."

"About how far out do you think this person, I'm sorry…this thing, jumped? Ten feet, twenty feet?"

"No, no, no. It was a pretty good distance, well over fifty feet. Cause on its second jump it disappeared into the fog."

"Really and that's where the wings came in?" Hunter said, his smarminess making an appearance.

"Yes sir." Gil said, not picking up on Hunter's doubtful tone.

They walked into the field a bit. The ground was moist and Hunter felt his feet sink into the soft, freshly tilled soil. He thought if anything could jump that distance, it would surely leave a footprint or marking of some sort. He looked over the field and saw nothing but a few scattered deer tracks.

"Would you say it jumped about here?" Hunter asked as they continued to proceed into the field.

"It's kinda hard to tell but this is a good guess, maybe a bit further out."

Hunter nodded. He thought the estimation was ridiculous. They had already walked almost a hundred feet. *What the hell could jump this far?* He really wanted to search the grounds and see if he could find that empty Jack Daniels bottle.

They walked a few more feet, scanning the ground carefully.

"How bout this," Gil said, his voice a little excited.

Hunter walked over and looked down. The ground definitely had a disturbed look to it. Immediately he began to look for deer tracks of some sort but couldn't find any. The depression wasn't much of a track but there were two definite disturbances of the ground, swirls, as if something landed and spun itself into the soil. He knelt down to examine it more closely; no defining marks he could recognize. No heel imprints, no animal type tracks, just the strange swirls as if whatever landed was able to twist and distort its track rendering it unrecognizable.

"I don't know if it's going to do any good, or if it's anything at all," Hunter said looking up at the farmer, "but I'm going to have someone come out and take a cast of this. I need you to not let anyone out here. This ground cannot be disturbed any more than it already has." He looked around for a stick and quickly found one to use as a marker. "I'll get some tape out here to mark this off."

Hunter stood up, and stretched a little. "I understand this thing said something,"

"If you consider a screech as saying something, then yes," Gil shot back.

Hunter smiled. That was something he might say but with more sarcasm. He was starting to like this guy. "Did anyone else hear it? Your wife?"

"Yes she did, though faintly. She woke after hearing the gunshot. She said she heard something but was more concerned about me firing my rifle," Gil said.

"Of course she was," Hunter added. "Who wouldn't be?"

CHAPTER 4

Casey Windall sat down at her small pre-fab pressed wood, assembly required light brown desk, a fresh cup of coffee in hand. For the last year and a half, she worked as a fulltime freelance reporter for the quarterly magazine and website, The Evening Door. The Evening Door devoted itself to paranormal disturbances, creepy folklore and ghost story history throughout the state of New Jersey and surrounding regions.

Casey enjoyed the spirited workplace. Having written for the local daily newspaper for a few years, she tired of the petty jealousies and ego trips, the politics of promotion and the drive for a picture in your byline. A friend had mentioned The Evening Door to her and upon meeting its creators, liked their work philosophy. They were equally happy to have her join them, someone who actually knew how to write articles. She learned their preferred style of storytelling and in a short time developed her own voice within their format. It didn't take her long to become a major contributor and one of their more popular writers, focusing on ghost stories along the Jersey Shore.

"Good morning Casey, here are your papers," an intern said putting a stack of various newspapers from around the state on her desk.

"Thanks," she said giving him a friendly smile. She took the top paper and opened it to the Police blotter. "Anything interesting?" she said lightly to herself and began to comb through the reports.

Once a week, like a ritual, she would go through police blotters. She was always looking for something out of the ordinary that could spark an idea or offer an interesting story. Mostly she just came across the standard DUI's, B and E's, domestic disturbances and drunken assaults.

*'Discipline'*, she told herself, *'keep the faith, good reporting, good investigating takes patience.'* She sipped her coffee as her eyes scanned every report. She stopped and zeroed in on one that jumped out, *Reported several goats mutilated the night of March 13 at the farm of Mr. Denten on Ridge Rd, New Egypt. Investigation pending.*

She had seen farm vandalizing reports before but never a pending investigation of an animal mutilation. It struck her as odd. She folded the newspaper, and put it to the side with a note to call the police station. A feeling stirred… a hunch.

"You're kidding me," Hunter said almost shouting. "I don't believe I actually have to follow up on this case. I filed an initial report and thought I'd take my notes and pass this on to Jackson, he's the junior member on this staff; shouldn't he handle this sort of case?"

Captain Morgan looked at Hunter with the kind of smirk that revealed he enjoyed this moment. "What can I say? The kid has enough on his plate just getting accustomed to how things operate around here."

Hunter scowled. "Since when has that ever mattered? I know I'm not your favorite guy but this reeks of favoritism."

"Watch it," the captain snapped, his temper instantly rising.

"I am watching. I'm watching how the mayor's kid is being coddled," Hunter said, then made a sad face while bringing an imaginary tissue to his eye, "because we don't want to upset the poor little guy. Heaven forbid he be asked to do anything beneath him."

The captain shot up from behind his desk, his chair slamming the wall. He had stuck his neck out for Hunter in the past; protecting him from termination (mostly for insubordination), knowing he was the best detective this county had seen in twenty years. "Sit down and listen," he shouted.

Hunter stood staring at the captain, not giving any ground.

"You listen to me you brass balled pain in the ass. Sit the fuck down or gather your shit and get the hell out of here." Swearing was not a usual part of the captain's demeanor but he hit his boiling point.

Hunter didn't release his gaze. He grabbed the top of the chair in front of him, shifted it and sat down. He wasn't going to win this standoff, but he didn't want to show weakness either.

"I don't have to tell you that your arrogance and attitude have had you headed up a creek for a while now. Well guess what?" he said not taking his stare off Hunter. "I'm tired of your shit. I know you've been trying lately but that doesn't excuse the past. This case is yours. Follow it up. Do it with a smile. Show me why I shouldn't give you shit work all the time. Prove to me that you don't deserve it. Put your stubborn pride in check for once and show a little humility and maybe then you'll get all you think you deserve."

Hunter's tense expression never changed but he knew the captain was right. He had to just shut up, take his lumps and work his way back into favor, if it was even possible.

"Are we understood?" the captain said, not really asking.

"Yes sir." Hunter stood up, turned around and left the office.

Back at his desk, Hunter shuffled some loose papers, searching for the paperwork on the Denten case. It had been three days since the mutilation. After filing an initial report, he hadn't given much thought to it. Now he was scrambling to find his notes. He glanced at a manila envelope sitting on the top of his 'in' basket. He knew it contained photos of the scene and cast pictures of the supposed footprints. He hadn't bothered to look, thinking he was passing off the case. Farm vandalizing never received priority status unless the damage exceeded a few thousand dollars, had a significant lead or deemed a hate crime.

*'How much could five goats be worth?'* he thought to himself as he laughed a sad laugh. "Who hates goats that much?"

He grabbed the envelope and opened it. The pictures brought back mental images of the gruesome slaughter. He looked at the casts. It was indeterminable to him, nothing more than smears in the dirt. Funny thing was there were two smears, both of equal size and shape, and far enough apart from each other to give the impression that something could have landed on the ground. He leaned back in his chair, smirked and tossed the pictures onto his desk.

"I can't believe I'm looking at tracks," he said.

The phone rang. He rolled his eyes. "Detective Matthews," he said with little enthusiasm.

"Good afternoon detective," the voice on the other end said in a sweet formal fashion. His ears perked up at the lilting tone of the woman on the other end. "I'm calling in reference to the farm incident I read in this morning's paper."

"Yes," Hunter replied unaware that the mutilation had become a story.

"I understand you're the lead investigator on this case?"

Hunter turned sour. "What can I help you with?"

"Well, I'm a reporter with The Evening Door. My name is Casey Windall and I was wondering if I could ask you a couple questions about the case?"

"You can, but right now I have nothing to say on it."

Casey continued, undeterred. "I was curious as to why the incident wasn't termed a vandalization? Is there more to this story I should know about?

"Well for one, there is no such word. It's either vandalized or vandalism."

She felt a twinge of embarrassment but pushed on. "Yes, it struck me as odd that the blotter didn't simply indicate a farm was vandalized and several animals were killed. Instead it specified 'mutilated', investigation pending?"

"Well Miss…" he stopped.

"Windall, Casey Windall."

"Well Miss Windall… it is Miss isn't it?" He didn't wait for an answer. "It just so happens, there is an investigation pending but it really isn't anything more than a vandalization of property."

"You just said vandalization," she noted.

"It was in your honor," he replied.

"May I ask what happened?" she said ignoring the attitude.

"Five goats were mutilated."

"Yes I read that. How were they mutilated?"

"Off the record?" he said waiting for a response.

There was a gap of silence. "Off the record," she said with less enthusiasm.

"Five goats were mutilated and it looked awful," he said, emphasizing the word *awful*.

"Yes, well…"

"There you go."

"Is there a means by which they were mutilated?" Casey kept her cool. She knew all too well that cops could be stubborn and less than forthcoming when talking to the press.

"I'll tell you what," Hunter said. "What paper did you say you were with?"

"The Evening Door," she answered without giving a hint that he may simply dismiss it.

"Never heard of it, is it new?" he asked.

"For the most part," she knew she needed to be coy in this matter and just keep asking the questions. Any allusion to the true nature of her magazine would most likely end the conversation with a dial tone. "So, is there any nugget that you can give me?" she asked.

"Really… is this some kind of prank? You know I have your number. If this is some shtick… I'm not amused." Hunter didn't mind the banter but thinking he would just divulge information to an unknown press person was insulting.

"No, no," she said in a hurry. "I'll e-mail or fax over my credentials if you like and you can do your own checking. I assure you this is above board."

Hunter nodded, enjoying having the upper hand. "Yes, send me your information."

Casey agreed but still decided to make a case for herself anyway.

As he listened, he tried to picture her. She sounded young but not college young, maybe mid or late twenties. Was she skinny, short, tall? It was obvious to him she had minimum dealings with detectives but she did possess a certain confidence that revealed maturity. It always took guts to cold call a detective and think you could just get answers. Meanwhile, he Googled, The Evening Door and the website came up. He half laughed in silence as he gave it a quick scan.

"So how about that nugget? Any chance?" she asked in a sweet whispered manner.

Hunter decided to dangle a carrot but knew he wasn't giving out any information. Besides, he could always deny it.

"Off the record?" he asked. She acknowledged his request. "It looks like they were pulled apart."

"Pulled apart?" Her voice belied some confusion. "Any suspects? Why? How were they pulled apart?"

He chuckled so she could hear it. "That's the part where investigation pending comes in Miss Windall," he said. "I have to go. This was fun, feel free to call back if you are still curious. Thank you and have a nice day." He hung up without a second thought.

# CHAPTER 5

Joe leaned forward towards the steering wheel. Cloudy skies made the night appear even darker than usual for driving. It looked as if his headlights had a tough time penetrating the thick of the evening. Thin wisps of fog occasionally drifted into his sight line as he cruised down the single lane road, not a streetlight seen for what felt like miles. Joe reached over and turned down his radio so he could concentrate more on the road ahead. His girlfriend Nell nodded on and off in the passenger's seat. Joe knew his eyes would start getting heavy soon; he looked at the clock on the radio, 2:45am. He reached for the coffee he bought soon after leaving the beach. The cup wasn't warm anymore but he needed a jolt of something and cold coffee offered a better alternative than nothing.

"Keep to the smaller sips," he said as he put the cup back into its holder.

"Hey honey, how ya doing?" Nell said, her voice groggy with sleep.

He looked over. Her nearly closed eyes met his with a reassuring smile. "I'm doin' alright. It seems a little harder to see tonight but not to worry; I'll get us home safe."

"I know you will," she said. She turned to look out the windshield. Her eyes popped wide open, "Watch out," she shouted.

Joe hit the brakes. All he saw was a large shape move across the road, and then felt a light thump at the front of his car. The car skidded, turned a hundred and eighty degrees and stopped, the engine stalling.

"You okay?" he said to Nell, his breath nearly gone.

"I'm fine" she replied, panting. "Did we hit it? I thought I heard something."

"I heard something too."

He tried to start the engine but it wouldn't turn over. "Ah shit," he said, banging his fist on the steering wheel. "Let me see what kind of damage I did."

"Be careful," she said as he opened the door to get out of the car.

*It's really dark out,'* he thought. Looking down the road, he saw the double yellow stripe on the pavement meld in with the night. He swallowed hard and felt a chill ripple through his body. He examined his car, running a finger along the quarter panel, then the hood. Everything looked in order. He started towards the passenger side of the car when he heard a rustle in the woods nearby. He walked up to Nell's window and lightly knocked on it.

"Everything okay?" she asked as she rolled down the window.

"The car looks fine; I heard something move just off the road. Maybe I did clip something. Open the glove compartment and hand me the flashlight please."

"Just be careful will you, it's really creepy out here," she said as she looked for the flashlight.

"It is creepy," he said glancing towards the sky, noticing the cloud cover. "What happened? It was all stars at the beach."

She handed him the flashlight. "Do you have to look, can't we just go?"

"Just wanna take a quick peek and see if there's an injured animal. Believe me; I have no desire to go exploring." He took the flashlight and turned it on. He heard the rustle again. He snapped the light in the direction he thought he heard the sound. Slowly he walked along the shoulder then felt the crunch of dried pine needles and leaves under his feet as he moved off the pavement. Joe still couldn't see the source of the noise. Then he heard a crunch sound as if someone else was walking along edge of the shoulder. It came from another direction and he whipped the light towards it. Joe's heart thundered. Another rustle came from back where he originally pointed the flashlight. He darted the light back to the original spot. He began to sweat. He couldn't see very far into the thicket of pines and undergrowth. His beam then locked onto a set of eyes. They looked reddish. A deep red. They were looking right at him. He turned his beam away to see if he could still see them. There they were. They appeared locked right on him, penetrating.

"Shaaah," he yelled waving his hands in the air. The eyes didn't move. He yelled again. Nothing happened. Then, just as he turned away, a great rustle came from the woods. He turned back and a large dark object rushed right over him knocking him to the ground. "Friggin deer," he mumbled, brushed himself off and stood up.

"You okay?" Nell half screamed. She was frantic, having just seen her boyfriend knocked to the ground.

"I'm fine. A friggin' deer shot out of the woods and knocked me over. We're getting out of here." He took two steps towards the car and stopped dead in his tracks. Standing on the roof of his car loomed a large dark figure, tall, thick but with a body that looked to have a sway to it. The thing hissed at him. Its eyes began to glow red. Joe couldn't move. The figure began to bend at the knees and raise its muscular looking arms. Then, to Joe's stunned amazement, he saw wings unfurl. The thing hissed again, its breath letting off a stench like a decaying body.

"Honey," Joe said softly. She didn't hear him. "Honey," he said louder. "Try starting the car."

"What?"

"Start the car," he commanded. "Just try starting it."

The creature locked its gaze on Joe. Joe heard the car turn over.

"Let's go, you're creeping me out," Nell shouted, seeing Joe's terrified face.

Joe took a step towards the car. The creature screeched and then leaped towards him.

"What the hell was that?" she shouted as Joe disappeared from her view.

"Get out of here," Joe screamed, his voice trailing off.

The creature tackled him, its force incredibly strong. Joe tried to hold its arms and wrestle free. He was, after all, a one-time varsity wrestler. The creature flailed wildly and Joe could not get a solid grip as they rolled around on the ground. Joe felt the things razor tip claws rip into his flesh. It stung. He grimaced with pain while trying to fight off his assailant. The creature hissed and screeched as its acidic saliva dripped all over Joe's face, stinging his eyes and mouth, blinding him and making him want to throw up all at the same time. Joe then felt something penetrate into his abdomen, a presence pulling at his organs. He began to weaken. It became harder for him to breathe. He felt the strength in his arms wane. Joe watched the creature lean its dark, snout like face closer to his. He peered right into its hollow red eyes. He couldn't resist anymore and let the creature pin him to the ground. Then he heard a pop. He looked to his side and saw his arm was gone. He looked back at the creature holding it in its clutches. Joe felt another thrust stab into his stomach. Everything became fuzzy… then nothing.

"Joe," Nell shouted. She opened the car door to see what was going on, taking a step out of the vehicle. All she could discern was two dark objects on the ground. Terrified, she got back in the car. The creature turned to her. It hissed. Her eyes met the red eyes of the beast. She heard it hiss louder. Quickly she positioned herself in the driver's seat. The creature jumped to the front of the car and stood in her way, screeching as it raised its arms and wings above its head. It was holding something in its hand. Then she realized it was

Joe's arm. Nell screamed and hit the gas pedal to the floor. The creature jumped straight up. She thought she heard a thump but didn't look back to see. Crying hysterically, Nell drove off. She couldn't stop screaming Joe's name.

# CHAPTER 6

Night began its inevitable fade into day. The once cloudy skies cleared revealing the last remnants of the evening's stars against a deep dark blue backdrop. Flashing lights cut into the remaining darkness as Hunter pulled up to the usually desolate locale. State Police, Sheriff's department, unmarked cars, local police, and ambulances, all had their sporadic prism of yellow, red and blue lights blazing in all their glory.

"How the hell can anyone see anything with all those lights?" he mumbled, still sitting in his car. He thought it was ludicrous that every vehicle had its lights going. "One car with lights usually gets the point across."

Captain Morgan greeted Hunter as he stepped out of his car. "Glad you could join us this morning, I know what an early bird you are. We've got a real strange situation here."

"I see the birds have picked the yard clean… now let's see if they left it so I can make heads or tails of the situation," Hunter said looking at all the personnel mulling around.

The captain guided him past a few vehicles. "A girl called screaming that her boyfriend was attacked. She thought they hit a deer but when he went out to check, someone tackled him. The assailant then tried to attack her but she took off."

"Attacked… out here?" he said while gazing at the endless line of trees that filled the scene from horizon to horizon.

"She said the attacker jumped in front of the car to stop her but she just floored it and sped away," the captain said.

"Really" Hunter said with a bit of surprise. "Did she get a description of him?"

"Yup," the captain said, as he handed over a pad.

Hunter read it. His brow curled and his face contorted into a confused expression. "Do you believe this?" Hunter asked. "What kind of description is this? Have you talked to her?"

"No, she's back at the local station. She's pretty shook up."

"Is she hurt?"

"No, but I called Carol in to take a look at her and help calm her down," Captain Morgan said with assurance.

"Your wife?"

"Yeah, she was a nurse for 20 years. I thought she could stay with her, help the girl out if she needed any immediate attention."

"I forgot she was a nurse," Hunter said.

"Of course you did, why doesn't that surprise me?" the captain shot back. "A good one too but she tired of being surrounded by death, so she left."

"Good for her. When are you leaving?" Hunter replied chidingly.

"Nice," said the captain. "Keep it up."

With all the flashing lights, Hunter found it hard to get a good sense of what occurred. He could see blotches of blood on the grass and surrounding ground clutter.

"Well there was one hell of a struggle, I can tell you that," he said as he continued to examine the scene, noting the patted down areas of grass and kicked up chunks of soil. "Is there a body?" he asked.

"Body parts," the captain said.

"Parts?"

"Yeah. It appears that after the victim was overcome, he was brought into the woods and ripped apart."

"What?" Hunter said trying to digest the report. "What's left? I imagine we are scouring the area."

"We have all that under control. K-9 is coming to comb the woods. We have other municipalities on alert as well as a working perimeter."

"No sign of another car?" Hunter asked half knowing the answer.

"No."

"So there's a chance our sicko is still in there?" Hunter said as he looked to the wall of woods in front of him.

"It's a possibility."

"What parts have been found?"

The captain jutted his jaw out. "We have a hand, a foot, part of a leg, a thigh I think, and some unidentifiable material that I'm going to assume was internal. Forensics is going to look further into it."

"Over here," a voice shouted from the woods. A stream of flashlights, in unison, all turned towards the voice. Captain Morgan and Hunter made their way into the woods. It wasn't far, only about fifty feet when they came to the scene. On the ground laid an arm. Hunter noticed the nub end of a Humerus bone sticking out from the flesh.

"This looks like it was ripped clean from the shoulder," the officer who found the arm said.

Hunter nodded in approval. "Thank you officer," he said. "Good job, continue looking around, there might be more."

"Yes sir," the officer said, and then soon faded from the scene.

Hunter knelt down to look closer. He couldn't get over how clean the break was from the shoulder joint. "That is some strong son of a bitch," he said shaking his head.

"Are you done with that," a voice asked breaking Hunter's concentration. Hunter looked up and saw a man with a large bag in his hand. "If you're not done that's fine, we just want to get this to the lab as soon as possible for a better look."

Hunter stood up. "No, I'm done, but I want to make sure this area is photographed."

"I'll see to it sir."

"Fine, good," Hunter said. He turned towards the captain who had walked a few feet away. "This is one sick fish, we're dealing with."

"It certainly is," the captain responded. "Any ideas?"

Hunter shook his head. "Not at this moment. This is peculiar." *There was that word again.* "I have to spend more time sifting through all this. Has anyone found any kind of footprint, boot, sneaker, any kind of track?"

"Not that I've been told but let's head back towards the cars and see if anyone has reported anything new."

Hunter and Captain Morgan approached two State Troopers standing by an ambulance, having a conversation as if on break.

"Gentlemen," Hunter said, "I'm Detective Matthews and this is Captain Morgan." Hunter smiled at the captain. He always got a kick out of saying the captain's name as if it was a put on. The captain on the other hand had no sense of humor for it. "Has anyone from the press arrived?" Hunter asked.

"No," one trooper said with a touch of attitude.

"I'm surprised…they are usually on this before the flies get to the remains," Hunter said, his eyes scanning for a camera of any kind.

"It's early and this is a kinda out of the way place," the other trooper said. "I wouldn't worry yourself too much. We got it all under control anyway."

"Yeah, well, not like all these lights wouldn't attract any attention you couldn't handle," Hunter said. He could see by the two troopers' smirks and raised eyebrows, they didn't hold his presence in high regard. He didn't really care. "Smoke'em if you got them boys. Don't work too hard holding up the side of that car."

Casey rushed to get out of her apartment. She knew arriving at a crime scene in the midst of chaos gave her the best chance of getting a story. If she arrived late, yellow tape and uniformed men would impede any chance at something 'exclusive.' Time was of the essence.

She had received an emergency scanner as a present from her aunt who thought it would be the perfect gift for an aspiring journalist. At first, Casey was thrilled with it. Every night she had it on. She imagined herself getting the jump on all the other media outlets to break the next big story. However, central New Jersey was not a haven for big breaking news. She didn't tire easily from listening to the various domestic disturbance calls, a few B and E's, fires, a missing person who always showed themselves before too long. For six months, she listened diligently. It was only after coming back from a weeklong vacation that she didn't turn the scanner right back on. From that point, listening became a random act.

On this night though, she had turned the scanner on as background noise while researching, The Woman in White, a ghost story that circulated in the early 19th century along the Jersey shore. Some recent reports of ghost sightings on Long Beach Island had a strange resemblance to those old stories and she was preparing to travel out there to talk with witnesses.

It was a little after four in the morning, when a flurry of voices crackled over the scanner and woke her up. Having not heard the initial call, she tried to piece the conversations together. She could tell something big happened by the rapid fire pace of the talk. *But what… where?* An instinct clicked. This was worth it. She turned the volume up and began to get dressed.

The voices on the scanner came and went. Some information she heard clearly, others, harder to hear. It seemed that all the vital information came through garbled.

"Where? Where? Where?" she shouted at the scanner as she pulled a sweater over her head. She heard the words, State Police. She didn't hear any calls for EMT but she assumed that she missed that transmission.

Finally a breakthrough; one of the State Troopers on their way to the scene missed where he needed to turn and asked for the road again. "537 – Down past Colliers Mills," came the response.

"Great," she shouted. "But where the hell is Colliers Mills?"

She looked at the New Jersey map pinned to the wall in her bedroom. She scanned it feverishly, running her fingers all around the central part of the state.

"There it is," she said. "Southwest of Six Flags Great Adventure." She looked at the clock and it was almost four thirty. She figured it would take a half hour to get there. *'Damn'*, she thought, *'they'll have that scene sealed tight by the time I reach it.'* Still her instincts told her to go.

The scanner crackled away laying in the passenger seat as Casey pressed the bounds of the highways speed limit. Voices on the scanner continued to overlap, cutting each other off. All the activity was shaping up into a huge manhunt, but she still couldn't tell what happened.

She spotted the exit she needed and turned off. Soon she was traveling down a dark road with no streetlights, just her headlights surrounded by blackness. Still, it was open road and she knew she could press the gas pedal.

The voices on the scanner grew louder but so did the interference. A flashing light broke her concentration. She looked in the rear view mirror and saw a cop speeding up behind her. She slowed down and eased off to the shoulder; the police car whizzed by. She marveled at how fast it went. *At least ninety miles per hour, had to be*, she thought. She brought herself back onto the road when another police car came out of nowhere and whizzed by.

"Where there's smoke, there's fire," she said aloud and hit the gas.

She neared 70 mph in a 45mph zone before realizing how fast she was actually going and slowed to sixty. After a couple minutes of speeding down the road, it dawned on her that she hadn't seen a turn off. She wondered if she passed it. She tried to calculate how long it had been since she had seen the last police car go by. *A couple minutes maybe?* She didn't recall seeing any of them turn.

"Damn it, I've got to get a GPS," she said.

She looked all around for flashing lights. "Another mile Casey and we stop to reassess."

She leaned forward on the steering wheel peering out the windshield. All around her, she saw twisted dark forms back dropped only by the darkness of night, no moon and just a handful of stars. Her stomach tightened. Her nerves heightened as unpleasant thoughts began to circle in her mind. "Stop it Casey," she shouted to herself. "You're a professional… don't let your imagination chase you out of here." But her mind wandered anyway - what if some psycho was hiding just off the shoulder, what if he jumped out in the middle of the road and waved her down. Would she stop, would she run him over? She again yelled at herself to get a grip.

Casey finally and to her relief, came to an unmarked intersection. She noticed double painted lines on the other road. "Wait, my phone has a map app," she said scrambling for it.

She tried to figure the app out but put it aside after a few frustrating seconds. She was wasting time. In front of her, the road just continued straight into the darkness, unlined. She turned the wheel to the right and went down the new road. "I'll take this for a mile or two. If I don't come across anything, I'll just turn around," she reasoned.

Voices picked up on the scanner again as patrolmen were reporting in. Casey looked in every direction, nothing, just darkness.  Then she heard something about K-9 units. She became more eager and found herself traveling at a quicker pace. She also became impatient, wanting to know her exact location, so she grabbed her physical map and opened it.

Through a series of glances, she followed her path. She located her general vicinity but felt frustrated that she couldn't pin point her exact whereabouts. *I have to learn the map thing on my phone.* She examined the map a little closer. This time her stare lingered longer than a fleeting second. When she looked back up, a dark figure filled her windshield, her eyes widened. She hit the brakes and screamed. The car skidded. She fought the fish tail and thought for a second the car might flip. It finally came to halt, just off to the side of the shoulder.

She let out a long breath and shook her head. "What the hell was that?" she shouted.

Casey tried to piece the moment back together. She then noticed flashing lights coming towards her. A few seconds later, a police car pulled up behind her and an officer got out and ran towards her car.

"You alright?" he said as he rapped his knuckles on the window.

Casey composed herself as she rolled down the window. "I'm fine officer."

"I saw your lights spin around. Did you hit something?"

"No sir."

"How fast were you going?"

"The speed limit," she said knowing it was a lie. "I may have been going a little faster."

"Have you been drinking?" He asked as he looked around her car with his flashlight.

"No," she answered quickly. "Sorry, but I was looking down at my map and when I looked up, this thing was in the road."

"A deer?"

She paused. She didn't know what she saw exactly. "No, it wasn't a deer."

The scanner started up again. It had slid off the passenger's seat and fallen to the floor with some other papers. The patrolman leaned in a little further after hearing the device.

"Can I see your license and registration ma'am," he said with purpose.

"Yes sir," she responded. She fumbled through her purse and produced the appropriate paperwork. "I'm a reporter," she said trying to explain her situation.

He said nothing as he took her paperwork.

"I heard a call on my scanner and wanted to get a jump on a story. Is there anything you can tell me?"

The patrolman turned away and mumbled into his radio before turning back towards her. "What was it you saw ma'am? Could you describe it?"

She looked straight ahead hoping something would come to mind. "I was looking at my map, I looked up and I saw this figure. It couldn't have been a deer. It wasn't on all fours. It happened so fast... I just didn't want to hit it."

"Could it have been a person?"

That didn't register as right either but it made more sense. "I guess it could have been, but I didn't think that when I saw it."

"Can you step out of the car please?" the patrolman asked.

"Have I done something wrong officer?"

"No ma'am, but we have had an occurrence out here tonight and I'm sure what you saw or may have seen, will be of interest to the investigators."

Casey stepped out of her automobile just as another police car arrived.

"We have a reporter here who claims to have seen something," the patrolman said to the new one.

"A reporter? What paper?" the new, older looking officer asked.

"The Evening Door," Casey answered

"What's your name ma'am?" asked the new officer.

"Casey Windall," she said. "And yours?" She squinted to see his nametag, "Officer O'Brien." She looked over to the first patrolman's tag, "and Officer Lawton."

"What brings you out here?" Officer O'Brien asked.

"I had my scanner on and was awakened by the flurry of activity on it. I listened and figured I would get a jump-start on what sounded like a good story. I am not familiar with the roads out here but when I saw a few police cars fly by me, I knew I was on the right track. I decided to follow them but they went too fast and I lost them. I came to an intersection a ways back and thought this must be the way. As I was driving, I checked my map. When I looked back up from glancing at it, I saw this thing and almost hit it."

"Thing?" Officer O'Brien asked.

Casey didn't know what else to say.

"A deer maybe," O'Brien said.

She shook her head. "No, it wasn't a deer. It wasn't on all fours that much I know."

"Well Ms. Windall, there's currently an investigation going on. You happen to be in the perimeter of the investigation. So, would you mind coming with me to answer a few questions?" O'Brien asked in a stern way.

Casey didn't know what to say. At first, she wasn't up for it but then thought, what better way to talk to those who are investigating the case first hand. "What about my car?"

"Patrolmen will be coming up and down this road all day. Your car will be fine." Officer Lawton said.

"May I grab some personal belongings?" she asked.

They nodded. Casey leaned back into her car. She grabbed her purse, opened the glove compartment and took out her voice recorder. She looked over at the scanner, switched it off and pushed it under the seat.

Hunter felt groggy. It would pass. It always did. He knew how his body clock worked when it didn't get enough rest. The sluggish phase usually lasted about an hour before a new wave of vigor arrived. Yet, it was in this fatigued hour that irritability usually consumed him and where he almost always found trouble. He knew he had to watch his tongue. He made a mental note to keep himself in check.

"You've got one person that may have seen something," an officer said as Hunter entered headquarters. Hunter nodded in acknowledgment, and made a line straight for the coffee maker.

"You've got one," he heard another voice say.

He just raised his hand in response and made a cup of coffee. "Hope it's strong" he said looking at the black liquid fill his cup. He poured in some milk and a pack of sugar, gave it a quick stir then raised it to his lips for a refreshing sip.

"You've got one waiting for you to talk to," a female voice said. Hunter closed his eyes, *'God help me'* he thought as he took a long slow sip of the coffee.

He went to his desk and sat down. He rubbed his eyes, yawned, stretched, and took another sip of coffee. He saw another officer walk towards him.

"I know," Hunter said. "Besides being human, can you tell me anything I should know?"

"She's a cute reporter who was picked up trying to find the crime scene. She says she was run off the road by someone."

"Interesting," he said. "What happened to the other girl – the one that witnessed the crime?

"Oh, she was brought to the hospital. She needed sedating."

Hunter nodded. "Oh that should make for a pleasant interview."

Hunter looked at a stack of paperwork piled on his desk. He had no interest in it. He didn't have a whole lot of interest in talking to the witness now either. Taking a sip of coffee, he stood up. "Okay, let's do this," he said. "What's our reporter's name?" he asked the officer standing by his door.

"Casey Windall," said the patrolman waiting on Hunter's instruction to bring her in. "She's a reporter for The Evening Door. She was trying to get out to the crime scene. A patrol car saw her spin out and responded."

"Where was this at?" Hunter asked

"Higgins Bottom-Chesterton Road."

Hunter squinted as he tried to see the location in his mind map. There were so many duel named roads crisscrossing the Pine Barrens, he just wished for a Maple Street or Fifth Avenue. "Send her in."

Hunter settled in to his chair when Casey Windall walked into the room. Hunter noticed she kept her head up and her eyes didn't dart all over trying to get a sense of her environment. She made direct eye contact and greeted him with a friendly smile.

"Miss Windall is it?" Hunter asked extending his hand to shake hers. "Please sit, can I get you a cup of coffee?"

"No thanks," she said. "I've had enough this morning." Casey sat down. "Your name is Hunter Matthews?"

"Detective." Hunter was impressed with her body language, a five foot five frame that stood tall, shoulders back, chin out not tucked in revealing insecurity or weakness. Usually people were nervous about having to speak with a detective and tended to fold up or slouch, cross their arms and avoid eye contact but not her. He also noticed that she was quite attractive; slim not skinny, brown hair, nice bright blue eyes. He didn't want to give her a complete look over like some hound at a bar. *No, save the rest for walking her out.*

"I understand you were a witness to an odd incident earlier this morning?" Hunter asked.

"Yes," she said but paused.

"You can elaborate, it's okay," he said with light sarcasm.

"Yes, I'm sorry, something just occurred to me," she said, now realizing this was the same detective she spoke to on the phone about the animal mutilations.

"Anything dealing with last night?" he asked seeing her momentary distraction.

"No," Casey said. "Last night… let's see, it was after four… I was listening to all the activity on the scanner. I was trying to find my way to the scene." She shifted in her seat and her tone changed. "Any leads on the murder?"

Hunter remained silent for a moment. "Murder?"

"Yes, the one that happened last night. The one you're investigating."

"Who said anything about a murder?"

She smiled a wry smile. "Detective Matthews, please… all that scanner chatter I heard is not for some B&E or drunk driving incident. Please give me some credit."

"That's right, you're a reporter," he said, her voice and name registering. "For what again?"

"The Evening Door and other freelance jobs for various newspapers."

Hunter shook his head, "never heard of it." He lied. He definitely remembered her now and had checked out her credentials.

"That's okay," she answered. "I was told someone was killed and that my incident may have some interest to you since it happened inside your perimeter."

"Yes, what exactly did happen to you?" he asked. He really wasn't up for playing the back and forth question game with a reporter, at least not now.

"In a nutshell, I was trying to find the crime scene. I made a right turn off route 540 and thought it would lead me to the scene. Since I only heard references to your location, it was a long shot finding you to begin with. Anyway, as I was traveling down some road looking at my map trying to figure out exactly where I was…the roads aren't well marked out there, as I'm sure you know."

Hunter nodded then said, "Is this a big nut?"

She stopped and stared at him, "sorry?"

"You said in a nutshell. It seems that this is a rather large nut," he said leaning forward, a smirk forming out of his Cheshire grin. "You should also think about GPS. Your phone probably has some kind of map app on it."

She shook off his smartass remark. "I was going along and glancing back and forth from the map. Then as I looked up from one of my glances, this person or thing, I don't know, was in the middle of the road right in front of me. I hit the brakes, lost control of the car and skidded off to the side. Within seconds your officer was on the scene."

"This person or thing, did you get a good look, anything of detail?"

She looked towards the floor. She just couldn't put any fine details together in her head. "No, I've been trying but it all happened so quick I just can't remember anything specific. It was dark."

"What was dark? The person or just in general?"

"Both really," she said looking back up at him feeling a little uneasy. She took a moment before speaking again. "It was dark, whoever it was, had to be dressed in dark clothes. But it…" she shook her head in confusion,

"It what?" he asked with calm interest.

"Why would a person be in the middle of the road, in the middle of the night?" she asked rhetorically. "Let alone, so close to my car that I almost hit him? I imagine you can see lights coming from quite a ways off. The road was flat and straight."

"It's a good question," he said in all seriousness. "Anything else, skin color, height, weight?"

"Dark. I'd say tall but it was so close and startled me so much that I just tried not to hit him. When I came to a stop, I saw nothing in the road and then your officer arrived moments later."

Hunter took a sip of his coffee. "The road is flat. How far could you see looking down the road?"

She thought about it for a second. "A couple hundred feet I guess."

"You didn't notice anything in the road the whole time driving? There was never anything peculiar? You know, like sometimes you see a deer off in the distance but you're not sure until you get closer?"

"I really don't recall seeing anything, that's why I felt comfortable looking at the map. The road was straight and unobstructed."

"Then it was suddenly right there in the middle of the road?" he asked. Hunter decided to get snide. "You know reading or texting while driving is hazardous?"

Casey nodded in agreement, ignoring his smarmy remark. "It seemed inevitable that I would hit him. I hit the brakes and the car locked up and spun around a couple times. I never heard a 'thump' or anything."

"Did you see it move out of the way?"

She was silent again as she tried to recall the scene. "It would have had to jump straight up to get out of the way because I was right on top of it."

"Jump?" He'd heard this before.

"I didn't see it jump but it's really the only way it could have avoided being hit."

Hunter nodded. "Did you get out of the car to check for damages or anything?"

A puzzled look overcame her face. "No, the policeman came, he got out of his car, while I stayed in mine trying to catch my breath." She paused. "He didn't check my car out for damage either. The only time I got out of the car was to answer the officer's questions and leave with him to come here."

"Alright," Hunter said. "We'll have to check out that car."

She could sense he was waiting for some kind of response. "That's fine with me."

A uniformed officer knocked on Hunter's door. "A few details you might want to check into," the patrolman said as he brought Hunter a piece of paper.

Hunter looked it over. "Miss Windall, would you excuse me for a minute. I have to make a call before we go."

She nodded yes, then whispered, "Okay."

"Officer Holis here will escort you to a waiting area," Hunter said as he stood up.

She turned and walked out thinking that this could work for her. If she could find out anything of note, it could lead to a breaking story.

Hunter smiled as he watched her walk out. *Not bad… nice movement.* Then he thought again – *okay pig, enough.*

Daylight created a completely different perspective of the Pine Barrens for Casey. Sitting in the passenger's seat as Hunter drove, thick oaks, tall cedars, and spindly pitch pines consumed the landscape set against the backdrop of a blue sky. The thorny bare undergrowth weaved like barbed wire in many places. Soon it would bloom into a pretty wall of green. Casey glanced into the woods but it was near impossible to see very far into it.

"You wonder how someone could hide out in these woods for days," she said as Hunter cruised down the long straight road.

"It's really not a wonder. If this guy is proficient, he can stay in there for weeks. Besides don't you know this area is the mafia dumping ground?"

"What?" she said with a confused look.

Hunter laughed. "Don't take it too seriously and please don't quote me but it's an urban myth; at least partially. In the 70's rumors swirled that the mafia would use this region to bury bodies. The area has developed a lot since but there are still sections that are remote and largely not traveled."

"Do you believe this myth?" Casey asked.

"It's not totally unfounded but it's been overly exaggerated."

"Well now that we are on the topic of mysterious murders, what else can you tell me about what I might be involved in?" she asked eager to know more. "Any suspects?"

"Suspects?" Hunter replied. "I can't say anything to you except that we are investigating all angles and appreciate any leads the public might be able to help us with." He paused for a moment. "Off the record," he turned to her. He had a stern look, "When I say off the record, I mean off. This is your test...We are investigating mental wards for possible suspects."

"Why mental wards?"

"Whoever killed that young man had to be strong as an ox," Hunter said. "This was so brutal I can't fathom a normal person committing the crime we're investigating."

"Normal people don't murder?" Casey said with a smirk.

"Of course they do but not like this; psycho's murder like this. My instincts tell me a mental patient did this." Hunter motioned as they came to an intersection. "This is the road you turned down," he said half question, half statement.

Casey looked all around. "It sure looks different during the day."

"About how far down would you guess you went?"

"I don't know. It looks so different now. Maybe a mile or so."

"Alright, let's see what kind of skid mark you left."

They had gone about a mile when he spotted her car on the shoulder. He also spotted a faint dark strip in the road. He pulled over. "This area is supposed to be secured," he said as he looked about.

"I was told they would be in the area frequently," Casey said.

Hunter continued to look down the road. The expression on his face didn't exude confidence. "If I don't see a car soon, someone's ass is going to fry."

Hunter exited the car and walked over to where the skid started and knelt down. He put his hand on the black mark. "This is where you hit the brake," he said looking at the mark.

"I was right on top of him," she repeated. "I mean he couldn't have been standing more than twenty feet from me, if that."

Hunter stood up and began to search the shoulder on the one side of the road, then walked over to the other side. He couldn't find anything resembling a clue. He decided to walk a little further off the road.

"What in the hell could get out of the way of a moving car like that?" he said looking back at Casey who stood on the shoulder, doing her own search. "You didn't happen to see which direction he went, did you?"

She looked back at him with a helpless expression and shook her head. She watched Hunter canvas the terrain. She hoped she would witness the discovery of a clue or even better…find one herself. It was nice to have the inside track but she knew one wrong step and she could find herself persona non grata.

"Nothing," Hunter shouted. "Not a friggin' foot print, piece of cloth, nothing." He came back towards her, "Let's check out your car."

Hunter marked the skid close to 175 feet in length. Casey's car faced them as they walked over to it. "You were going at a good clip I can see. My guess is over 60 miles per hour."

"I guess," she said following him back to her car.

"More than a guess," he said. "Little fast for night driving in an area where there's a lot of deer."

"I was in a hurry."

"What you were was lucky. You could have easily flipped your car or worse," he looked up to meet her eyes, "this could have been a real mess."

Hunter walked around the car. There wasn't a scratch on it. He ran his finger along its contours. "You keep it in nice shape."

"Thanks. I figure on my salary, I'll need it for a while." She continued to watch him look over the vehicle. "You see anything?"

He shook his head. Not a scratch. He made his way back to the front of the car. "It's hard to believe, you didn't hit this guy."

"I'm amazed myself. I thought it was over, I really did."

Looking at the front of the car, he spotted something in the grill. He kneeled down to get a closer look. *Fibers.* "Pop the hood."

She quickly grabbed for her keys, unlocked her door and pulled the hood release. "You find something?"

"Maybe," he shouted as he jogged back to his car. Opening up the glove compartment, he took out a small kit. He pulled out a pair of surgical gloves, a clear baggie and a pair of tweezers. He ran back to the front of Casey's car. He opened the hood to see if there were more fibers.

"What is it?" Casey asked spotting what grabbed Hunter's attention. "It kind of looks like fur doesn't it?"

"Kind of," Hunter said while looking at the evidence. He ran his hand slowly along the edges of the grill and just inside, but could not find anymore. "I'm afraid I'm going to have to hold your car," he said.

"Are you kidding?" Casey said, exasperated. "What am I supposed to do about work?"

"I can tell you or ask you not to mention any of this in your writing," Hunter said. He was quite serious. "If you want to mention your car was impounded that's fine. But the evidence; well if you could keep this to yourself for the time being, I would appreciate it."

"You ask an awful lot. There is journalistic integrity you know."

"There's also jeopardizing an investigation," he shot back.

"How's mentioning hairs jeopardizing?"

"For one," he said. Hunter was always extremely serious about information given to the press. "I don't need any leaks about what we have on this case until I can get a closer fix on what we're dealing with. Besides, we have no idea if this has anything to do with this crime. The last thing I need is misinformation getting out into the public."

"The public has a right to know," Casey said. She knew it was a weak declaration but felt she couldn't just stay silent.

"You're absolutely right. They have a right to know about the facts, of which we have very few. The worst thing that can happen is rampant speculation that does nothing but distract and waste a lot of time. I need time to formulate a lead, a trail. I need answers."

Casey looked at him with understanding. She had a good conscience and wanted to do the right thing but she also wanted this story. She felt it was hers to tell.

"I need at least another forty eight hours. Give me forty eight hours to put something together and I will give you a story," Hunter said.

Casey agreed. She even put out her hand to shake on it. As she released his hand, a patrol car arrived.

"Oh good, the Calvary," he said. "I need to head back to headquarters and I will have this officer bring you home or to work, whichever you prefer."

He would have preferred to take her. He enjoyed her company and wanted to talk some more but now wasn't the time. He turned and focused his attention on removing the fibers from the grill, placed them in the baggie, sealed and marked it.

"Can we talk later?" she asked.

"We'll talk for certain," he answered smiling.

"When?" she asked just as his phone rang.

He put up a finger gesturing her to hold on as he answered his phone. He spoke for a few seconds before pausing. He looked towards her, "I've got to go... we'll talk soon."

## CHAPTER 7

Hunter spotted the media trucks well before he saw the police station. He expected some press but not as many as had lined up along the street leading to the building. TV crews were setting up their satellite feeds, reporters were jockeying for their best standup position. Both New York and Philadelphia stations as well as local TV, and radio had sent someone to report on the mysterious murder.

He could see a podium set up at the top of the small staircase that led into headquarters. Hunter casually walked through the throng of press gathering, trotted up the stairs and went into the building without a question asked, much to his relief.

Captain Morgan stood just inside the entrance as Hunter passed through the doors. "Hunter, we need to talk after I make a statement. Standard stuff; we are following all leads, and the obligatory promise to keep everyone posted on information as we get it. But when I'm finished we need to discuss a more detailed plan on how to handle this case."

Hunter heard him. "The podium looks nice all cleaned up. How far back did you have to dip into that closet to retrieve it?" he said with a smile.

The captain didn't appreciate the snide remark. Hunter regretted his comment, seeing that his stab at more playful humor failed. He wished the captain good luck and said he'd be at his desk.

New photos of the crime scene lay on his desk. He pulled out his baggie with the fibers. He looked it over, turning the small bag around and around. He couldn't make out the fabric. It looked like a heavy flannel or some sort of faux fur. He picked up his phone and dialed a friend at forensics to let him know what he had and when he would be dropping it off. No sooner had he hung up the phone, then it rang.

"Detective Matthews," he answered.

The voice on the other end was pissed. "You never mentioned there was going to be a press conference today. I thought you were going to be up front with me. Remember the play ball bullshit you tried to sell me?" It was Casey.

"Hold on Ms. Windall… Casey. I was just as surprised, when I arrived, to see all these people gathering around. You think I expected this? I don't think anyone here expected this coverage."

"Don't give me that. You knew there was going to be a press conference when you received that call."

She wasn't wrong but Hunter had no idea it would turn into a big event. He also didn't like her tone, so he shot back, "Hey listen. Where the hell was I this morning? Or did you forget that I was out with you, checking out the scene, giving you a personal escort, giving you more information than any journalist could ask for. You see all those mic monkeys out there… they're getting nothing but an official statement. I'll fax you a copy of the statement if that'll make you happy."

Her anger didn't abate so easily. "I still don't have much of anything. I thought we were going to have a partnership here."

Hunter worked to temper his anger. "There's not much of anything to go on. You are currently part of the investigation. There's nothing but theory and you know more than anyone else about it."

Casey maintained her displeasure. "Still, I feel like I've been sold a line of crap."

"Tell you what… Keep it up and you'll get the scraps of this investigation. I'll see to it you have to beg the other reporters for information. What should I have done, delayed the press conference so I could contact my personal journalist?" He paused to take a breath before continuing. "I told you, you play ball with me and I'll play ball with you. You know these press conferences are nothing but a dog and pony show. You'll get your story."

Silence filled the line. Casey boiled but she believed him. She felt she could trust him. She had that instinct about people and it usually worked in her favor.

"Okay then," she said finally, her temper easing. "Just understand my position. We make an agreement then I'm no sooner back at my desk and bang, I hear about a press conference being held. Naturally I felt betrayed."

"Understandable," Hunter replied. "Let's chalk it up to bad timing. I told you I'd keep you up to date. As far as press conferences, well, I can't control them. We have an information desk for any updates and briefings that will take place. Call them; they'll have a better idea than me as to when official briefings will take place, unless of course I'm asked to say something or stand there and look good for the camera."

"Fine," she said. Her tone softened. She didn't want to blow it with the lead detective. "I'm sorry for yelling."

Hunter responded quickly, "Don't mention it, we're fine, okay?"

"Yes," she replied.

"By the way, just to let you know, I'm sending those fibers over to forensics this afternoon for testing, if anything comes up that I can share, you'll be the first to know." He paused. "I promise."

"Thanks," she said. "I've taken up enough of your time. I'll let you get back to work." Casey hung up the phone.

Hunter reclined in his chair. His hand lingered on the receiver. He never let a pretty face interfere in the past. Could he have a soft spot for a reporter trying to make a name for herself? "You're thinking too much," he mumbled to himself. He grabbed the new reports on his desk and began to sift through them. He needed to concentrate on the case not his social life, what little there was of one.

Hunter wasn't two minutes into reviewing his evidence list when the phone rang again. He didn't want to answer it. He wasn't in the mood, especially if it was some annoying press person looking for information he wasn't going to release.

"Detective Matthews," he answered finally.

"Hunter," the voice said hurried and soft. "She's coming around. You might want to come down here now. I can't say she won't fall apart again. They had to sedate her last night. I hope they don't have to again. So please get here quick." It was the captain's wife Carol. She had stayed with the victim's girlfriend all night.

"Have any newspaper or TV people been around?" Hunter asked.

"No"

"Good, I'm on my way."

Hunter did not like hospitals. The first smell of alcohol triggered all the past visions. As a child, he had to visit his dying grandfather nearly every day for a month until the inevitable occurred. The image of his grandfather lying motionless with tubes in his arms, up his nose and down his throat had long left an indelible scar in his consciousness. He could envision the bloodshot hollow eyes of his grandfather clinging to life, his withering body, the hand that never seemed to stop trembling; a shell of a man he once knew. The image haunted him. His stomach churned while walking through the corridors, peeking into rooms, seeing feet, bare and motionless while the volume of tinny televisions roared too loud. He felt like he was walking back into his childhood. *'Get yourself together man!'* he shouted at himself. *'You're a professional, suck it up.'* He made another turn down another identical hallway, the same gray walls with the same colorful prints of flowers and landscapes but nothing overly striking or artistic. Hunter started to count the numbers on the wall next to each room. *'Here it is, 316.'* He stood outside the door, and took a couple deep breaths before entering.

"Carol," he said as he smiled wide and opened his arms to her. She looked tired. He could see she had a long night.

"How are you Hunter?" she asked returning the smile and embracing him.

"I'm fine, how are you holding up?"

"Good. It's been a while since I've been in this situation," she said.

"Thank you for doing this."

She shrugged him off. "I feel like it's part of my duty when called."

"How's she doing?" he asked.

"She came around when I called but quickly went back to sleep. She's more restless now. The drugs are wearing off. She should be coming around soon."

They both looked at the girl. She appeared ragged, her cheeks sunken, complexion pale, her shoulder length brown hair disheveled.

"She was hysterical last night… crazed. She had to be sedated," Carol said.

Hunter nodded. "Did she say anything?"

"She babbled. Mostly incoherent," Carol said sitting back down. "Poor girl really lost it."

"Well if she witnessed half of what I saw, I'd be babbling too."

Carol looked at him with a touch of confusion.

"Her boyfriend," he said dropping his voice to a whisper. He paused as he looked at the girl, then leaned in and whispered in Carol's ear. "He was ripped apart."

Carol's face contorted as she jerked her head back.

"Limb from limb," he said, his voice barely audible.

"Oh my God," she gasped. "My husband didn't say anything about that."

He nodded. "Not pleasant." He was quiet for another moment. "So she hasn't said anything to anybody?"

"Not that I'm aware of. Police picked her up outside of a Wawa not too far from the scene. She made a 911 call reporting the attack on her boyfriend. Then it seems she began to fall apart." Carol looked at the sleeping girl. "I don't know how she could operate a car or make a call after witnessing something like that."

"I'm going to have to listen to that 911 call."

"By the way, her name is Nell," Carol said.

"Nell?"

"Yes, Nellie Mae Johnson."

"Nellie Mae?" Hunter said with surprise.

"Yep."

"Come on," he said, in whispered exasperation. "I used to pay my student loans to Nellie Mae."

"You mean Fannie Mae," Carol said with an eyebrow cocked. "Did you get the boyfriend's name?" she asked.

"Yeah, his name was Joe… Joe West." It then hit him. He couldn't believe it. He saw the engagement ring on her finger. "Are you kidding me? Nellie Mae West, that's too much."

Carol held back a laugh, turning her head away to hide her expression. "I feel terrible," she said. "This poor girl is lying here traumatized because of the brutal murder of her boyfriend and we're laughing at what her married name could have been."

A few minutes passed and Nell started to come around. She turned her head from side to side a couple times then slowly opened her eyes. "Where am I?" she asked. Her voice was groggy. She rubbed her eyes and tried to push herself up in the bed. She made eye contact with both of them. Her eyes began to well up. "He's dead isn't he?" she muttered, knowing the answer.

Hunter leaned forward and touched the top of her hand. "I'm Detective Hunter Matthews, this is Carol Morgan, she's been by your side the whole time you've been here."

Nell offered a grin of appreciation. "Is he dead?"

"Yes," Hunter said as compassionately as he could.

Tears began to flow down her face but she kept her composure.

"Do you think you could answer a couple questions for me?" Hunter asked. He gripped her hand and gave it a reassuring tug. She nodded.

"Last night," he said with a soft voice, noticing her bite her lower lip trying hard to hold back another wave of tears. "Can you tell me what happened?"

Nell did her best to hold her composure. "We were coming back from the shore." Her words were slow and unsteady. "I think we were on 537. I was in and out of sleep. Then there was this thing in the middle of the road. Joe hit the brakes and we spun out of control."

"Did you hit what you saw?" Hunter asked.

"I don't think so, we may have bumped it. I'm not sure."

"Was it a person...a deer?"

"It happened so fast, I don't remember. It was just there."

"So you spun out and stopped."

"We were both shaken up but okay. Joe got out to check the car because it stalled and he couldn't get it started." She stopped and again her eyes began to well up.

"It's okay dear. Take your time," Carol said. "Just relax."

"He started yelling for me to start the car," she said as she closed her eyes. A few big tears streamed down her cheek. "I didn't know why he was yelling but I didn't like it. He was scaring me," she continued.

"Did you see anything?"

"No," she said as she began to tremble. Carol now held her hand and Nell shifted in the bed to move closer to her. "There was a noise."

"A noise?" Hunter said.

Nell shook her head and took a deep breath. "I heard Joe yell... he was in pain." Nell sat up. Hunter could see she wanted to battle her fear. "I went to see what was going on and I saw Joe and someone else fighting on the ground."

"Did you see what he looked like?" Hunter asked.

Nell shook her head. "But there was this screech."

Hunter nodded. "A screech?"

"It was awful." Nell began to shake again and her voice drifted as she lost control. She started to shake her head back and forth and mumbled Joe's name repeatedly.

"Can you describe this person?"

Nell's body trembled. She curled her knees up to her chest.

"I understand you went through a traumatic event and it's still hard to process but any kind of information you have could be of tremendous help. We can catch this guy and make sure he doesn't do anything like this to anybody else," Hunter said.

Nell whimpered. Her eyes widened as if she was reliving the scene. She clutched the bed sheet. Perspiration rolled down her face. She didn't move to wipe it away.

"It's okay dear, you're safe here," Carol cooed. She looked up at Hunter, "I think that should be all for now."

Hunter acknowledged her but didn't leave. He hoped she might recall a few extra details.

It wasn't long before Nell calmed down. She let go of Carol's hand and relaxed back into her bed. She closed her eyes and took a few deep breaths. In a matter of seconds, they watched her fall back to sleep.

"I'll leave the rest for later," Hunter said. He really didn't want to go but he didn't want to wake her either. He looked at Carol. "Stay a little longer please."

Carol nodded.

"Have her parents been notified?" he asked.

Carol nodded again. "They are in transit coming back from a trip to China. They don't know all the details yet."

"Alright," Hunter said and as he turned to leave the room, Nell woke up.

"No, let me get through this," she choked. Nell wiped her eyes. "This will sound crazy... but when the man or thing stood in front of me, it looked like he showed wings or a cape. For a second I thought I might have been looking at a..." she paused, her lips quivered as she tried to say the word. "A vampire."

Hunter stiffened. He didn't expect that kind of answer.

"Wings?" he asked.

She could see he was perplexed. Her eyes remained locked on his as she nodded in agreement.

"Vampire?" he asked not expecting an answer.

Again, she looked at him with tear-filled eyes and nodded. "But the face...it didn't look like a man's face." She shook her head. "I got into the driver's seat and took off." She looked off to the side, dropped her head and whispered, "Why Joe, why did you get out?" Another tear rolled down her cheek. She raised her head and looked at Hunter. "It all happened so fast. I didn't want to leave Joe but I couldn't stay. I thought it would attack me too. I just hit the gas and drove off as fast as I could."

"Did you happen to look back or see anything else?" Hunter asked.

Nell curled her knees up once again. She shook her head. She looked at Carol. "I want my mommy."

Carol grabbed her hand and looked over at Hunter. "I think that should be all for now."

Hunter agreed. He said thank you to both of them and told Nell she was incredibly strong and had been extremely helpful. He asked if they could talk again. She nodded yes.

"A Vampire?" he said as he shook his head. Hunter had contacted the regional psychiatric institutions and none of them reported anyone missing. He continued to tap his fingers in random sequences. "Vampire," he repeated. He needed more to work with than wings and vampire. He would try Nell again. *Tomorrow*, he thought. *I'll leave her alone today.* Carol had advised him to wait a couple days but he didn't have that luxury and by then she'd be home with her parents creating another obstacle. He knew he couldn't file reports stating that a possible vampire attack had occurred.

The phone rang and he picked it up quickly. A voice greeted him before he could say anything. "Hunter," the voice said excited.

"Charles," Hunter shot back. Charles Fortney was the county forensic expert. Hunter liked him. Charles had a sharp sense of humor. Hunter also liked that they could go toe to toe on topics and neither of them took it personally.

"Tests are back on your fibers," Charles said.

"What do you have my fine scientist friend?" Hunter replied.

"Well, Mr. Holmes, what we have is a mystery," Charles replied.

"You mean like a Scooby Doo mystery?" Hunter said, eliciting laughter. "Do tell. What are we looking at?"

"We ruled out any kind of synthetic or natural clothing fiber."

"Yeah, and," Hunter said.

"So we ran other tests to see if it's some kind of animal."

"Animal?"

"Yeah, well if it isn't a fabric and it isn't human then that's our only alternative, right Sherlock?"

"Okay smart-ass. Anything turn up?"

"Strangely no… that's the mystery. I can't identify it yet, so I'm running more tests."

"More tests? You just said if it wasn't synthetic or human, it had to be animal. Are you suggesting alien," Hunter said with sarcasm. "I always knew you had connections to the men in black."

"Oh my naïve friend…I am a man in black," Charles returned.

"What kind of extra tests?" Hunter asked, skipping the sarcasm.

"Trying out some other DNA type tests. I can't divulge anymore. I'm not sure your brain could handle it," Charles said, continuing the banter.

Hunter wanted straight answers. "So you're saying the samples match nothing?"

"Horse," Charles said. "The closest thing in the realm of what I could draw a match to."

"Horse?" Hunter shot back rather stunned.

"Believe it or not, you may be looking for Mr. Ed's evil cousin," Charles said.

"I'm having a hard time believing it," Hunter said.

"Well yes, I would hope you would have a hard time believing Mr. Ed had an evil cousin."

Hunter laughed. "Alright, thanks for getting to me so quickly Charles, I appreciate it."

"I'll let you know what further tests indicate… probably in a day or two."

"Please do and quicker if possible," Hunter said.

"You got it," Charles said and hung up the phone.

Hunter leaned back in his chair perplexed. He really

thought he had retrieved some sort of clothing fiber. It didn't make sense. He went to make a cup of coffee. He made it slowly as he organized information in his head. He walked back to his desk and spotted a folder marked Denten. *The farmer,* he thought. *Those animals were butchered to pieces…ripped apart.* He sat back down and flipped through the folder. *Screech. That's right… the farmer said he heard a terrible screech. This couldn't be the same thing? Could it?*

Hunter decided to compare notes from the farm case and the murder scene when his phone rang again. He picked it up and before he could say anything, the voice greeted him promptly. "It's been over 48 hours." It was Casey.

"What?" Hunter said, not getting her drift. "Casey?"

"48 hours. You said to give you 48 hours and you'd have something for me to work with," she said.

Hunter let out a long exhale and bowed his head low. "Well, to tell ya the truth, nothing has come up yet." Again, he lied but the fiber/fur information was unconfirmed news. He didn't want that known, at least not yet.

"What about the samples you took from my car?" she said. Her voice grew agitated.

He continued his ruse. "I called the lab and they're still running a synthetics check. I should have something by the end of the day or tomorrow," he paused then added, "I hope." Her momentary silence was a good sign.

Casey didn't like the answer. "End of the day huh?"

"I hope or tomorrow," he said. "By the way, I checked out your website and reviewed some of your work. I see farm vandalizing is a popular topic, or as you and others so eloquently put it – mysterious animal mutilations."

"You did?" she said. It impressed her that he took time to look at the site.

"Yes. It is quite a site for those looking to get their fill of mysteries and assorted tales of bluster."

"How do you mean?" she asked, her attitude shifting to protective.

"I mean, there's a lot of cat chasing the tail kind of material on there," he said.

Casey caught his drift. "Not unlike a lot of what you are presently giving me."

Hunter laughed. "Quick. I like that. By the way, did you ever go out and speak to the farmer, Mr. Denten?" Hunter was curious about how much information the farmer may have given her.

"I did, the next day after talking to you," she said. "I had mentioned the story idea to my editor and he wanted me to follow it up. We have a lot of farmer market people who advertise with us and that same crowd seemingly likes these kinds of stories."

"What did ol' Gil say?"

"He told me what he told you because he prefaced everything with, 'as I told the detective.' He also showed me the barn and described some of the damage done."

"Yeah it wasn't pleasant," Hunter said. "Anything I might be interested in knowing," he asked coyly.

"Yeah, he thinks you're pompous," she replied in a playful way.

"He did? I didn't think a word like pompous would be in his vocabulary," Hunter shot back.

"Yep. Well… I took some creative license."

"Cute," he said. "Very cute." He enjoyed the conversation but knew he had to get going. "Listen, I'd love to chit chat and exchange recipes all day but I've got some work to take care of here."

Her voice returned to serious. "I understand. Can I call you at the end of the day to see if the lab results came in?"

"Yeah, sure. I should be here." He thought about asking her out for dinner, but didn't. "Call me later."

# CHAPTER 8

"Whatcha see boy?" Carl shouted to his dog Pup. Pup, a Cocker Spaniel with an off-white coat dotted with several black spots, had dashed about 30 yards ahead of him deep into the underbrush of the woods. It was small game season. Carl, a thin gangly sort who always wore clothes too big for his frame and his friends gathered to hunt in an area just south of Lebanon State Forest, the center of the Pine Barrens.

The sun began to dip below the treetops, casting long shadows throughout the woods. Carl had already bagged three rabbits and was looking for another before heading back to camp for the night. He saw Pup was onto something after dashing into the woods. He called out after losing sight of him in the scrub. Carl felt he had strayed too far away from the field they were working most of the afternoon. He could never get a good shot off this deep in the woods.

"Whatcha see boy? Trying to flush something back this way?" Carl yelled.

Pup was a good small game dog but at times, larger animals, like deer could easily distract him. Carl worked hard to break Pup of the habit, but now the dog was off after something.

"Pup!" he yelled. "Let it go boy, let it go."

He waited another second. He couldn't see much in the dimming light. He turned around, took a few steps back towards camp and whistled. A few seconds later, he heard Pup rustling through the undergrowth coming closer.

"That-a-boy. Now what in the hell were you after, huh?" he asked the dog playfully. Pup wasn't ten feet away from Carl when the dog suddenly stopped, turned back towards the direction that he came from and froze. Carl could see the hair on Pups back rise.

"What's wrong boy?"

Pup stood still then lowered himself and began to growl. Carl grabbed his rifle and pulled it up to a firing position. He had never seen Pup react like this. Carl popped off the safety on the rifle. He scanned the woods but could see nothing. Then he felt something, a presence, like someone was watching. His grip tightened on the rifle, he could feel his blood pulse against the wood stock of the weapon. Pup continued growling.

"I sense it too boy," Carl whispered. "Whattaya think it is?" Carl moved a little closer to Pup, hoping to scare or flush out whatever lurked in the brush ahead.

Pup barked.

"What boy?" Then Carl heard a rustling overhead in the trees, about fifty feet away. He aimed his rifle. He couldn't make out the form but something moved up there. Carl fired a shot in the direction of the sound but knew he missed it; whatever it was had disappeared or stopped moving. Pup began to relax and was soon wagging his tail for Carl to pet him.

"What ya suppose that was?" he said to the dog. "Mountain lion, cougar? Never thought one could be in these parts." He started to rub Pup's head. "Yeah and it scared the hell out of me too."

Carl and Pup returned to their streamside camp. Carl told his two hunting buddies, Lenny and Hank, who already had a fire going and a meal in the works, about the strange encounter.

"I certainly don't recall ever hearing or reading about cougar or mountain lions out here," Lenny said. He had quit early that day after bagging a big eleven-pound woodchuck. His love of hunting didn't run as deep as the other two. He simply liked getting outdoors, camping, sitting around a fire and having a couple beers.

"There have been mountain lion sightings reported up in the Adirondacks of New York," Hank added. Hank was the most devout of the three hunters, a big barrel chested man who stood nearly six feet four inches with thick forearms his friends had nicknamed 'the crushers'. He nearly always arranged their excursions. Hank had bagged three woodchucks and two rabbits. His dog Max had tired and lost focus, so instead of pushing the animal, Hank opted to come back to camp early with the idea to start fresh again in the morning. "Could have been a Bobcat, maybe a Lynx," he added.

"What about bear?" Lenny added.

"Bear?" Hank said. "There are no bear down here, let alone running around up in trees. They climb but they don't swing from branch to branch," he added with a laugh.

"I guess it could have been a Bobcat but that doesn't fit right either," Lenny said. "Do Bobcats run through tree tops?"

"That's a good question," Hank said. "They're cats, so I suppose they can climb'em but I don't know about going from branch to branch. They're a pretty scarce creature. They know how to keep a low profile."

"Pup got spooked by whatever it was," Carl said. "You shoulda seen his hairs, all standin' up and all. As a matter of fact he had all my hairs standin' on end."

"Sounds creepy," Lenny said. "And you took a shot at it?"

"Yeah," Carl answered. "Kinda stupid now that I think about it. Should have kept my cool but it was freaky. I've never felt like that out in the woods."

---

"Yeah this place has that effect sometimes," Hank said as he tended to the meal cooking over the fire. "I've heard a number of weird sounds out here. The place closes in on ya in a hurry when strange thoughts get a hold of ya."

"Well this was more than strange thoughts I can tell ya that much," Carl said. "Ya think we should take extra caution with stowing the food in case it was a cougar or some other large animal? We could be attracting trouble."

Hank rolled his eyes. "If it'll make you feel better there Little Bo Peep."

They chuckled but Carl had it in his mind to take more care with the way he stored his food. Lenny meanwhile decided, for the first time, to leave a magazine in his rifle as a precaution.

"Well if there is a big cat out there, the dogs will get wind of it first," Lenny said, surveying the area. Twilight made the woods feel more ominous, the tall oak trees and looming spindly branches of the pitch pines. He began to get uneasy.

"Dinners up!" Hank shouted.

Lenny's concentration shifted and he was thankful for it. He didn't need or want to let his imagination get out of hand. He grabbed his plate and hurried to the fire to get his share of Hanks wife's delicious beef stew. As he ate, he relaxed, forgetting about big animals in the woods.

As night set in, stars pierced the dark canopy to shine bright in the clear sky. The crackle of the fire was music to their ears as they relaxed. The steady noise of nightlife in the woods provided a comforting backdrop of white noise. The stream next to their camp trickled in a perfect rhythm.

"Man it sure is dark," Hank, said breaking the silence. He decided to bust Carl's balls. "Oh boy… I think I see a flying bear coming out of the trees," he said in a creepy but playful voice.

"Kiss my ass," Carl said. "Whattaya gonna do, ride me about this the rest of the weekend?"

"Well if I had a hanky, I'd give it to ya so you wouldn't get all misty on me," Hank shot back.

"What was that?" Lenny shouted in a hushed manner, going completely still.

"What," Carl said, his voice shaken.

"Just jerking your chain," Lenny said.

"You're an ass too," Carl said, picking up a small stick and throwing it at Lenny.

"Listen, the dogs, will pick up on anything before we do, so just relax, take it easy will ya. The largest things out here are deer anyway," Hank said. He stood up and stretched. "I think I'm gonna hit it gentlemen."

"Goodnight," Lenny said.

"Goodnight ass," Carl chimed.

Hank disappeared into his tent.

"Another log?" Carl asked while picking one up.

"Sure, why not," Lenny said. "Don't let Hank bother you. You should know by now he just likes to bust your stones."

"I know" he said and got up and headed towards the cooler. "Want a beer?"

"Yeah sure, it's been a while since I've had one."

Carl tossed him one and then opened one for himself.

The smell of meat and fire floated in the air and into the woods. The creature was feasting on a rabbit it had pounced on when the smell from the men's campsite caught its attention. The beast stood erect, almost seven feet tall, darted its long snout back and forth sniffing several times. It locked in on the smell. Lowering itself towards the ground while curling its back almost into the shape of a 'C,' it leapt. The creature sailed through the myriad of branches upward, never touching one, perching high on an upper branch of a pitch pine as if it weighed the same as a small bird. It sniffed and hissed. Turning back and forth, the creature then climbed to the absolute top of the tree. It exposed itself to the night sky, a lone dark shape poised atop the flat black roof of the forest. Then its gaze locked in on a distant point. The creature could see the flicker of the fire from where it balanced. It stood motionless, just watching. Then without notice, it crossed the tops of the trees for several yards, unfurling its long wings to help it glide from treetop to treetop. Stopping about two hundred yards from the campfire, it stood silent, swaying with the breeze, just watching. It could see the campfire more fully and hear movement and voices. The creature's eyes began to glow. It dipped its dark head and let out a low hiss. Saliva dripped from between its sharp teeth, like thick syrup, onto the pine needles on the ground below. Its spindly long claws tightened around the branches it held. Continuing to observe the activity around the flickering fire, it sniffed several more times while remaining motionless, inspecting. One of the campers disappeared from view. Without a sound, the creature let loose its hold on the branches and floated to the ground, landing on its hind legs in silence.

"So not much action today huh?" Carl said, while he stoked the fire.

"Nope. Early on there was some but it seemed to all go away. I didn't even get a shot off the last couple hours out there," Lenny answered. "I decided to come back here and throw a line in the creek."

"Anything?" Carl asked.

"A small brook trout that I threw back," Lenny said before taking another sip of his beer, finishing it. "Want another?" he asked as he got up and headed for the cooler.

"I'm good. If I have another, then I'll have another, then I won't want to get up in the morning. If I don't get up in the morning, Hank will pitch a fit," Carl said half joking.

"What about this cougar? You really thought you saw a big cat out there?" Lenny said sitting back down. He opened his beer and took a good gulp.

"I never *actually* saw anything," Carl replied. "Pup saw it. Whatever it was… right Pup," Carl said looking over at his dog whose eyes remained half closed with sleep. "All I know is Pup had me scared shitless. His hairs were all up. I'd never seen a dog do that. Hell, I'd never seen a cat do that."

"You saw nothing?" Lenny asked fishing for some kind of reassurance to ease his growing nerves.

"When I looked, all I heard was scurrying in the trees," Carl said. He felt goose bumps come over his body. "I couldn't locate it. My mind was racing and my eyes darted all over the place." He stopped for a second, looking around their own camp. "Then I saw this dark shape bustling in the tree tops but it was already a good ways off. I took a shot but knew I missed. I couldn't tell what the hell it was but it was strange. I've never seen anything like that in the woods."

"So you think they're mountain lions or cougars out here?"

"Well that's what ran through my head at first but it doesn't make sense," Carl said. "Remember a couple years ago, there was that lady who owned tigers and other exotic animals and one got away and it caused a big uproar?"

"You think something's on the loose?" Lenny asked.

"Could be. Why not? Hell, out here who knows who owns what," Carl said.

"Wouldn't one of our wives have called us or texted if something like that happened?" Lenny asked.

"Yeah sure but first they'd have to hear something before they could call. Or how bout if something did get loose and the owners didn't know yet or maybe, they haven't reported anything because they thought they could get it back on their own?"

"You make some good points Carl," Lenny said. He took another sip of his beer.

"Besides, like Hank said, if anything outta the ordinary happens, the dogs will react to it first."

They fell into relaxed silence. The crackle of the fire soothed their nerves. Lenny looked up into the sky and stared at the thousands of stars that lit the night. Carl's eyes became heavy in a hurry and he began to nod off. Lenny looked over at the dogs. He instantly noticed the dogs all sitting at attention staring in the same direction. Lenny sat up quickly and peered off to where the dogs were looking. "What is it boys?" he whispered. They seemed not to pay any attention to his words.

Carl heard Lenny and immediately snapped out of his trance. "What's up?" he whispered, noticing Lenny's alarm.

"Look, the dogs see something," he said. They both stared in the same direction as the dogs.

"Whattaya see boys?" Carl said.

The dogs didn't move.

"Yeah, they didn't respond to me either," Lenny said.

Both men continued to stare into the wall of darkness that was the woods, only about fifty feet away.

A stick snapped. Lenny felt a rush of adrenaline flow through his body. Keeping his eyes fixed on the woods, he slowly moved closer to his rifle. When he felt it, he picked it up and nestled it snug under his armpit. "Whatever the hell it is, I'm gonna blast the shit out of it."

"Alright cowboy, calm down, it could be a raccoon or deer," Carl said while picking up his own rifle. "It'll pass."

They were silent again and then another snap pierced the dark just a few feet from the first sound. "Why don't you give it a yell and scare it," Carl said.

"Why don't you?" Lenny shot back. There was a definite tremor in his voice. The rifle started to shake in his hands.

Seeing how uncomfortable Lenny acted, Carl warned him that he was going to stand up and yell. "HeeYaaa, HeeYaa," he shouted jumping up and down waving his hands.

A rush of noise ensued, then out of the dark three deer bolted through edge of the camp. Lenny ducked and Carl fell over startled. The dogs started to bark because of all the sudden movement and noise. In seconds, the deer were gone.

Carl stood back up and started laughing.

Hank rushed out of his tent. "What the hell is going on?" he yelled.

"Lenny thought the cougar was out there," Carl said trying to catch his breath and stop laughing. "I'll tell ya, he had me pretty good too."

"Idiot," Hank snapped.

"Well the deer seemed to scare you pretty good too," Lenny said pointing to Carl.

"Deer!" Hank said. "Friggin' deer. What the hell else do you expect out here?"

"Sorry Hank, I think we freaked each other out with the mountain lion, cougar thing," Carl said. "It's really kinda silly now that you think about it." He took a deep breath to get his wits back but then locked eyes on the dogs. They all stood frozen in place, staring from where the deer had just come. Carl could see Pup's hair begin to rise. Hank and Lenny saw it too.

"What boys?" Hank said to the dogs.

A dark figure then rushed through their camp letting out a terrific scream. The men nearly fell over as the object jetted by. They heard a quick yelp and noticed that Hank's dog had disappeared.

"What the hell was that?" Lenny shouted before a sharp pain tore through his ribs. He became woozy. Another sharp jolt ripped into him, this time in his lower abdomen before curling up towards his chest. He felt his feet lift off the ground as his ribs cracked.

"Lenny!" Hank yelled.

The rifle fell out of Lenny's hand. His body went numb.

Lenny dropped to his knees. His body paused for less than a second before toppling face first onto the hard ground.

The creature didn't pause long. It heard the barking of the dogs, hissed, and then leaped towards them.

Carl stood stunned. Lenny laid motionless, blood-streaming out onto the grassy pine-needled ground. It wasn't until he heard Pup yelp in pain that he snapped back to attention. A swirling dark figure circled like visible wind around the remaining dogs.

"Pup!" Carl stammered half confused - half terrified. It was too late as the creature ripped Pup's head off and tossed it into the stream. Hank's other dog was next but this time the whole rear end looked as if a shark chewed it off. Hank and Carl watched in a daze as the dog's torso flung about, spraying blood all over. Neither man could make out any detail of what was attacking the dogs.

Hank rushed into his tent then came out screaming with his rifle in hand. "Bastard!" he yelled. He took aim at the creature, though he couldn't get a proper fix on it and fired a shot. He aimed and took another but couldn't tell if he hit it or not.

The creature stopped and stood still. It looked at Carl, then over to Hank and locked its deep maroon glowing eyes on him. It let out a slow hiss. Hank felt a rush of fright consume his body. "Oh mother of God," he uttered, his rifle falling from his grip.

The creature screeched and charged Hank.

Carl stood petrified as he watched the creature become a blur of movement. He heard Hank scream to him, "Carl, shoot it! Shoot it."

Tears streamed down Carl's face as he watched Hank's arm get ripped clean out of the shoulder socket. Hank's screams echoed around him, his pleas for help unanswered. Carl then heard the snapping of bones, like thick branches and Hank's screams turned into cries of mercy.

The creature then turned to Carl and locked eyes with him. Carl could see blood all over the creature's black, near featureless face. Within the bat of an eye, the beast came face to face with Carl. He could smell the stench of blood and flesh on the creature's breath.

A shot rang out. The creature screamed and hissed, disappearing as quickly as it came. Carl turned, saw Hank and ran to his side. Hank had a hole in his stomach, and his left arm was missing. Yet in his right arm, he clutched a rifle.

"Hank, I'm sorry," Carl said kneeling by his side unsure of what to do for him.

Hank could barely make a sound. He managed to form a glimmer of a smile before coughing up some blood.

"Hang on buddy," Carl pleaded.

Hank's mouth opened but no words came out. His eyes closed. His body went limp.

# CHAPTER 9

Hunter arrived at headquarters already briefed on the double murder. He made a cup of coffee and settled in at his desk. A report on the lone survivor sat square before him. He picked it up and began to review it. Before he had a moment to absorb the new information, his phone rang.

"Hunter Matthews," he answered.

"Hello Detective Matthews," Casey said. "It has come to my attention that the murderer decided to go south a few towns."

He played coy. "What are you talking about?"

She didn't bite. "Don't pull that with me. The latest murders, they're related."

"You think so," he said. "What makes you think that?"

"Limbs ripped apart," she answered.

"And…" he said.

"Well I just happen to have a friend who is a fireman there and he said the scene is an awful mess. Body parts all over the place. Any comment?"

"No comment," he replied.

"Sounds similar to the farm incident, any comment?"

He put his finger in his coffee and swirled it, waiting for her to continue.

"It seems a pattern might be emerging, any comment?" she asked.

"A pattern?" he asked.

You know this little game that you play works only for so long," she said. Her voice remained calm. She knew he would never show his cards first, so she opened. "Nell's parents are very nice and concerned people."

"They are?" he said continuing to play coy.

"Yes, they were very fond of Joe. He treated her well. It was a shame that their daughter had to see some psychopath show off a prize in front of her."

"I could have you arrested for tampering with an investigation," he said.

"I've been a good sport with you," she said, her voice becoming indignant. "I've played by your rules. Besides, chatting with her parents is not against the law."

"Okay, your point?" he asked, making her work for it.

She tempered her tone. "My point is… what's going on with this case? I think I've been patient. I've played ball and I think there's a distinct pattern developing."

"You have been a good sport, I'll give you that," Hunter said. "You're on the right track." He could hear her breathe a sigh of relief on the other end of the phone. "I'm heading down to the new crime scene. When I return, I may have something for you."

"What?" she asked.

Hunter sighed. "A theory."

"What good is that going to do for me? It's about as good as the non-information you have given me about the hair sample."

"A theory needs some valid information, before you can present it…how's that?" He blew off the other remark hoping she wouldn't follow up on it.

"So you'll have something for me then?"

"It's possible."

"Possible means BS and you know it. Why can't you give me something?"

"Oh please, you know why. Listen, I want to help you but I can't jeopardize this case."

"I'm not asking for that," she shot back. "Right now it's all wild speculation. Somebody needs to add two and two together. I want to be that person."

Hunter shook his head as he audibly exhaled. "So do I. I have your number. Let me figure this out. I'll call you." His voice softened. "We'll meet. I'll have something for you to work with."

"Promise?"

He rolled his eyes at the childish question. "As much as I can promise; pinky swear," he replied and immediately hung up. He stood up to leave, shaking his head; *what am I getting myself into?* The phone rang again. "I told you I'll do what I can," he said frustrated.

"Detective Matthews?" the voice said a little taken aback.

Hunter apologized, realizing his gaffe.

"My name is Doctor Howlentz from the Klingler Hills Center of Psychiatry in Connecticut. I believe you may be after one of our patients who escaped here ten days ago."

"I see," Hunter said sitting back down.

## CHAPTER 10

Hunter arrived at the crime scene early afternoon. The walk through the high grass of the field reminded him of his days when he used to hunt with his dad. He brushed his hand along the tops of the almost waist high grass as it swayed in the breeze and tickled the palms of his hands. He hadn't thought about his dad in…

"Right over here sir," said the young officer escorting Hunter to the scene. Hunter observed several police personnel moving around the campsite area. He noticed another at the edge of the clearing, investigating the woods. As he walked closer, he spotted one of the bodies, face down in the dirt.

"I thought these bodies would be gone by now?" he said to the officer walking with him.

"The one is. Then a call came in about a bad accident that needed immediate response. EMT will be back as soon as that is taken care of." The officer looked at his watch. "Which should be any time now."

"I guess this is what you get with budget cuts and shared services," Hunter said noticing another detective approach him.

"Hunter Matthews?" the man asked.

Hunter nodded.

"Detective David Grossman."

"Yes, my captain said to meet up with you," Hunter said while shaking the detective's hand.

"I understand we have similar cases," Grossman said.

"Apparently," Hunter responded. "I e-mailed a folder of images for you to review and I understand you'll be doing the same."

"Yes and thank you. I got a call on my way here that it came in."

"So what can you tell me that I might help you with?" Hunter asked.

"Well, as you can see by these wounds and the report about the other victim, it was a brutal killing. Just a few yards away, several dogs were mutilated. You can't tell which part belonged to which dog because it's such a mess," he said pointing over to the spot. Detective Grossman then pointed out the small fire pit. "As you can see the hunters made an unauthorized fire but that isn't uncommon as I'm sure you know."

Hunter wrinkled out a wry smile. He had come across enough of these fire pits in his own time, not to mention the ones he made as a kid. He wondered how the Pine Barrens had even survived this long without the whole place turning into a tinderbox.

"The one victim, Hank Tresser, was found here," Detective Grossman said pointing to three small orange cones representing the victim. "From what we could surmise from an initial examination, he was impaled and had his left arm torn off. The other victim, Lenny Turlington, he had several ribs broken as well as an impalement. He also has a hole in his stomach that I haven't quite figured out how that happened."

Hunter looked around. "Jezz, what the hell is going on? This is one sick bastard."

"You ain't kidding," the detective added. "I'm not sure but more than one person had to have been involved to pull this off."

"How many then?" Hunter asked.

"My guess is that three extremely strong and brazen men did this. By the amount of carnage, one or two people couldn't pull this off."

"Has the lone witnessed talked?" Hunter asked.

"No, not yet. He's at the hospital under sedation and treatment."

"Maybe we can take a ride over there after this and see how he's doing. I'd sure be interested in an eyewitness report," Hunter said still scanning the site to see if he could notice anything more.

"What did your witness say?" Grossman asked knowing about the case involving Nell.

Hunter looked at him straight away. "To be honest, I think it'll be better to hear what your guy says, then compare notes."

"Alright, I'll take your word for now," Grossman answered with little emotion.

Hunter then asked. "Have the State Police been called?"

Grossman nodded.

"What's their position?"

"We haven't heard one yet. They have a guy at the station gathering information. They were here briefly. I'm sure they'll be back."

Hunter knelt to the ground. "Any theories aside from the three man one?"

"Four men?" Grossman answered knowing all he had were guesses. "We haven't found any clues. I'm waiting for a K-9 unit to arrive and see what it can find out."

Hunter looked up at him. "K-9 found nothing on our site."

"Really?"

Hunter continued to glance around. "I got a call this morning before coming here… from a psych ward. Our suspect could be one Henry Staffen. He escaped from an east Connecticut facility over a week ago. He isn't considered dangerous but he is supposed to be quite strong; abnormally strong I was told."

"Really? One guy to do this?" Grossman questioned.

"My case, one guy could have done. In fact the witness only claims to have seen one suspect kill her boyfriend," Hunter said. "I also have a farm mutilation that has some eerie similarities."

Grossman nodded, intrigued. "The state involved in yours?"

Hunter shrugged. "Not so much. A couple troopers arrived on the scene to help secure the area but otherwise they left it to us to handle. They'll keep an eye on it but we'll be doing all the work." Hunter paused a second before continuing. "You have two victims and a bunch of dogs. If they start connecting the dots they may take over the whole thing."

"Couldn't hurt to have their help," Grossman added.

"Or just make a bigger mess of it," Hunter said. "I've been involved with them a few times. They are the definition of red tape."

"Not denying that." Grossman said. "What of this Staffen guy?"

"The interesting note is that he is from south Jersey. He grew up down here. I'm expecting his file today. After I process it and look it over I will see that you get it."

"That would be helpful, because right now we have nothing to go on. I just hope K-9 is able to get us on track."

"Like I said, don't be surprised if they don't," Hunter replied as if he already knew they wouldn't.

"Something is always left behind; it's only a matter of seeing if the dogs can identify it." Grossman looked around and then up at the clear blue sky. "Especially when you get these kinds of conditions – the scent is fresh."

"No doubt," Hunter said. He knew they would find nothing out there. "When we're done here, let's check out the survivor."

CHAPTER 11

Back at his desk, Hunter pondered whether to call Casey or not. He leaned back and pulled out his pocket video recorder. He purchased it last minute on the way to see the lone survivor of the attack, Carl Messing. Detective Grossman needed to stop at an electronic store to pick up a new wireless card for his laptop. While in the store, Hunter happened to notice the small handheld video recorders and decided to record what Carl had to say rather than use his phone.

As it turned out, what they heard from Carl baffled the two detectives, neither one quite certain what to do with the account. It was just too bizarre. Both had looked at each other and couldn't comprehend how they would explain themselves to their superiors.

Hunter stared at the phone on his desk. *She could be useful, I don't know how yet but she could help us out.* He pulled out his cell phone instead and dialed Casey's number.

She answered quickly but Hunter didn't even let her say hello. "I have something you may find interesting," he said. "But the thing is we have to agree on how you are going to work with the information I give you."

"So you want to dictate my journalistic integrity?" she responded.

"Not dictate, negotiate. This could work out well for the both of us," he said. "I'm rather certain you'll agree that the information I have is delicate. If we don't proceed carefully we could, I could, jeopardize our careers."

"Really" she said with suspicion. "And how's that?"

"Tell you what. Let's meet for something to eat and I'll show you."

"Okay," she said. "I'll listen to what you have to say and we'll take it from there."

"That's all I can ask," he said.


Hunter arrived at the diner early. He felt antsy, nervous, especially since he checked her report and learned she was twenty-eight. He had just turned thirty-four. *Not too old for her.* He couldn't help but think about his attraction to her. She had shape, nice hips. He liked a woman with some curve to her, someone who didn't mirror a pencil. He also had to remember that this was a professional meeting, not a date.

He fussed in his seat. He took a booth by a window overlooking the parking lot so he could spot her coming in. It wasn't long before Casey arrived. He couldn't believe the anxious feeling that took over his body.

Casey walked in and glanced around. Hunter noticed she wore a sweater that nicely hugged her upper body. He stood up and gave a casual wave to signal her. Returning a friendly smile, she came to the booth.

"Coffee or something cold to drink?" he asked as she settled in.

"Coffee would be great," she said. Casey positioned a workbag onto her lap and took out a pad, pen and a digital voice recorder.

"Prepared are we?" Hunter said as he watched her set up a small workstation while signaling for a waitress to come over.

"Preparation and opportunity, the best recipe for success," she responded.

He nodded his head in agreement while noticing that he liked the way her sweater shaped itself around her not too large but full breasts. *It's been too long. Get it together, think straight.*

"So what interesting information do you have for me?" she asked, looking him square into his eyes, confidence brimming.

"I have some speculation, I have some facts and have a big bucketful of the surreal," he said matching her gaze and confidence. "What I need from you is a fair assessment, balance and discretion."

"Sounds like terms," she said.

"We'll get to those. I'm sorry. I just can't have full disclosure hitting the public. Besides what I have to show you isn't something people are readily going accept," he stated. "That's why it may work best for your market."

Casey sat back. She wore a quizzical look. "Enough of the cryptic stuff please. I think I should have earned your trust by now. I don't know what else you want from me."

Hunter knew she had done everything he asked. It was his job to protect information. He could have simply locked her out and made her stand in line with all the other journalists but he didn't. He felt he could trust her. He just needed time to feel comfortable with her. Trust was something he didn't offer easily.

A hint of relief came over him when the waitress finally approached and asked to take their order. It gave him the moment he needed to regroup. He ordered coffee for Casey and a refill for himself. He asked her what she wanted to eat.

"BLT, whole wheat, no mayo, please," she said not asking for a menu.

"Toasted bagel, butter and a side of fires," he said.

Casey raised an eyebrow. "Got enough carbs there?"

"Yeah... it balances my coffee intake," he replied.

She smiled. "So, what do you have for me?"

Hunter grinned as if trying to pick where to start. "I got a call you might want to check out. You could certainly work it. To what end I'm not sure," he said as he twisted his way through his thoughts. "The name is Henry Staffen. He escaped a mental facility in Connecticut, Klingler Hills it's called." He patted his chest pocket, let out a deep sigh. "I didn't bring the name of the town it's in."

Casey waved it off. "That's easy enough to find out. What about this person, Henry Staffen. Is that with an 'a'?"

"Yes, S.T.A.F.F.E.N" he said. "Born in Hammonton, New Jersey 1968… grew up in Shamong Township. A true Piney. Parents lived in the woods. Father was a handyman, an alcoholic, mother didn't work and she died when Henry was around ten. It doesn't say from what or how. The facility doesn't have a complete record on his early childhood. Don't know if he has brothers or sisters. We are trying to compile a better profile than what they have aside from his criminal record, which we are still compiling. This is where you come in. How do you feel about digging into his background?"

"He's the prime suspect?" she asked as she jotted down notes.

Hunter made a non-committal grimace. "He's a suspect but we have nothing concrete on him."

"What does that mean?" she asked.

"It means, he escaped the mental facility a week and a half ago and no one has seen him since. He has some violence in his past, nothing like what we're dealing with but some previous convictions and now he's a person of interest."

"What about the hairs you took from my car or any of the other scenes, do they link up with this guy?"

Hunter hesitated. "All samples have come back inconclusive at this time." He didn't know what else to say.

"Inconclusive?" Casey said with suspicion. "How can that be? Are you saying the sample you took off my car didn't match up with anything?"

"That's exactly what I'm saying," he said, giving up on DNA as a source of hope.

"Seems conveniently vague," she said.

"Believe me I'm not thrilled with it either. Anyway, he's a big guy," Hunter said wanting to move on to leads that might actually point to something productive. "I received this brief summation earlier today," he said pulling out a piece of paper from his workbag. "I'm supposed to get something with more details tomorrow." He skimmed through the notes. "He's six feet six inches and roughly two hundred and fifty pounds."

Casey's eyes widened as she mouthed a wow.

Hunter continued. "The director of the facility, Doctor Howlentz said that Henry wasn't a violent or disruptive patient but wouldn't rule out the possibility."

"How long has he been there?"

"Just under three years," he said looking over the information on the page.

"How did he get there?" she asked, double-checking that her voice recorder was on.

He put up a finger as he continued to glance at another page, "a series of disturbances, erratic behavior and vandalism back in his hometown. He did a small stint in county for assault but I don't have the specifics. It's all in a detailed report that is coming to me."

The waitress brought their food, which disrupted his flow. The two of them quickly positioned their plates so they could get back to business.

"So, after he was released from county, he went back home. He has no skills and soon enough, with no guidance or direction, he was out getting into trouble. It was only after destroying a neighbor's barn..." he paused as he glanced over the information. "He was picked up but not before causing a hell of a scene. Again, I have no details on this," he said flipping the page over. "Anyway, he was declared mentally unfit and after jumping around a few of the local facilities he was sent up to Klingler Hills where they were supposedly better prepared to handle a patient like him."

"Apparently not," she said. "Details on that barn incident would be nice."

"Yes it would," Hunter said. "I can only imagine what a detailed report is going to look like." He looked up at her and handed over the papers. "If you can find out anything more it would be nice to see how your findings compare with the official report."

Casey could feel the excitement brimming. "I'll see what I can find out."

"That would be helpful," he returned. "What do you plan on doing with this information?"

She looked at him with a blank stare. "I have only supposition at this point. I don't have anything concrete." She looked at the papers. "My editors aren't going to be interested in this. It isn't what they do."

Hunter grinned. "Yeah, they may not be into that but I've got something to show you." Hunter reached into his sport jacket and pulled out his video recorder. "As you know, there was a double murder and not only were the victims ripped apart but the dogs were all mutilated as well. Anyway, I went to the hospital with the detective who's running the case there." Hunter paused, looked around to make sure no one would overhear him. "We had an interesting interview with the lone survivor." He then got up from his seat and moved over to her side. "Don't mind me."

Casey smiled and slid over to make room for him.

He held the camera low to the table and in front of her. He hit play.

When the footage ended, she sat in silence with her mouth open. It took a minute for the words to sink in. "Oh my God," she gasped. She turned to him and he nodded a surprised confirmation. "Are you kidding me?" she said.

"Right out of the Book of Odd," he said low key. "I have no… we have no idea what to make of it." He got up and went back over to his side of the table.

Casey tried to process what she heard. "Why did you mention vampires to him?" she asked. "Were you trying to be clever?"

"Actually, Nell, the first victim's girlfriend mentioned a vampire when we spoke," he said. "As you heard Carl say, he had no idea what was going on, just that a whirlwind of death stormed through the camp."

"But he said he went face to face with it," she said still stunned.

"And yet he could not describe one thing about it, except that he felt it breathe into his mouth and its eyes looked through him."

"Red eyes," she whispered. "What's that?"

"Hence vampire," he said as if completing a logical reasoning.

"I'd say he needed to spend some time in an institution if the circumstances were in anyway different. How can any of that be believable?"

"He hasn't been ruled out as a suspect," Hunter said.

"You have to be kidding me," Casey shot back. "That guy did not kill his friends."

"Yeah I don't think so either but until he's cleared, he's on the list."

"Yeah... well... that's crazy stuff what he described... vampires, monsters. What's next, werewolves?" she said her voice flummoxed.

"That's why I thought you might be interested in it. This sort of thing falls far more into your current line of writing," he said.

She nodded. "You're right. It's just... too real."

"And that's the difference between what I do and what most of today's reporters do,"

She looked at him and met him eye to eye. "What's the next step?"

Hunter smiled. *I like this girl.*

## CHAPTER 12

The chill of the night air bit into the bones of Henry Staffen. His body twitched trying to shake the cold but to no avail. He had been living outdoors for nearly two weeks. Only two of the nights, he managed to sneak some sleep in abandoned barns. It was dangerous to sneak into a barn; no good of it had ever come to him for as long as he could remember but the last few nights had been chilly and he sought warmth.

Visions of beatings, straps, needles, and screaming filled his mind. He rarely ever felt at peace lying on a bed inside a place. The outdoors had always provided solace. His best childhood memories all took place outside, him and his dad camping and fishing. Those tranquil times were distant to him now especially after his father succumbed to the bottle. His father's smile was vague in his mind but the image of the two of them sitting along a lake on a sunny day, talking and casting their rods was all he needed to bring him comfort in times of anguish.

The hollowed cedar tree he fashioned into a bed was damp. He wore some extra shirts he had stolen off a laundry line and he covered himself in as many leaves as he could. He had even spread out pine needles to act as a cushion but he still couldn't get comfortable and the chill made him restless.

Looking up through the trees, he could tell overcast skies kept the stars from shinning. He felt it might rain. He didn't usually mind rain but now the thought of it made him feel anxious. With every passing minute, he became more restless. He began to think of where he last saw a barn or shed or some structure where he could seek warmth. Places and days all blurred together now. He couldn't remember if he passed a barn yesterday or a few days ago.

Finally, he got up from his hovel. He looked around trying to remember which direction he had come from. With no moonlight, it took more time for his eyes to adjust to the darkness. He tried staying off the trails but needed to remember where the closest one was in order to move quickly through the woods at night. He scanned back and forth a few times and the shapes of the woods became clearer to him. He started to walk, *yes, this way*. He headed towards two pitch pines that formed a unique V shape. It's what initially drew him off the trail. He quickened his pace. *This is the way.*

The cloudy night began to produce a light rain. Henry didn't know how long he'd been walking but he thought long enough that the sun should start to come up. His legs ached. His chest heaved to take in air. He felt exhausted.

As he made his way along the sandy trail, his feet continually slid in small movements. At times, it was hard for him to keep his balance. It also tired him more than a normal hard dirt trail would.

Henry stopped at hearing the faint sound of sheep bleating. He couldn't see them. The sound floated from all directions like a soft echo. He continued, but slower and more aware. His legs stopped aching and his breathing eased as he mustered all his attention to listening for the sheep. He knew wherever they were, shelter would follow. He smiled at the thought of warmth.

It only took a few minutes before he spotted a fence line. The fence bordered the woods and an open field. Then he heard the sheep again. Now it came from a discernable direction. He still couldn't see much in the dark. The sound came from his right. He proceeded at a quick pace and within a hundred yards spotted the sheep and even better…a barn.

The old barn looked perfect to Henry. He could smell the hay and that was a good smell to him. As he crossed the property, he saw that the sheep did not mind his presence. Looking around, he spotted the main house. Partially hidden by several large trees, he hoped no one saw him.

The mist picked up into a steadier rain. He wasn't sure if the temperature was dropping or the chill in his bones was setting in. Henry moved closer to the barn. When he got to the back door, he turned the knob and to his delight, the door opened.

Henry quickly looked for a safe place to lie down. The animals inside stirred a little but nothing that would attract attention. He spotted a ladder going up to the top loft and climbed it. Once there, he lay down on the hay. His eyes went heavy and he breathed a deep breath of relaxation. *This is warm. This is nice.* Within a matter of seconds, he was fast asleep.

Henry woke to the rustling of animals and two voices that were clearly inside the barn. He froze. The voices didn't betray alarm or anything out of the ordinary. Frightened, he hoped the voices would go away but they didn't. Instead, the voices carried on; talking about subjects he couldn't quite make out. From time to time, he heard them break into laughter.

Whomever they were, Henry could tell they were working. He could here metal bang and other noises that wouldn't occur on their own. He felt himself sink deeper into the hay.

He then heard the big barn doors squeak open and felt a rush of crisp air and bright light fill the place. The noise of the animals began to fade. *They're letting them out.* Henry's tension began to ease but his relaxed state awakened his hunger. He also realized that he had to pee. The urge wouldn't diminish and before he knew it, he found himself out of the hay and standing in the loft. His eyes darted around looking for a place to relieve himself. Spotting a bucket, he walked over to it and saw it was empty. He listened as best he could to hear any voices but none came.

Henry felt much better as he finished but then noticed the flooring around the bucket started to discolor. His eyes widened. He leaned over and looked more carefully at the bucket. A crack in the bottom allowed his urine to leak out.

A voice suddenly came closer. From his angle, he could make out a figure entering the barn. Henry began to shake.

The person who entered the barn stopped and slowly scanned the surroundings. The person sensed something was not quite right.

Panicky voices began to fill Henry's head. They became louder and louder. Some were saying *Get out! Get out!* Others were screaming *Run!* And in the distant recess of his mind, he could hear the faint chant of *Kill*. Yet he stayed frozen, paralyzed in place. Through the cracks in the floor, he watched the person move with caution. Henry's voices began to speak in chorus; *Run, run, find a window, any opening and fly.* He turned, and spotted two possible exits; one was an ordinary window and it was open. The other exit was the closed gable where the hay loaded in. He couldn't tell if it was locked or not. He wanted to fly out that open window but he knew if he moved he'd give himself away.

The footsteps below Henry stopped. Silence followed. Perspiration started to fall off his face and hit the floor. For Henry, the splats of sweat resonated like cymbals crashing. He began to breathe loud.

"Shit," said the man below. "What's this?"

When Henry heard the footsteps come towards the ladder, every voice that screamed in his head earlier went silent. There was nothing. His world became an empty void. His body oddly began to relax.

The person below began to make his way up the ladder. With each pull of the rung and footstep up, Henry knew he was closer to his escape. His panic turned into a feeling of ecstasy. Adrenaline pulsated through his body. The taste of it brought a smile to his face. His muscles began to tighten but in a familiar way that gave him joy. As the top of the persons head made itself visible, Henry kicked the bucket towards the ladder, splashing the remaining contents onto the person. The voices, like thunder in his head, screamed *FLY!*

"What the f… who the hell! Stop you piece of… jeez," the person cried out. It was too late. All he saw was a figure crash open the gable door and jump out.

The farm hand ran to the opening, wondering what the hell that odd smell was. Looking out the window, he watched a large figure of a man run, with the swiftness of a deer, into the woods. He stood stunned. It was at least a fifteen or twenty foot drop to the ground below. Surely, the person would have hurt an ankle, a leg or a hip, from a jump like that. Yet at the rate in which the figure ran, it certainly didn't appear as if he hurt anything. Then, remembering the strange barn slaughtering that had occurred a few weeks back; he wondered if this was the same person.

Henry ran hard. The voices in his head said nothing as his body kept running. His legs just kept going. He leaped over every log and object that he encountered. His breathing was controlled and focused. This was only the second time in recent memory he could recall running this fast. The first was when he left the hospital and all the straps and needles and, of course, the nightmares.

The woods became denser, and the under-brush grew thicker. He slowed his pace. He had run through a lot of brush. When he finally stopped to catch his breath, he noticed all the cuts in his pants. Traces of blood had soaked through. He knew he couldn't stay still for long. He needed to get far away. Far away was better, safer. The voices would tell him when it was safe to stop. The voices always told him the right thing to do.

# CHAPTER 13

"You're saying he flew?" asked Hunter. "Like flying flew or the 'ran so fast' it's as if he flew?"

The farmhand needed a moment to think. The whole incident had happened so fast. He was at a loss for details. He stammered as he tried to put the pieces of the incident together.

"You said it flew, Jack," chimed in Paul Hackett, the owner of the farm and the other person who was there that morning. "And when I asked if you meant, like in flying you said yes."

"I did? It was just so weird. It was like a flash and it or he was gone. When I looked out the doors, he was off and running like nothin' I've ever seen before. He was damn near the fence when I finally saw him."

Hunter watched Jack's body and facial expressions, the slumping shoulders, the befuddled squint of the eyes. He wasn't lying, of that much Hunter was certain. *No one gets that dumbfounded, unless of course...* "So there was no flying when you looked out the window?"

"No sir, just a lot of fast running. I'd never seen no one ever run like that 'cept a deer."

"Okay, that's good," Hunter said. "Now... you said 'it'. Why do you think you said that?"

"Well," Jack said scratching his head, then the back of his neck. "Well, cause... when something like that moves as quick as it did and just shot out the doors after spilling a bucket of piss, you have to wonder what the hell that was? Who holds a leaky bucket of piss and flies out gable doors?"

Hunter scrunched his brow at this new tidbit of information. "That's true. Holding a leaky bucket of pee is certainly not the kind of thing you'd call normal." He paused. "How did you know it was a bucket of piss?"

"Yeah, well I guess, because piss can sometimes have a smell to it. And I just don't reckon there's a whole lot of things in the world that smell like piss."

Hunter nodded again. "There's certainly truth to that. Now, can you show me where this happened?"

The nip of the morning's fresh spring air was even colder when the wind picked up. Hunter gazed out into the woods before entering the barn. Thick grey clouds hung over the scene adding to the already mysterious aura. *Was Henry here or was something else…*

"Right in here sir," Paul Hackett said pointing towards the big open doors of the barn.

Hunter acknowledged him and followed the two men in. The smell was the same as every other barn he had ever stepped into, hay, animal, feed and shit. The layout was almost a duplicate of the Denten farm where he examined the first slaughter. Slowly, looking over the stalls he scanned all the various tools, straps, buckets and enough spare parts to build another tractor. Nothing looked out of the ordinary, unlike the Denten place where blood and body parts littered one of the stalls.

"Up here sir," said Jack. The farmhand pointed to the wooden ladder that led up to the hayloft.

"You go first," Hunter said. Then, one after the other the three men went up the ladder. At first glance, the loft didn't look out of order. It was a basic hayloft; lots of hay, a variety of rakes, ropes, pitchforks, tools and miscellaneous items that he couldn't identify and was sure he would never have an occasion to use.

Hunter spotted the bucket on the floor and could see the residual stain. He approached it, kneeled down and examined it further. There was no smell, for which he was thankful. He had no desire to smell the spot either. Still, he had to have someone come out and take a sample as well as comb through the hay for DNA.

Hunter walked over to the gable doors. One of the two large swinging doors was open. The other had closed. "So he went out here?"

"Out and down and gone," Jack said as he nodded his affirmation.

Hunter got closer to the opening and looked down. It was a serious leap. *That is one desperate man.* He peered off into the woods beyond the fence line. Looking back down, he couldn't conceive of 'just jumping.' If you landed the wrong way, it was an easy broken leg if not worse. "And you're saying he just took off for the woods?"

Both Jack and Paul approached the opening. "Yes sir," said Jack. "When I got this far, he was nearly at the woods."

Hunter examined the dimensions surrounding him. He looked back at the ladder and then the distance covered between it and the gable doors. It wasn't more than thirty feet at best.

"Let me get this straight," Hunter said, looking to clarify. "You are saying that from the time you saw this figure leap out these doors, until you got to this spot, he was near the woods?" Hunter looked back out over the land shaking his head in disbelief. The distance between the barn and the woods looked to be close to a football field in length.

Jack nodded his head.

"So it was a man?" Hunter asked.

"As much as I could tell."

"What was this person wearing?"

"It was darkish. I really don't know what color you would call it. It looked dirty."

"Brown?" asked Hunter.

"Like dirt color I guess but not the whole thing."

"Okay," Hunter replied. "Can you show me the path he ran?"

Jack nodded and pointed out the direction the suspect went. It was a straight line right into where a group of pines looked to cluster together, just beyond the fence line.

"Alright then, let's head out there and take a look at the ground."

Outside they walked around in the area where the suspect could have landed. Hunter asked them to stay back a bit as he walked along the mostly bare area gazing back and forth from the window to the ground. He looked carefully for any disturbance that resembled a depression. The ground was moist dirt with sparse grass spots. The area saw a lot of traffic by machine, man and animal.

"Have either one of you been walking through here since the incident?" he asked the two men standing about twenty feet away from him.

"No sir," said Paul Hackett. "We even managed to keep the animals from roaming around back here. Can't say if one of the dogs hasn't been sniffing around though."

Hunter didn't see any fresh dog tracks. He bent down and checked out what looked like a depression but not a discernable footprint. The best he could determine was it *might* be a landing spot but he didn't hold out much hope for that possibility. He turned in the direction of the fence line and followed a path with his eyes that led towards the cluster of trees he had seen from the hayloft. It was a straight line. He stood up and then looked for a trail of some sort. Hunter had learned some basic tracking skills as a kid and then some more after he joined the force. In this instance, he was coming up blank. *Surely, someone would leave a track of some sort.* He turned back to the depression in the dirt… maybe. Looking back up towards the loft, he estimated the trajectory to the spot was feasible. He continued inspecting until his phone rang.

"Detective Matthews," he answered. "Yes. I need this farm declared a crime scene. I want to determine whether Mr. Staffen was the person who was here. I'm certain there will be fingerprints to work with as well as DNA." He listened. "Yes, put out a bulletin for the area." He looked at his watch. "It's been almost 3 hours since the incident occurred. A healthy person could do maybe 10 miles max in this environment given proper water, food and resting times. The region is quite expansive but at least we have a quadrant to work with." He looked up at the sun. "Based on the information I have, I'd concentrate the patrols to the southeast, south and southwest." He paused again before talking, "the suspect is in dark clothes, dirty clothes. It would seem that he's been sleeping in the woods a lot, it's about all I can give you at this time aside from the descriptions we already have." He listened to the officer on the other end before interrupting, "Yes there is something else. I would like a K-9 unit to come here and see if we can pick up a scent."

He hung up the phone and looked back at the men. "A crime unit is on its way to look for fingerprints, hair samples, and check out that stain. So please do not touch or disturb the area. Now I'll ask you again. Did either one of you touch anything in that loft?"

Both of the men looked at each other and said no.

Hunter nodded. "Alright, if you have any questions call me," he said as he reached for a business card. "If you remember anything more, you call me. And another thing, if anyone from the press comes around, you say nothing. You just refer them to the police. Anything more than that is only asking for trouble and possible legal consequences and I don't think either of you want to deal with that?"

They both nodded that they understood.

"What happens if that suspect should come back?" Paul asked.

"He won't," Hunter said.

Henry watched several police cars go by. There seemed to be a lot of them. He kept low behind a pair of fallen trees. He needed some rest. His legs ached after running nearly nonstop through brush, crossing over a few creeks, and stumbling into a swamp, before coming to his current location less than a hundred feet from a road. *Just need a little rest.* He knew he couldn't stay in one place too long. He needed to move on. He looked out at the road. The voices told him to stay put and keep low. He liked the advice.

Henry jerked, realizing he had fallen asleep. Whipping his head frantically from side to side, it took a few seconds for him to get his bearings. Once settled he carefully scanned his surroundings. He listened for cars but didn't hear any. He stood up and walked closer to road. He ditched behind a thick oak that hugged the shoulder. Then he heard the drone of a distant car coming towards him. He fell to ground and squirmed back towards some underbrush. *You're safe* said a voice. A few seconds later a State Trooper zoomed right by him. He watched the car disappear down the long straight road. Once it was gone, he got up and made his way to the woods edge again. Taking a slow methodical step out onto the shoulder, he looked both ways up and down the road, saw nothing and darted across into the woods on the other side. Once again, his legs began pumping hard and he was off and running at full speed.

Hunter received an e-mail from Casey with a link to The Evening Door and a piece she wrote about the farm mutilation. He felt his stomach wince. He spun the cursor over the link.

Looking across his desk, a litany of paperwork awaited his attention. He picked up the folder marked Joe West, the young man killed on the side of the road. He thumbed through one of the folders to reread how the K-9 units couldn't find a discernible trail. The dogs had given the officers mixed signals as to the direction the perpetrator could have gone. None of the directions led anywhere.

Hunter looked back at his computer screen. The link pulled at him like something from Edgar Allen Poe's, *The Tell Tale Heart*. He tried to divert his attention by reading some reports but time and again, he would look up at the screen to see the link there, begging him to open it. Finally, like an addict caving in, he clicked it. A moment later her story popped up titled, *Mysterious Mutilations in the Pine Barrens*. He skimmed through it looking more for inconsistencies than content or style. All the facts lined up. He grinned reading her creative license but he couldn't find fault with the facts. He was relieved that she kept her word. Then he read the last sentence and paused. He read it again while shaking his head and biting his bottom lip. He pulled out his cell phone. He had to call her.

The sun sank lower in the sky. Henry began to feel safer but his stomach screamed for food. It had been over twenty-four hours since he last ate. He looked for some old dead trees. It wouldn't be the first time he ate bugs to relieve hunger. He scrounged along the ground and overturned a few rocks to reveal a couple beetles. He scooped them up and swallowed them. After spotting a large branch that was in obvious decay, he rolled it and pulled out a few juicy worms. He didn't care for the taste or squishy texture but he knew it would have to do.

Henry soon came to a dark cedar creek. He decided to follow it for a while, occasionally walking into it to clean up a little and take a few sips to refresh himself. He knew he would run into a farm, backwoods house or small town at some point. It wasn't as if he was out west when he had hiked in Colorado as a kid with his dad. Out there, you could disappear into the mountains and just live without seeing anyone, forever, if you really wanted. He remembered his dad loving it out there. When they returned home, his dad tried to teach him as much as he could about surviving out in the woods.

Henry remembered lots of the lessons and it had helped keep him hidden, safe and alive. What he needed now was something to eat but he also knew he had to locate or erect some kind of shelter before nightfall.

It didn't take long for him to find a place to bed down. Locating a partially fallen tree, Henry assembled a crude lean-to. He then padded the ground with leaves and pine needles. As he finished, he was quite happy with it and wondered if his dad would think it worthy of sleeping in. *Of course he would, he loved me so much.*

While he still had some light, he went to the creek he had been following. He wanted to see if he could find anything to eat. He took off his dirty clothes and waded into the water. Carefully, he upturned some rocks to see if he could find any crayfish but quickly gave up on the idea. He set his sights on locating frogs. He knew he only had about an hour of light before darkness would envelop the forest. As he waded through the creek, he came up on some fishing string entangled on an overhanging branch. He eagerly started to work the string hoping he could use a decent length of it. *Ten feet, give me ten feet.* His eyes darted around the creek and into the woods, always listening for anyone who might see him. He was deep in the forest, but if fishing string could find its way to here then he couldn't be as far away from a trail or road as he thought.

He untangled almost fifteen feet of line, when it dawned on him to look for the hook. He became frantic, thinking he may have wasted all this time in hopes of fish when he could have been looking for frogs. His stomach roared with pangs as his hopes briefly sank. Henry breathed a sigh of relief when he located a small hook. Cutting the line with his teeth, he retied the hook to the line he had salvaged. Excited, he scrambled out of the water, making more noise than he wanted. Turning over some rocks and larger branches, he found a few worms. Fastening a worm to the hook, he tossed his line into the water while roping some around his hand. Gently, he tugged at the line, nothing. The current was soft and he knew the spot wasn't the best place for fish. Seeing the muted sunlight cutting through the trees, he guessed he had a half hour of light left. Locating his shelter, he tied off his line then made a rough cairn on the shoreline to mark his location. Taking a guess, he walked up stream with his line to see if he could find quicker waters where he stood a better chance at catching a fish.

Henry waded naked through both shallow and shoulder deep water but it was all slow moving and calm. It didn't take much effort to walk up stream. All the time he kept aware of his surroundings. He also kept watch for any frogs that might make for an easy catch. Wood Frogs began to fill the forest with their call but they weren't a viable option: too small and hard to find.

Holding a couple worms in one hand, and the hook and line in the other, he finally spotted a stronger current. He worked his way out of the creek and walked the water's edge. He found a section he thought looked promising and gently tossed his line out. Pulling, tugging and then letting the line drift back again, he followed this routine for a few minutes before a fish hit the hook. With a solid yank, he knew he had it. He pulled the line, turning his wrist like a reel to bring it in. His eyes lit up, a trout; not big but it wasn't a baby either. Looking for the sun once again, he saw it disappearing near the horizon line as darkness began to settle in. Henry plopped back into the water, sticking a finger in through the trout's gills and out its mouth, he headed back to his shelter.

When he reached the cairn, he pulled himself out of the creek. Without hesitation, he picked up a rock and crushed the head of the trout. When it didn't move anymore, he bit into it. It tasted both wonderful and slimy. He moaned a little as he chewed it. In less than five minutes he was done. Rinsing his hands in the creek, he took the remains of the fish and tossed it to the other side of the bank. He knew if it was anywhere near him it might attract a raccoon and he didn't want to deal with that.

Back at his lean to, he nestled into the pine needle bedding. Satisfied and not as hungry, he fell fast asleep.

## CHAPTER 14

Hunter walked into the diner, angry. He visualized throwing stuff, dishes and coffee cups smashing into little pieces. He thought his fingers might cramp from how hard he clenched them into a fist. *Breathe easy Hunter.* He looked back and forth to see if Casey had arrived. After a second look around, he spotted her waving him over to where she was sitting. She flashed a friendly smile. That dented his mood some. He also noticed she was wearing another form-fitting sweater that accentuated her figure. *Does she do this on purpose?*

"I got here early this time and got you a cup of coffee," she said.

Hunter tried toning down his anger but couldn't hide it in his face. "Thanks," he said as he slid into the booth.

"Something's wrong," she said.

He raised his eyebrow and looked at her with a sarcastic, master of the obvious, stare. "Yeah something's wrong," he nearly barked.

Casey held firm. "Listen, I didn't agree to come here to get my ear chewed off."

He gave her another look, not as angry. "Please. It isn't about you," he replied as if blowing off her response.

"Then what?" she blurted, expecting an explanation for the attitude.

Hunter turned to look out the window. *No point exploding.* He picked up his coffee and took a sip. "I wanted a K-9 unit to go out to a farm I investigated earlier today to check out a possible lead."

"Another bizarre killing?" she said softer but straightforward.

"No," he said. "Staffen may have bunked down for the night in a barn. A farmhand scared him and he took off into the surrounding woods."

"I don't understand why your prime suspect wouldn't warrant a K-9 unit," she said suspiciously.

"Turns out the witness couldn't I.D. him. Turns out the suspect jumped out a window and took off for the woods."

"Jumped out what window?"

"Not a window, sorry but from what I can gather, he slept in this hayloft, second floor and when he was discovered, jumped through these gable doors. How he did it without breaking something is beyond me but supposedly he did." Hunter took another sip of coffee. "By the time this farmhand, the witness, looked out the door, the guy was sprinting into the woods."

"And no one else saw this?"

"That's right," he said.

"And that's why they aren't sending out a K-9 unit?" she said, easily following the logic of his superiors.

"You pick up quick," he said more reserved.

She shrugged. "It's not hard to see. You have nothing but an eyewitness who can't give you much and no evidence to go on. I guess I can see wanting to focus your resources elsewhere."

He nodded. "Normally I can see that. But I had urine to work with."

Casey laughed in confusion. "What?"

"The guy pee'd and there was a residual sample that is being checked out. So there is a chance for DNA and they may have found some other hairs and fibers in the hay."

Casey became exasperated at hearing this turn of events. "And they wouldn't send out a unit for that? At least you have something tangible. There's a possible murderer running around out there."

"I know," Hunter said happy someone empathized with him. "Currently the K-9 unit is busy with the double murder. Those folks don't have a unit to work with so there are a lot of shared services with other towns in the county. My boss can't justify reassigning manpower and dog power for what may simply be a trespassing vagrant."

Casey shook her head with disbelief. "I guess."

"Bureaucracy can suck," he said half under his breath.

They both sat in silence, letting the tenor of their situation soak in. The clicks, clinks and murmurs of the diner floated through the air like white noise. It acted as a soothing tone and they both sat comfortably in a brief moment of peace.

Casey was the first to break the silence. "You know," she said pointing with the spoon she had just used to stir her tea. "I have a friend who trains dogs. In fact, I know he has trained dogs for tracking. He's even done some work for various police departments."

"Really?" Hunter said perking up.

"What do you think about me seeing if he can help us out?"

Hunter found the use of 'us' amusing. He nodded. "I have to double check my schedule. Is he going to want a fee or something?"

"I don't know. I know he's good at what he does and maybe he can use this as a training tool."

Hunter straightened up in the seat. He liked this new option. "Let's make it happen."

"I'll make the call," she said. They both looked at each other as if they had just closed a successful business deal.

"By the way," she asked half forgetting why they were getting together. "Why did you ask me to meet you here? I know it wasn't for this."

Hunter remembered why he called her and his annoyance started to resurface. He pretended to search his mind so that he wouldn't snap at her. "Oh yeah, I nearly forgot. What the hell was that bit about the Jersey Devil in your article?"

"You liked that?" she replied smiling.

"Not really," he quipped. "Stuff like that just encourages the fringe whackos to get involved. It means more goofy phone calls, more dead ends. It just adds a lot of noise where I don't need it."

Casey nodded agreeing with what he said. "But what if it's true?"

"What if *what's* true?" Hunter shot back.

She shrugged. "What else do you have? A lot of odd stuff adds up to a pretty odd analysis."

"And this coming from the lab of Doctor Who Dunnit and Ran? I know there are a lot of odd circumstances but come on," he said, not believing how the conversation turned.

"Listen," she said calmly. "I did some digging around and this isn't the first farm mutilation that's been associated with the Jersey Devil. In fact there have been quite a few over the years."

"What?" he said with disdain.

"Yeah," she continued. "Most of the cases I found happened further south in the state but as for the brutality, this isn't out of line. It seems more brutal because we're up close and personally involved. But this isn't such a big leap."

"Okay, okay. Did a brick just fall and smack you on your head?" he said.

"I'm serious."

Hunter closed his eyes, took a breath and couldn't believe he was going to indulge her. "When did these occur? News of some kind would have made its way up here at some point, so you need to give me an example or three," he said.

She shuffled. "Well, the last one that I came across was from 88," she said with a sheepish delivery.

"1988?" he said with derision.

She took a more defensive posture. "Yes, 1988, but there have been reports of this sort going back to the nineteenth century."

"I know there have been all kinds of weird stuff that happens on the edges of dark and spooky woods all over the world. Hell, I've watched *MonsterQuest* on the History Channel. Lots of tales, no evidence, no proof but some good music and great narrating," he said.

She stared at him. "I'm just saying. This is what I do and I have plenty of resources. Do you think I went into this field believing all this stuff? Hell, I needed to work and I can write. It also turns out that I'm pretty good at this stuff. But let me tell you something; there's a whole lot of weird crap going on in the world that the average person is blind to. Not everything is easily explainable with perfect, tangible reasoning. I'm simply saying it's possible that some weird shit is afoot here and you need to at least keep an open mind about alternative possibilities."

"This is a bit too alternative for me. I guess my intuition with you was off, I thought…"

Casey interrupted his flow as she slid a small stack of 8x10 photos across the table.

"What are these?" he asked picking up the photos.

"Those are remains of what you saw at the Denten farm but it's not the Denten farm, its three different farms. They're pictures that resemble the same type of incident you investigated, just at different points in time." She paused to let him absorb her words and look over the pictures. "All these reports talk about a strange creature menacing their animals, strange screeches in the night. Some have reported seeing a flying creature bounce along the air, wailing as it disappeared into the night. Many of them have blamed the Jersey Devil for what happened. I have taken the liberty of obtaining a few old police reports and I'm waiting on others. Would you like to see the rest of them?"

He waved for her to handover what she had. He said nothing as he took the folder, opened it, thumbed through some of the paperwork and then went back to checking out the pictures. The similarity in the style of killing piqued his curiosity. The pictures were essentially variations of what he had witnessed, with limbs cleanly ripped from sockets, lots of blood, bowels gutted, and body parts strewn about.

Hunter replayed in his mind the evidence of the latest double murder, then Joe, then the farm mutilation. Comparing those mental notes with these pictures, it was hard not put the two together. *Detectives don't think this way. This can't be. This is wrong, get a grip.* Still, something in his gut told him not to blow this off. He clenched his teeth while closing his eyes. *Tell me I'm not considering this because of a pretty face.*

He dropped the photos onto the table and scooted out of the booth. He stood, almost as if standing to attention. "Call your guy," he said. "Call him. If he can do this, we'll meet at Jersey Joe's Tomatoes out on 571 in New Egypt. I'll call with an exact time. The earlier the better… you know the place?"

Casey nodded.

"Good."

She could see he was serious. She knew she was witnessing a change in his perception of reality. "You okay?"

"A little wierded out to be honest, but I'll be fine," he answered. "Remember, meet at Jersey Joe's Tomatoes."

"Got it. Would you like to check out these reports?" she asked.

"Not now. I have to go," he said as he took ten dollars out of his pocket and placed it on the table. "I'll see you tomorrow."

# CHAPTER 15

Casey walked out of Jersey Joe's, the scent of warm chicken parmesan soothing her nasal passages. She brought the bag closer to her face one last time before getting to Troy Brock's car. She needed to embed any kind of refreshing scent into her olfactory glands because the stench of dog embedded in the fabric of Troy's car overpowered her to the point of nausea. Twice on the trip, she felt a touch of vomit run up her esophagus. She choked it back down, trying her best to hide the wince of disgust. She liked dogs but wasn't a dog person per se'. The thirty-minute ride to the meeting place didn't help change her opinion. Troy owned beautiful dogs and the two he had in the back of his faded silver station wagon were gorgeous, brown coated, happy tongue hanging Coonhounds who kept a keen eye on Casey waiting for her to pet them.

Troy stood along the side of his car as Casey approached. His lean, almost gaunt frame made him look taller than he was. He dressed in bulky clothes to give the impression of more size but it didn't work. An older man in his late 50's, his face showed weariness, deep cut lines along his cheeks and forehead, as if the world had dealt him a hard hand. His dirty blonde hair was disheveled but not to the point where he looked unkempt. Casey had met Troy a number of times through her job at another newspaper writing human-interest stories. The editors often assigned her to do people and their animals. Troy became a good go-to story. They struck up a friendly relationship. Casey had a soft spot for people she thought looked lonely and could use company. Any time she interviewed or talked with him he never mentioned anything about family, wife, children, or friends. While talking to him once in his makeshift office inside an old motorhome, she noticed all the pictures hanging on the walls only had him and his dogs in them.

"They didn't have any hot turkey available for a sandwich," Casey said as she approached the car. "So I got you a chicken parm."

"Thank you," he said. "That's perfectly fine."

She opened the bag to take out the sandwiches and the aroma brought a relaxing expression to her face. "You don't mind if I eat this out here do you?" she asked.

He reached out his hands to take the bag, "No no, put the bag right here on the hood. It's a nice day, let's enjoy the sun."

In her mind, she let out a 'Thank God'. She looked towards the back of the car and saw the dogs panting heavily as they watched the two of them start in on their early lunch. "Will they be alright?" Casey asked looking back at the dogs.

Troy turned to them and saw how eager they looked. He told her they'd be fine and that he would give them something to hold them over when they got to the site.

Casey pulled out her phone and saw that it was ten minutes to eleven. She wanted to text and let Hunter know they were waiting but didn't. She had an urge to hear his voice but kept her emotions in check and decided just to enjoy the sandwich.

It was a minute before eleven according to Casey's phone when Hunter pulled up. He got out of the car and immediately came over wearing a big grin. "Beautiful day. I see you guys are finishing up eating. Sounds like a good idea. Hope you don't mind if I grab something real quick?"

His enthusiasm caught Casey by surprise. "Hunter, this is Troy Brock and in the back are Petey and Bower."

Hunter reached out to shake Troy's hand. He turned and gave the two dogs a quick wave. "Beautiful dogs," he said. "Good to meet you Troy, thanks for coming out. I appreciate you doing this for us."

Troy stood tall. "It's my pleasure sir. I gotta work these two when I can to help keep them sharp."

"Who are you training them for?" Hunter asked as he took off his sunglasses.

"Oh no, these two are mine," he said.

"Keep the best for yourself?" Hunter said with a grin.

Troy shook his head. "Not really. Actually, these two didn't make the cut. When they don't, I either sell them as pets or keep them."

"What do you mean, didn't make the cut?" Hunter asked his grin fading.

Troy could see the change in expression. "No, they are fine trackers. Just when it comes to official work, they don't make the cut because of their personality." Troy walked to the back of his car. "You see Petey here," pointing to the dog with the light brown coat and dirty white spots, "he's kind of A.D.D. He can get distracted easily but if you stay on him and keep him focused, he's great. And Bower here. Well let's just say, he's too friendly. Police like their dogs a bit more formal. He's not formal. You'll see when I let him out."

Hunter regained his confidence. "Alright then, sounds like we have an interesting team. Let me get something to eat real quick and we'll be on our way."

Casey had wished Hunter offered her a ride to the farm. Even though the trip was only ten minutes, it took roughly a tenth of a second for the stench of the Troy's car to toss Casey's stomach into revulsion. When she noticed Hunter turn on his directional to pull into the property, she rejoiced inside, anxious to cleanse her lungs and senses with clean air.

After pulling up close to the house, Hunter made sure they both knew the game plan; he'd do the talking and as far as the farmer was concerned, they were part of the investigative team. Hunter reminded them if they acted the part, no one would ask any questions.

Casey and Troy stayed near the car waiting for Hunter to call them over. They watched as Hunter talked with two men who glanced over at them with curious anticipation. Casey quickly found out what Troy meant about Bower being friendly as she caught a face full of dog tongue when Troy said it was okay for her to pet them. He quickly admonished Bower as Casey worked to wipe off the sticky spit from her face. Troy apologized but she laughed it off and said she hoped the dogs brought that much passion into tracking the trail.

They only had to wait a couple minutes before Hunter waved for them. He introduced Troy, Casey and the two dogs. Once again, Bower needed some restraining from his over eagerness to meet new people. The farmers found it funny and enjoyed the playfulness. Troy asked, in a professional manner, for the men not to encourage the behavior.

"I hope the trail hasn't gone cold?" Paul Hackett asked half joking in a worried way.

Troy reassured him it hadn't. "It would have to rain an awful lot for these two not to track a scent. A day old trail won't be a problem but I understand you don't have any kind of sample for them."

"Partly right, we have a hayloft where the suspect was but no clothes or anything like that," Hunter interjected before anyone could answer. "But I was under the impression you didn't need one; that if I brought you to the loft, they should be able to pick up a scent and track the trail."

"Yes. They often can." Troy said, "As long as the sample area has stayed relatively uncontaminated, they'll be fine. But before we go any further, I want Bower and Petey to sniff your hands, this way, they will have no problems differentiating the scent."

"Good. Let's do this," Hunter said as they all put out their hands for the dogs to smell.

When Paul Hackett swung the barn door open, the dogs immediately calmed down, their tails stopped wagging and their tongues no longer hung out the sides of their mouths. Troy led them in.

"The hayloft you said?" Troy asked the farmer.

Paul nodded. "The dogs can use the dumb-waiter to get up there," he said motioning towards it.

"I think we can take it from here," Troy said. The dogs entered cautiously but obediently. Paul made sure the dumb-waiter lifted properly as Troy made his way up the ladder, followed by Casey and Hunter.

The dogs worked their way through the loft, immediately smelling where the suspect had urinated. When alerted to what it was the dogs were sniffing, Troy had them move on. They spent a significant amount of time roving through the piled hay.

"They have something," Troy said as they watched the dogs narrow their circling. "It's a tough scent to distinguish unlike say a mattress where so much of a scent can be absorbed. But they can pick up on something to work with."

"I hope so," said Hunter, watching and studying the dogs work. He had observed K-9 units work in the past and these dogs worked with a similar pattern. Yet, unlike most trained dogs that will sit or bark to show they have located something, these two dogs paced in a narrow circle. Then Petey broke from the hay, scampered to the gable doors, and sniffed around that location.

"He got 'em!" Troy exclaimed.

"Great!" Casey shouted enjoying the moment.

Hunter was thoroughly impressed. He hadn't been sure if the dogs could pull it off. Now he hoped they could track the scent.

Eager to get out of the loft, Troy ushered the dogs into the dumb-waiter. When they all descended, Hunter led them around to the back of the barn where the suspect had landed.

The dogs immediately began to work the area. They watched as the dogs circled the suspected landing spot. Petey started to stray from the scene and off into the direction of the woods. Then he made his way back to the original spot and circled again. A few seconds later Bower left the circle and began to walk the same path Petey did. The two dogs alternated this ritual a few times, each time taking the suspected path further and further.

"That is amazing," said Casey.

Troy beamed as he watched his prized dogs work so diligently. "They've got a scent, and they are working it."

The two dogs soon left the plot of ground they were circling and steadily made their way in the direction the farmhand had said the suspect went. Troy, Hunter and Casey followed. The dogs picked up the pace, until they came to the fence line, where they stopped and again began to circle. Bower, stood up on his hind legs, placed his front paws on the fence, and began to sniff around.

Hunter turned to Troy. "Can they stay here for a minute or do they need to immediately follow the trail?"

"Are you going somewhere?" Casey asked, looking perplexed.

"A map, I want to retrieve my maps, so we can have a sense of where we are headed," he replied.

"They can remain here," Troy said.

"What? No GPS?" Casey interjected with a tone of sarcasm.

"You have a GPS on you?"

"No", she replied. "What about your phone?"

"I don't have anything topographical or that shows finer detail of this area," Hunter said. "Besides, I like maps. You can call me old fashioned." Hunter turned and headed for his car.

It only took a couple minutes for Hunter to retrieve the maps and make his way back to the fence line. He opened a booklet that had sections of the county divided up into detailed quadrants.

"This is us," Hunter pointed as Casey looked on. "And that is the direction we are looking," he continued tracing his finger along the page and into an expanse that was clearly defined as woods on the map.

"It's all woods," Casey said, her tone not hopeful.

"Yes it is, swamps too but thanks to smart highway planning, we can make up a lot of time by car where our suspect is fighting his way through wilderness," Hunter said. He studied the pages of maps, mostly looking at seasonal and back roads that twisted their way through the expanse of woods that made up the Pine Barrens.

"Shouldn't you call for backup and have an alert out for this guy?" Casey asked.

Hunter continued to stare at the map. "We already have one out, a description, the whole work up."

"What's with the whole deep focus on the map there Columbus?" Casey quipped trying to add a touch of levity.

Hunter ignored her comment and called for Troy to come over. "Listen, I want to establish a baseline of a direction our suspect may have travelled. I think he wants to head south towards where he grew up. His profile states he has outdoor experience so he can survive out here on his own. Do your dogs need to stay on a direct line or can they keep a scent if we staggered our approach?"

Troy understood what Hunter was getting at. "They can hold a scent. Reinforcement would help but they can do the job."

"He's got a whole day on us, so I want to see if I can head him off," Hunter said before Troy jumped in.

"You want to see if the dogs can pick up his scent in different places? Absolutely," Troy said.

"Superb," Hunter shot back. "Then let's do this. Take the dogs into the woods. Give me a ten to fifteen minute trek. If Staffen's path isn't erratic, I'll plot a course based on his line, then we'll head over to this road," Hunter said pointing to the map of another county road that cut through a swath of forest. "We'll see if we can find his exit point and new entry point, then recalculate. My guess is he keeps it simple and direct."

Troy grinned. "You got it." He whistled for his dogs who instantly obeyed, gave them a treat then signaled for them to start into the woods.

Casey and Hunter stood along the shoulder of county road Rt. 541. They watched Troy work the dogs along a stretch of pavement Hunter pinpointed as a possible exit point where Henry Staffen may have emerged before crossing the road into a larger expanse of woods.

"That was a pretty smart move to grab a bagful of hay from the loft for the dogs," Casey said as she casually scanned the woods on either side of them.

"Well... I get paid for stuff like that," Hunter said as he watched the dogs methodically work sections of the woods just off the road.

Casey kicked some sticks off the shoulder into the road. The standing around began to bore her. A thought surfaced. She tightened her lips as a chill shook through her. "What happens if we run into him while we are out here?" she asked.

"My plan is to bring him in for questioning," Hunter said, as he continued to examine his map.

"That's all good but what if it doesn't go as smoothly as you want it? What's the backup plan?"

Hunter pulled aside his jacket to reveal his holstered pistol. "That's the backup plan."

"Oh," Casey said. She hadn't thought about the possibility of a violent clash.

Hunter had not put much thought into that aspect either. He hid his worry. He even considered calling off the search. The thought of using his weapon didn't even occur to him until he revealed it. He had only used it a handful of times in his dozen years on the force, first as a cop, then working as a county detective, mostly assisting smaller towns who did not have the budget to afford full time detectives.

Troy broke their trains of thought when he yelled, "Got it."

The dogs circled in a frenzy near a downed tree just off the road about three hundred feet from where they parked.

"Great," Hunter said. "Now… can they pick up his trail and if so, follow it for fifteen minutes or so to establish another line of direction."

"My boys can do that," Troy answered while walking back to Hunter and Casey.

Hunter continued. "You see, what I'm looking at here is this creek," he said pointing at the blue line that weaved through the forest. "I want to see what he did if he came to this point. Establish that, then call me if you have a signal, if not, get back here so we can coordinate our next step."

"You got it," Troy said. He called to his dogs, praised them, gave them treats, and then had them resume tracking the scent, quickly disappearing into the thick of the woods.

With Troy out of sight, Casey wanted to revisit the possibility of Hunter using his weapon. "Were you serious about the gun?"

Hunter half forgot about his weapon comment. "I certainly have no desire to take this out of its holster. What I want to establish is the direction he's headed. This guy can handle himself out here but I think he's heading home. I think he needs to make some connection that will make him feel secure. If I can narrow that path down, I can let other departments and the state police know where to be on the lookout."

"Do you really think this Henry guy murdered those people?"

Hunter said nothing for a moment. His gut instinct said no. "The only way to rule him out is to question him."

"What about all those red eye descriptions? That doesn't make any sense. People don't have red eyes," Casey said.

"Bloodshot eyes," Hunter countered.

"Yeah but I don't think that Carl guy you had on video meant that," Casey said.

"I know," Hunter said. "But people can imagine all kinds of stuff in a delirious moment. Did Carl look like someone who was mentally all in one piece? And my other eyewitness wasn't in the most stable condition either, when I interviewed her initially."

"It just doesn't seem like one person can do all that damage," Casey added.

Hunter hung his head. "Please… don't give me the Jersey Devil bit. I've got enough mystery here with this case without adding coincidental nonsense to the list."

Casey knew better than to press her luck. "I understand."

## CHAPTER 16

Hunter spotted the opening for the unmarked seasonal road and pulled into it with Troy, Casey and the dogs following. The dogs tracked the trail to the creek as Hunter expected, located a makeshift camp before following another relatively straight line. Troy said they took the scent for another ten minutes before turning around, believing the suspect kept a steady course.

Hunter plotted a line out to a rural area that led to a few large farm properties. He wanted to see if they could pick up the trail there. If so, he could once again establish a path and issue a report with his findings.

The wheels to his car slid slightly as they drove slowly down the narrow, partially overgrown road. A four-wheel drive car would have zero issue with the hard sand surface of the road but both Hunter and Troy found themselves working their respective steering wheels harder than expected. After about a three-mile drive Hunter pulled off to the side.

Troy got out of his car followed by Casey. They looked in both directions at what appeared to be mirror images of underbrush and trees.

"Want me to get the dogs out?" Troy asked.

Hunter nodded. "And if they need some hay for a scent, let me know."

It took almost fifteen minutes before the dogs picked up the scent again. An uncomfortable feeling came over Casey. She felt woozy. Taking in a few deep breaths, she shook it off and caught up to Hunter who was trailing Troy and the dogs.

"How did you know this was the area to come to?" she asked Hunter.

"Sometimes I have a good feeling about these things," he answered. "And I've always been a good judge of locations using maps."

"Spot on, I'd say," she said as they watched the dogs dart in and out of the low brush on the side of the road.

Hunter was the first to notice a field through a row of trees to their right, farmland. A wave of protective caution began to overwhelm him. He realized Staffen could be hiding out in any one of the farms in the area. The magnitude of his little adventure hit him like a truck; he was responsible for the safety of these two civilians assisting him on unofficial business. It was too late. They were here. They had come this far. The thought of calling for backup ran through his mind. He worried more for Casey than Troy. During the day, he learned that Troy had assisted on criminal investigations over the years. Casually, he took his phone out and noticed he had no service. His hand brushed his pistol nonchalantly, for security.

They didn't walk far when the dogs veered to the other side of the road. The three of them slowed to watch. Petey and Bower disappeared into the thick brush. Hunter again grazed his hand over his sidearm.

"If there was something there, they'd let us know," Troy said with an even tone.

A few moments later Bower came out of the woods about fifty feet further up with Petey right behind, noses to the ground. The three of them trotted to catch up.

The woods bordering the farmland thinned to a small thicket. They could easily see the expanse of farmland that stretched out from beyond their current spot. Hunter looked back and noticed their cars were nearly out of sight. They continued to walk a little further when the road began to bend towards the interior of the thick woods. Hunter noticed what looked like a large shed on the border of the farmland and woods. He motioned for them to stop.

"Up ahead," he whispered, "there's a structure, a shed or something," he said waving them back behind him. "Let's stay back here and see what the dogs do."

The dogs moved ahead and began to work an area just short of where Hunter had pointed.

"Something's going on there," Troy said.

Hunter acknowledged as he began to take careful steps towards the dogs. As he approached closer, his view of the shed improved. He took a few more steps towards the dogs when he saw Bower sit perfectly still. He stopped. He looked back to Casey and Troy, making sure they hadn't followed. The bend in the road obscured their view. He saw Casey wave. He put up a finger and made the gesture to stay put. By her reaction, it didn't appear that they could see Bower had stopped.

"What do you think boy?" Hunter whispered. Bower flinched at his voice but stayed in place. "Is someone in there?"

Petey, the more active of the dogs, calmed down. No longer did the tail wag like a metronome on crack. Hunter took a few more steps trying to get a better view of the surroundings when Petey walked over to Bower and nudged him a few times. Finally, Bower got up and followed Petey. Hunter watched as the dogs went ahead another fifty feet. When both dogs sat at the same time, Hunter knew they had something. Slowly and quietly, he maneuvered towards the dogs. He unsnapped the holster protecting his pistol, keeping an eye on the shed and its immediate surroundings.

Hunter looked at Bower. "You ready boy? Let's sniff this guy out." Hunter looked at Petey. "You protect the rear... if someone comes running through, you get him." And, as if Petey knew what Hunter said, he began to pant with his long tongue drooping over the side of his mouth.

Hunter took out his pistol. It felt strange now, the metal somehow colder. It had been over a year since he had used it on duty. Looking straight ahead, he stepped into the edge of the woods. He winced at the cracking of sticks and leaves under his feet. He marveled at the silence at which Bower maneuvered. Meeting the dog's eyes, he motioned for Bower to lead and without hesitation, Bower did.

Hunter kept a close watch on his environment. Every few steps he would stop and scan, the pistol leading the sightline. He didn't notice anything unusual. Yet in his gut, he felt something was near.

A sharp crack made Hunter spin towards the sound. He saw nothing. Bower didn't react at all, so they proceeded. The two of them approached within twenty feet of the shed. It looked handmade, old, withered and worn; stained dark by nature and time. In the distance, he could hear farm animals. As they closed within ten feet of the shed, Hunter could see the structure looked abandoned. Again, he scanned. When he turned to Bower, the dog was lying low, frozen to the ground, his eyes locked in a dead stare but not on the shed. Hunter looked around but saw nothing. He looked back at Bower who now exposed his teeth and churned out a low guttural growl.

"What do you see boy?" Hunter whispered trying to spot whatever set Bower on high alert. "What's going on boy?"

Bower's body jerked at the sound of Hunter's voice but kept his eyes locked into the thicket.

Hunter darted his eyes all around but saw nothing.

Suddenly a crashing sound echoed, followed by the wail of goats and sheep. Hunter tried to see what made the noise but couldn't. Bower didn't flinch, still focused on whatever he had spotted.

Hunter repositioned himself trying to get a better view of the situation. He moved over to the other side of the shed when he heard Bower bark a vicious yelp. He glanced back to see Bower growling, eyes wide.

"What?" Hunter said louder while still making his way to the other side of the shed. Bower barked again. "What?" Hunter repeated not seeing anything while trying to locate the source of the crash.

Out of nowhere, Hunter felt a thundering force smash into him. He fell to the ground with a thud. He quickly oriented himself and spotted a figure on the run.

"Stop!" he shouted as he got up. He began to pursue the figure. "Come on Bower," he screamed at the dog.

Bower stood frozen. The dog paid no attention to him.

"What the hell dog, come on," he shouted as he ran. The suspect closed in on the trail and Hunter hoped Petey would slow him down. *Shit... Troy and Casey are that way.* He picked up his pace leaving Bower to take care of himself, when he heard a grisly scream come from behind him. He looked and saw nothing at first before spotting a flash of a figure swoop from the trees continuing to make horrific screech. It dove right for Bower. Hunter spun around with his pistol; he wanted to fire a shot but froze as he watched the flying figure dart back up into the trees with the dog in its clutches.

"What the fuck," he stammered.

Regaining his composure, he spotted Staffen, now on the trail, holding something in his arms. "Freeze Staffen," he yelled.

The man clearly heard Hunter and reacted to his name. Turning, he also saw that Hunter had a weapon trained on him.

"Freeze or I'll shoot," Hunter shouted. Again, the piercing shriek echoed throughout the woods. Hunter swung in the direction of the sound but could see nothing.

Hunter saw that Staffen had slowed. Whatever his suspect was holding, it clearly kept him from moving fast. Hunter bolted double time and began to catch up. He then watched as Staffen stumbled, dropping a chicken.

"Freeze," he shouted again.

This time Staffen stopped and put his hands into the air. Hunter heard Petey running through the brush and barking. Staffen dropped to his knees, when the scream sounded again.

Both Hunter and Staffen looked up into the trees. This time, the dark figure flew out of the trees like a flashing dart and pummeled full force into Henry Staffen.

Hunter didn't move. He had no idea what was unfolding before him. At first, he thought it might be a mountain lion. It was the only explanation that made sense. But this creature had wings. It was tall, big but not hulking, and it was dark. Hunter couldn't distinguish its form into a reasonable conclusion. It moved with incredible speed.

The creature ripped into Staffen's flesh, tearing him into pieces. Just then, Hunter saw Petey jump into the scene and with one swoop of its wing, the beast swatted the dog off to the side. Hunter screamed "freeze" again and pointed his gun at the creature approaching it in staggered steps. The beast turned towards him. Hunter met its glance. Terror overtook him as if the creature reached into his soul and grabbed the essence of his life by the throat. His hands went cold and he thought he might pass out.

The beast turned its body towards Hunter and leaned into an attacking crouch. Its eyes blazed a deepening, evil red. It hissed.

Hunter saw the discolored fangs dripping with blood and flesh. In an instant, the beast shot toward him. He could hear Casey screaming *NO!* as everything became a blur. In half a trance, he fired a shot. The beast screamed, altered its course and disappeared into the woods. Hunter fell forward, catching himself with his free arm. He gained some composure, enough to look up into the trees. The creature bellowed again. Hunter fired a shot into the treetops. Another scream echoed but this time it was more distant and moving away.

Hunter slumped forward. He took a moment before looking back over at Staffen. The body laid motionless, blood oozing out of it and seeping into the sand.

"My God," Casey cried out as she came closer. She walked by the man on the ground. She glanced at the large pool of blood before proceeding to Hunter. She leaned down and whispered to him, "Was that what I think it was?"

Hunter gathered himself. He reached for her hand and squeezed it. He let out a heavy breath, "I don't know what that was."

"Are you alright?" she asked, seeing he hadn't looked at her.

He nodded though he wasn't completely telling the truth. "I'm okay." He used her shoulder to lean on as he pushed himself up. He made his way over to the victim. The man had a large gash cut into his abdomen, and some of his organs spilled out onto the ground. Blood continued to drain from the body. The sand drank it up like a sacrifice. Hunter pulled out his phone and saw it had two bars. *Now I have service.* He dialed 911. As the line rang, he spotted Troy rustling in the woods trying to find his dogs.

Casey waited for Hunter's conversation to end before she locked eyes with him. "You know what that was...I know what that was... now what do we do about it?"

Hunter didn't answer. He shook his head. "We're in a different realm now. And we're going to be doing this on our own."

"No," Casey countered. "They have to believe us."

Her response was the remedy he needed to snap back to reality. "Sweetheart, no one is going to believe what happened here."

## CHAPTER 17

"Suspended with pay," Hunter mumbled with a nod. He wasn't about to question the captain as he stood before him.

Captain Morgan sat motionless, his hands balled into fists on his desk. He was pissed. He gnashed his teeth as he stared at Hunter, barely containing his anger.

Hunter was grateful he wasn't completely relieved of his duties, though that matter wasn't a certainty. He accepted his fate, something that caught his captain off guard, half expecting an argument.

Captain Morgan lowered his head. "I can't believe you endangered those people."

Hunter could see the color leave the captains clenched fists as he spoke.

"Do you understand the friggin' mess you've caused?" Morgan said, this time looking directly at him.

"I understood the implications of my actions," Hunter answered.

Captain Morgan's face tightened. "Then maybe you should buy some friggin' lottery tickets, because you are one lucky S.O.B. Unfortunately I am now responsible for the mess you left behind."

"I understand sir," Hunter said.

"I really don't think you do genius," the captain shot back, his jaw clenched. "If you knew, you would not have put those people into that situation. If you knew better, there would not be a dead man out in the middle of some backwoods road. If you knew better, then this conversation would not be taking place, so don't fucking tell me about things you know, because it appears to me that you don't know shit. Right now, you are the prince of stupidity. Thank God, nothing happened to those two civilians."

"Yes sir," Hunter replied.

"I'm telling you, you better pray that neither of those two sue us. Your one pal lost his dog in that melee and if he sues for damages and whatever else some opportune lawyer thinks up, that will be the end of you."

"Yes sir," Hunter said.

Captain Morgan looked at him, half expecting a reply of some sort. He wanted Hunter to say something. He even contemplated baiting Hunter into saying something so he could razz his ass more.

Hunter swallowed his words. He wanted to explain his actions. He wanted to blame ineptness on the department for not following up his suggestion that the vagrant at the farm was Staffen. He wanted to rant on about how budget concerns let a possible murder suspect roam freely around the Pine Barrens. He wanted to express how he thought his actions might have actually saved lives.

"So," Hunter said, catching the eye of his captain, "What now? What do I do from here?"

"You go home," the captain said. "You go home and wait. Someone will contact you. You'll have an inquiry. But mostly, stay out of trouble. If all this goes smoothly, you may actually still have a job in a couple weeks."

"A couple weeks?" Hunter replied.

Captain Morgan stood up, his shoulders and jaw tightened. He stared at his detective then spoke through his clenched teeth. "A couple weeks. Do you have a problem with that?"

"Sir," Hunter added with humility, "I just want it known that I defended Troy Brock and Casey Windall. Had I not acted they could have been harmed."

"I see denial and stupidity run hand in hand," the captain shot back. "Had you not entered into your adventure at all, there wouldn't have been a need to defend them. What... you don't think a police department would have apprehended this man?"

Hunter leaned in, "If actions speak for themselves then no, not anytime soon." He knew he pressed his luck.

"A couple weeks damn it," the captain shouted. "Now get the hell out of my office."

Casey typed at a frenzied pace on her laptop. After all the questioning, the attitudes she received, the confusion of the day, she still wanted to write everything down while it was fresh in her mind. The ideas and images flashed through her brain in a cascade of garbled thoughts. Writing it down helped her organize it and make more sense out of an otherwise surreal day.

She had a story idea to craft. She knew it would draw criticism but also lots of attention if done right. Then Hunter popped into her head. She knew this story could hurt him. She didn't want that. She needed to work her angle with precision and care. *How can I do this without getting him into deeper trouble?* She continued typing for quite a while. When she felt she was finished, she looked out her window and noticed that it was light outside. She glanced at the clock, 6:05am. She got up from her computer, laid down on her couch, turned the TV on, and fell fast asleep.

The thundering knock on her door woke Casey up, not quite sure what it was that she had heard – *did someone get into an accident in the parking lot?* She looked out her window, when another knock pounded. Startled, she walked to the door. She peered through her peephole to see Hunter standing there. Another round of loud knocks shook the door.

"Okay, okay," she said as she opened the door. "What's going on there Hercules? What's with the banging?"

"I've been knocking for five minutes," Hunter replied.

"Okay, so you could've called," she said.

"I tried calling, nothing," he said. "I saw your car out here, started knocking lightly and even rang the doorbell but nothing."

"Okay, okay, come on in," she said turning away and leaving the door open for him to close. "Wow that was some sleep. What time is it?"

"I'm sure it was," he answered. "Just about one o'clock."

"Can I get you something, coffee, tea, soda, water?" she asked.

"Coffee."

"Good idea. Sounds great," she said as she sat down rubbing her eyes. "It's in the fridge and the filters are in the cabinet left of the sink."

"Well okay then," he said as he made his way to the kitchen having entered many a garden apartment.

"I like mine with milk and a teaspoon of sugar. The sugar is in the same cabinet as the filters," Casey said as she lay back down on the couch.

"Can I make you a muffin?" he said. "Or crumpets, a scone maybe?"

"I don't have," she said before catching on. "Hey smart guy… what are you doing here anyway?"

"Suspended," he shot back.

Casey sat up. "What?"

"SUS - PEN - DED," he said louder, slower and clearer.

"Are you kidding me?" she said getting up and going into the kitchen.

"Ah… no" he said as he put the filter into the coffee maker.

"What are they thinking? They can't do that," she said, her voice growing angry.

"They can, they did," he said as he put coffee into the filter.

"But that's insane."

He just gave her a blank stare as he closed the coffee lid. "Insane, not insane, one thing is certain... their reality and yours are on different wave lengths. And yes, they have every right to do what they did."

She was aghast. "But Troy and I are fine. Nothing happened to us. I told them again and again how this was not your fault."

"Again," he said, "you can say it anyway you want, serve it as candy wrapped in thousand dollar bills while dressed as a French maid and I don't think they would have done anything different except smile more, and stare like a bunch of morons."

"Still..."

"Doesn't matter, it's all procedural," Hunter said as he took out two cups from a cabinet. "I'll get reprimanded and in a couple of weeks, if all goes well, I'll be back on the job."

"A couple weeks?"

"Hey, at least I'm getting paid," Hunter replied. "So," he said wanting to change the subject, "I can only imagine you have a story ready to go?"

"It's not ready. It will by the end of the day. I don't want you to get into further trouble."

Hunter shrugged. "I made my bed. I appreciate your concern but if you want to make it as a serious journalist you can't concern yourself with things like that."

"True, but this isn't a story that's going to shutter the halls of the state house or bring down a governor. Besides, I didn't see much of the actual action."

"Don't kid yourself. You saw enough," Hunter said as he handed her a cup.

"Not really," she said. "What I saw was a wild flash of something shoot past you and then disappear into the trees. I was coming around that bend in the road, so it wasn't like I caught sight of the whole thing unfolding. I only witnessed a second of the action."

"Well I can tell you, it happened just as fast to me, except with one notable difference. I met eye to eye with that thing. We had a brief, albeit terrifying stare down. At least it was terrifying for me. I'm not sure it was remarkably affected," Hunter said as he poured the nearly finished brewing coffee.

"Really," Casey said. She felt goose bumps roll up her arm. "What was it, what did it look like?"

Hunter bowed his head and shook it in dismay. "It looked other worldly. I don't know. I'm still trying to get a handle on its features but I know one thing. It had red eyes. Deep red eyes. Angry. Evil. They were piercing, hypnotic. To be honest, my shooting at it must have been instinctual because I barely have a recollection of discharging my pistol. For those few brief seconds I was staring at it, I was lost, somewhere else, in a trance."

"And if I write that, what will that do to you?" Casey asked. "If that gets back to your department, they'll have you chatting with shrinks while drawing up paperwork to have you removed permanently."

Hunter nodded. He knew a story like that would not help his case. Yet he also knew that what he saw was no mountain lion or large wildcat and it most certainly wasn't a vampire. A part of him just wanted to say, *screw them*, but he understood taking two civilians to help track down a suspect was beyond sensible. He knew as well as anyone in the department that a cop needed to follow the rules. There were always ways to bend things but his actions and decision-making went beyond bending. Without the rules and procedures in place, it would open up every cop to go rouge anytime they wanted. He knew the best option was to let the process run its course.

"Write your story as you need and we'll just wait and see," Hunter said with a hint of dejection. "And if I'm out on my ass, you might have a roommate." Hunter smiled to himself. It was a thought that had crossed his mind a few times. He was attracted to Casey and he liked her wit. Even though he had kept her at arm's length, he enjoyed their playful banter. This was his big gesture to signaling his attraction. He wasn't sure if he flubbed it but he also didn't care either.

Casey smiled back, a touch embarrassed. She too had felt an attraction but wanted to keep their setup professional. "I have a rough sketch of a story about the incident but it feels weak. My earlier story was stronger."

"The last story was good," Hunter said. "It was entertaining."

"Entertaining?" Casey questioned. "What do you mean by that?"

"Well, like you said." Hunter began to back pedal. "For a piece based on a lot of speculation, it was a solid read. You can see how your story can appeal to your base and how it could certainly fuel the conspiracy theory crowd."

"Uh, huh," she said barely cracking a grin. "Nice rebound."

Hunter returned the expression. "Hey I knew it was a bad word choice as soon as it stumbled out of my mouth. But now I know better. I'm a convert. What took place out there was nothing of this world, and I've seen some weird stuff."

"You got a better look at it than I did and I've now seen it twice," Casey said referring to her night incident on the way to the initial crime scene. She was convinced now that what she had seen wasn't some person in the road barely escaping a collision with her car.

Hunter sat silent for a minute, staring straight into her living room. "Listen, how many stories have you written?" But before she could answer, he rephrased his question. "How many stories on the Jersey Devil have you written?"

Casey had to think. The Evening Door liked Jersey Devil stories, because they always attracted reader response. "I've written two but they were some time ago. There are at least a dozen others that have been written."

"Two," he repeated softly.

"Yes, one was a general article for Weird NJ where I rehashed the history and then talked about some speculative sightings in the last twenty years. The second was on the documentary from the History Channel that did a Jersey Devil episode on *MonsterQuest*. I tied it in with a group that went to find the Jersey Devil and a murder took place."

"I remember that case. Do you have a plan for how you want to write future stories?" he asked.

"Well, I have our incident," she said. "I thought of going down to Leeds Point and seeing what I can find there. It's the birthplace of the thing. I thought about getting some local thoughts on the subject."

"That's good, anything more?"

"Well there are historical stories that are archived I thought I'd look at them again to see if I missed anything. As you may know in the early 20th century there were lots of stories that circulated in the south western part of the state where the Jersey Devil made multiple appearances."

Hunter didn't look particularly interested in that angle.

"I thought I'd try to collect names of recent witnesses and see if any of them would like to elaborate on their experiences," she said. "I also know that the possible birthplaces of the creature are on lands owned by private citizens. I'd see if I can get any comments out of them."

"Not bad," Hunter said.

Casey looked at him with some confusion. "What are you getting at?"

"What I'm getting at is that, instead of trying to write one big story, you should be blogging, Facebooking and tweeting and any other social networking thing out there. You should hit your audience with quick, exciting pieces, revealing up to the minute discoveries. That's what they want, isn't it? Half these folks already have their own conspiracy theory. You can feed that while at the same time formulate the bigger story. You want to generate buzz. You want to attract the people to come to you rather than you always running after them."

Casey felt excited. The notions had bounced around in her head before, but Hunter was laying it out far more clearly than she had. "Are you sure you weren't an editor in a previous life?"

"Do you think your editor will go for that?" he asked.

"Go for it?" she cried out. "He's always dying for that kind of stuff. He'll love it. But first I need to get organized on this."

"It's okay, take a breath," Hunter said. "Finish the coffee then jot down a rough plan. Nice and easy."

"Finish the coffee, that's a good idea. I'm just so excited about this. This is going to be good," she said.

"I think it's going to be far more interesting than you could have imagined," Hunter added before leaning back on the sofa and taking another sip of his coffee. All thoughts of his suspension drifted away. He had an energy he hadn't had in a long time. He felt good. Relaxed, he quickly tried to give her the once over as she walked towards her dining table. He wasn't done when he realized she caught him. A sudden rush of embarrassment came over him.

She turned away and smiled.

## CHAPTER 18

The Pine Barrens cover a significant amount of the central and southern region of New Jersey and the Garden State Parkway cuts through its eastern border. As Casey sped along in the slow lane of the parkway, cruising just above the speed limit, her mind wandered to thoughts of how intimidating it could be for someone to break down along this stretch of road at night. The parkway has many exits but from Toms River to Atlantic City, they become much further apart and the few exits that do come along lead to small, remote towns. If one doesn't know where to turn when exiting, they could find themselves meandering into the darkness of the Pine Barrens forest. A chill went up her spine as her imagination turned sinister.

Unlike the stereotype of New Jersey - over population, traffic and attitude - many of the towns in the southern region of the state are small enclaves where families have known each other for decades. Few people move far away and the myriad of mom and pop businesses are a testament to generations of family owned ventures. For many of these towns, Jersey shore tourism often added more distrust than it did appreciable revenue.

Casey spotted her exit and as she left the major highway, she felt a twinge in her gut. As she turned towards the little town of Leeds, a sensation of going back into history overcame her. She made her way slowly through the town, eyeing anything that might reference the Jersey Devil. She glanced from side to side at the small stores that lined the streets. *There has to be at least one Jersey Devil souvenir shop* she thought. As tacky as the thought was, she felt it was her best chance at getting some 'local' information.

Making a left at an intersection, she spotted a small antique's store. Its dust-coated window front and faded wood exterior made it look like a place straight out of a nineteen twenties time warp. At first glance, it looked closed but she spotted a dim light through the tinted window. She decided it was a good place to start, found herself a parking spot near its entrance and headed in.

The door handle clanked with a metallic snap as she opened it. There was nothing silent or smooth about Casey's entrance as the old wooden floor boards creaked in varying tones. She grimaced with each step not wanting to attract immediate attention. Glancing around, she didn't see anybody in the store. The musky smell made her nose wrinkle. She slowly moved through the soft-lit room where all the collectibles looked to be a shade of brown or old yellow, covered by a fine layer of dust. *How can a place like this be in business* she asked herself as she browsed the old lamps, small tables, and the myriad of trinkets that adorned every bit of space. She made her way along a glass-encased counter. Inside, in organized rows, she saw old hats, knives and even some antique looking pistols. The place reeked of local history.

It wasn't long before the noise from the creaky floorboards brought an elderly man out from behind a worn curtain. The old man was short, had a little bit of hunch and wore an aged brown and yellow flannel shirt with suspenders holding up a pair of dark gray pants. He moved slowly, staring at the floor, shuffling short steps towards her.

"Excuse me," Casey said with a soft tone, not wanting to frighten the old man.

The old man clutched his heart at hearing her voice and gasped. He staggered a little as he began to force his weight onto the counter, staring into the casing.

"Oh my God" Casey cried as she hurried over to him. She

grabbed the old man's arm. "Sir, I'm sorry," she said. She fumbled for her phone and whispered, "I need to call 911. You're going to be okay."

The old man reached a hand over and touched hers lightly, patting it. She smiled noticing the old man looking up at her. His eyes, bloodshot and nearly closed, met her eyes. He tried to say something. Casey leaned a little closer to hear. The old man then jutted his jaw out towards her. With a burst, he opened his eyes wide and barked, "Boo!"

Casey screamed and fell back, nearly knocking over a couple of chairs and an old end table. "What the hell," she shouted, totally taken by surprise and not amused.

The old man stood up straight and had a big grin on his face. "You don't get too much of that from an eighty-eight year old," he said with a chuckle.

Casey looked at the old man with suspicion, wanting to rail into him but refrained. Instead, she straightened her clothes, ran her hand through her hair and presented herself. "Hi, I'm Casey Windall. I'm looking for some information."

The old man's smile faded. "What then, my dear, is the information you seek?" he said.

"Well, it's an odd request really," she said before noticing the old man's hand rise up to stop her.

"You are seeking something to do with the Jersey Devil?" he asked. The old man stood a little taller, his voice grew a little stronger. "Well... that is a prickly pear in these parts."

"Yes, I thought it might be and I assure you I mean no disrespect." she returned.

The old man looked at her. His eyes did a quick scan of her body language. "You seem alright. Good enough for honest I guess."

"Thank you, I think," Casey responded.

"I'm sorry... I'm being rude, you introduced yourself and I have lost my manners along with some of my mind. My name is Arthur Leeds."

"Leeds…" Casey said rather surprised by the name.

"Yes," he said with a sarcastic tinge. "If I had a quarter for every reaction like that, I could have left this town while I was still young enough to do so."

"Sorry, the name…" Casey stammered.

Arthur gave her a reassuring look. "It's okay dear. So you are here to find out something about the Jersey Devil." He paused. "Is it something you believe in?"

Casey hesitated, caught by surprise at the question. "I've always been open to the idea and intrigued by the stories. But recent events have caused me to think it may be more than just a myth."

"Recent events eh," Arthur said warily. "I see. Would these events have anything to do with that massacre that took place with those hunters out in the woods? You know…the one they blamed on that escaped mental patient."

"That mental patient," Casey said wanting to stop there but couldn't, "he's dead." Then, as if to cover her involvement, she continued. "I heard the news of it on the radio."

"Dead," Arthur said as he moved away from the counter, seeming a bit surprised. "Dead," he whispered.

"Yes."

"That's too bad," Arthur said. He paused a moment looking off at nothing in particular. He turned back to her. "Now my dear, how exactly can I help you?" But before she could speak, he continued. "No, no, let me guess. You want to visit the birth place?"

Casey looked at him with an odd apprehension. *Either he's psychic or he's been asked about this way too many times.* "I understand it is on private land."

"Yes it is," Arthur said.

"I've heard there are two possible sites."

"Yes, I've heard that as well," replied Arthur.

"Are there?" Casey asked.

Arthur smiled. He didn't say anything.

"But I am in the right town," she said changing her tactic, trying to confirm information.

"You are most certainly in the right town."

"I thought as much," she answered.

"Why?" Arthur asked leaning in and placing his hand on top of hers.

She looked down at the old wrinkled hand. It was softer than she imagined for a man that had such distinctive lines on his face and hands. She looked back into his eyes, "Woman's intuition," she said with a steady, solid voice.

Arthur didn't flinch as he held his stare. "Yes. That doesn't surprise me in the least." He paused, still holding his hand on top of hers and looking deeply into her eyes. His voice became softer. "Tell me truthfully. The dead man... he died at the hands of the beast?"

Casey felt herself fall into his gaze, her mind focusing solely on Arthur's stare. She felt herself begin to perspire, as all outside noise went quiet. She felt his hand hold hers firmly. Her mind drifted back to that moment in the woods. She could see a blurry image of the beast ripping away at Staffen. Her vision went further, seeing more clearly Hunter firing his weapon and the beast disappearing off into the depths of the woods. She gasped and tried to take her hand away but couldn't.

"You were there. You witnessed it," Arthur said, his blank stare holding steady.

Casey tried to pull away again and felt his hand release hers, "Yes."

"You witnessed it," Arthur said again. "It's okay. There are only a few who have seen it."

Casey looked deeply into Arthur's old, heavy eyes. She saw pain and horror. "You've seen it?"

"No," he said shaking his head just a touch. He lied.

"No?" Casey repeated surprised. Her instinct told her different. His eyes could not mask his lie. "You were spared by it."

A tear fell from his eye. "Please," Arthur couldn't maintain his ruse. "Make no mention of this," he pleaded, his voice sounding more like an eleven-year old boy than an eighty-eight year old man.

Casey was confused. "Who would I say anything to?"

Arthur stood up straight and stepped back. He flicked away the tear that had run down his face. "Forgive me," he said rather matter of fact. "The subject can sometimes conjure up things I wish to keep to myself. Please forget my words." He paused another second before speaking again. "You seem like a sweet girl, what was it again you wanted of me?"

"What did you experience?" Casey asked, not wanting to let go of the moment.

Arthur shook his head and waived her off. "No… not now, not yet" he mumbled.

"Please," she said stepping back, then realizing it was no use pressing him on the subject. She regrouped. "I was simply looking to check out the two supposed sites that are the believed birthplaces of the Jersey Devil."

"Yes, yes, that's right. Well… those properties are privately owned. And neither owner is a fan of curiosity seekers or reporters of any kind," Arthur said, looking away, trying to busy himself with other matters.

"I understand that but I was hoping to possibly have a word with them," Casey pleaded.

"I could tell you where the properties are," Arthur said. "One of them has a good sightline from the road, the other is buried deep in the woods and, if I recall, the structure collapsed some years ago."

"Still, if you could give me the contact information I would greatly appreciate it. It's very important," Casey said.

"Is it so important? What drives you to them?" Arthur asked reasserting eye contact.

"What do you mean?" Casey responded.

Arthur remained silent.

Casey asked again with a stronger tone. "What do you mean?"

Arthur looked away. "I can see it in your eyes as you saw it in mine." He took a second before making eye contact that once again enraptured her. "I have felt the breath of that beast more than once in my life. I have seen its shadow haunt my windows. It is always near. I wish it never knew of me. I wish I could erase it from my mind." He continued to lock his stare into hers. "Others have come in search of it but it chooses who it will reveal itself to." Arthur paused again. Casey stood motionless, absorbed. Arthur continued. "The few who have a knowing … we talk in whispers as I do for fear that it will hear me tell my tale and then haunt me once again… or… worse. Yet you my dear, you want more. I don't know if I should tremble for you… or before you."

Casey wasn't quite sure how to gauge his words. He certainly spoke from the heart but she wondered if he was in fact, losing his mind. As the weight of his words sunk in further, she sensed this man had experienced something extraordinary, and that a dark shadow haunted his soul. Yet, she desired a 'knowing'. She yearned for more.

"I can't say that I'm not afraid, but I feel certain this is what I need to do," Casey said.

Arthur's shoulders sank but he did not flinch from her eyes. "My dear, the beast is cursed. Its soul is dark. It is not some ghost or imaginary monster. This is of a spirit that knows no good. It is evil incarnate."

The words sent a chill through Casey's body. The pull to know more grew greater. "I understand," she said. "Are you saying that if I pursue this, that the Jersey Devil is going to hunt me down and kill me?"

"There is a belief it keeps watch so that our tongues stay silent," Arthur said.

"Then what of this conversation?"

"It knows of the ones who have experienced its presence. It takes pleasure that we fear it. It has us in its spell."

"Who's us?" Casey asked. "How many others are there?"

"Enough to know," Arthur answered. "I have said too much already."

Casey wasn't sure what to make of Arthur's claim. A part of her was beginning to think the whole episode was some bad charade. Yet another part of her believed this man was sharing an absolute truth, a truth so terrible that he almost welcomed finality to it all. Her desire to know more continued to grow. She had to see it through.

"If this is my destiny, then so be it," she said, the words coming out of her mouth without much thought. "If I run away from this, what does it say about my character in the face of a challenge?"

Arthur touched her hand. "Beware of what you seek is all I can offer you. Destiny can offer futures we might otherwise turn our backs to."

Casey spotted a diner as she drove down the town's main street. Her stomach reminded her it was time to eat. She pulled into the lot. Before getting out of the car, she looked at the name and address Arthur had given her. He told her that Dorothy Asuras was someone she needed to meet and impress if she had any chance to investigate the properties she sought.

Dorothy owned a quaint old library just outside of the town proper. Arthur said that the library had many old documents pertaining to the Jersey Devil and local history. She was native to the region and considered the authority on the area's storied past.

Casey looked forward to meeting her but first she needed to eat. She also needed to regroup after the emotional rollercoaster she experienced at the antique shop with Arthur.

The coffee smelled fresh. She could always tell fresh coffee by her body's response to its aroma. Old coffee repulsed her but this cup eased her tension. She checked out the menu as she stirred the dark liquid. A light breakfast looked like a good choice but so did a hot turkey sandwich with gravy. As she mulled her choices, her phone rang.

"So, how did you make out?" Hunter asked.

"What, no hello how are you?" Casey joked. She could hear him sigh.

"How are you, is everything going well? I pray and hope that good health has followed you on your endeavor," Hunter replied.

Casey liked the good-natured teasing they could do so comfortably with each other. "I had an unusual encounter earlier," she said. "I met an older man at this antique shop." She lowered her voice to a whisper. "And he knew that I had an encounter."

"An encounter? How did he get that?" Hunter asked.

"Well it all started off casually as I asked some simple questions but then I found myself in a stare down with this man. He held my hand."

"Held your hand," Hunter interrupted. "How the hell did he hold your hand?"

"All that isn't important now," she shot back. "It was weird but he just knew. He told me he's seen it and that it continues to haunt him."

"Haunt him...how?"

Casey found her voice getting softer. "As if it were some kind of shadow... he thinks the creature keeps an eye on him."

"Really?" Hunter answered. "What do you think of it?"

Casey felt a chill. "I have to admit, I believed every bit of it. Even now I'm sitting at this diner and a rush came over me when you asked."

"You okay?"

"I'm fine," she answered. "It was an odd meeting but I feel fine." Casey waited a moment to see if Hunter would ask anything else but he didn't. "He gave me the address of a woman. She supposedly knows the people who own the land I want to see. If I make a good impression, he says that she'll put in a good word and that would be my ticket for checking these places out."

"And you think this is on the up and up?" he asked.

"I don't get the impression that he was leading me on to get rid of me or trying to put me in harm's way," she returned.

"Good. So are you going to see this woman?"

"Right after I get something to eat."


Within minutes of leaving the downtown area, Casey noticed how fast dense woods lined both sides of the road. The radio station she had tuned into suddenly lost its signal. Instead of tuning to another station, she turned it off. The quiet heightened her senses. She could smell the salt of the marsh that was nearby but couldn't see it. She began to feel uneasy.

A speed limit sign read 40mph. Looking at her speedometer, she noticed she was going over fifty. Slowing down didn't ease her nerves. She even wondered if she was on the right road. It felt so desolate she had a hard time imagining anyone wanting to venture down this way. The road twisted some and she began to notice that she was crossing over little tributaries and creeks. Soon the woods thinned and she began to see more open water and marsh area.

Another sign appeared and it took Casey by surprise, No Outlet. She slowed down and glanced at the paper with the address, 29 End Point St. There were no other signs around and she didn't see an immediate end to the road.

Peering ahead it seemed the road narrowed. As the eeriness increased, she noticed she was barely driving 15mph. Her hands gripped the wheel tighter as the paranoia mounted. "It's the middle of the day for God's sake," she said out-loud to herself. Still, she couldn't shake her uneasy feeling.

Relief swept over her when she finally spotted a street sign. Another glance and she could read End Point. The street appeared as if it was a random, haphazard cutout in the woods. Grasses grew in the old pavement that hadn't seen a coat of tar in decades. There was no shoulder, just scrub and trees. It reminded her of a road in a horror movie, the kind that makes the audience yell at the screen warning the victim not to turn. She couldn't believe this was the street she was looking for. She wanted to call Hunter but there was no cell signal. Her stomach sank and she began to reconsider whether this trip was worth the effort.

*BEEEP, Beep* cried a horn from behind her. Casey jolted hard, banging her skull on the ceiling of her car. She grabbed her head and leaned forward on her steering wheel in pain.

There was a rap on her door and she heard a woman's voice, sweet and concerned. "Are you alright dear? I'm so sorry I startled you."

With her head partially resting on the steering wheel, Casey turned to see a thin old woman wearing a faded blue toned flower print dress, her white hair pulled back, looking at her with worry. Casey didn't think she could answer at first because the pain was dizzying. "I'm okay I guess. I just wasn't expecting that," she groaned.

"I saw you jump so hard, I nearly jumped out of my skin myself," the old woman said bringing a hand up to the neckline of her outfit.

Casey sat up. Her senses began to come back to normal except for the light throb in her skull. "I'll be alright. I just need a minute... please."

The woman gave a small chuckle. "Take your time dear. You need to have your wits about you."

Casey had a clearer look at the frail old woman who was standing by her door. She could smell the woman's perfume. It was the typical fragrance associated with old women and she wondered, *at what age does one think… this is the scent that works for me?*

"I was looking for 29 End Point," Casey muttered, trying to be pleasant.

The old woman laughed. "That's me. That's my place. I'm Dorothy. You must come in. I'll get you an ice bag and then make you a cup of my special tea."

"Oh thank you," Casey said. Normally she would refuse the hospitality but she really thought that an ice bag would help not to mention some refreshing tea.

Dorothy's place was only about two hundred feet off the main road. The antiquated three story Victorian looking house, sat at such an angle to the road that it looked hidden. The long, hard packed stone driveway widened as it led right up to the house. As Casey drove closer, she saw that the house was much bigger than at first glimpse. Finely trimmed hedges bordered a wooden wrap around porch. The shingles were off white and in need of a new coat of paint. The once baby blue shutters looked as if it had been even longer since a paintbrush graced them. The house resembled a smaller version of a southern plantation home.

Dorothy parked her car close to the steps leading to the front porch. Casey pulled up beside her.

"This is a beautiful house," Casey said as she stood outside her car before closing the door. "This must go back to the 19th century at least."

"You're a very observant girl," Dorothy said with a great big grin on her face. "This is the second house," she said. "The first one was destroyed by a hurricane back in 1845."

"When was the first one built?" Casey asked as she headed up the stairs, following Dorothy's nimble pace.

"I believe, but there is no proof, that it was built in the early or mid-18th century."

"Wow," Casey said.

"It is kind of wow, isn't it," Dorothy said turning back to Casey. "I like to believe it was built that early. I feel in my heart that it was."

Casey found Dorothy's sweet demeanor comforting. She glanced about the long wooden porch. Baskets of early spring flowers rich in blues, red, white and orange adorned it. "Do you live here?" Casey asked.

"I do my dear," Dorothy said as she looked for her keys. "I've lived here for over 50 years."

Casey was impressed with that fact. "And I understand this is a library or historical society?" Casey asked forgetting exactly what Arthur had said.

"Well dear, it's both. I used to have a sign by the entrance to the road but it disappeared a while back and even though the town says I should have one up, they have never replaced it."

"That's a shame," Casey replied.

"Here they are!" Dorothy said with an element of glee as she held up the keys. "It's okay. I don't get many random visitors out here."

Casey nodded. "I guess I can see why." Casey regretted the words, hoping that Dorothy wouldn't take it the wrong way.

"The schools in the area all know where I am and the kids come once or twice a year to do reports on the town's history and such," Dorothy noted. "And other historians come now and then to do research. The place doesn't seem busy but it also never goes so long that you wonder if anyone's forgotten about you."

"As long as you are happy," Casey replied.

"Yes, I am very happy. Tired a lot these days, but happy for sure," Dorothy said as she put the key in the door and opened it. "And see… now you have come. And that is a pleasant surprise, because it's been almost a month since a visitor last dropped by." Dorothy stopped one-step into her house, "Can I ask how you came to find this place?"

Casey felt a twinge, a pang of caution. "I spoke with a man in town. An older gentleman," she said hoping her attempt to be coy was working.

"You must be looking for something unique then. My place is generally not at the tip of folks tongues," Dorothy said finally walking into her house. "Are you a historian?"

"Not exactly," Casey said.

"Well you can tell me all about yourself in a minute," Dorothy said dropping her keys into a small Depression glass bowl. She then flipped on a switch and a few bulbs lit up the dark painted walls. Casey followed her in. Dorothy put her purse down next to the little table that held her keys. She turned to Casey as if blocking her from going any further. "I'm going to make us something to drink dear. Why don't you have a seat on the porch, it's such a beautiful day, the fresh air will do good for that bump on your head."

"Okay," Casey said as she stood in the foyer watching Dorothy walk away, and then disappearing behind another doorway. She took one more glance about the place noting an opening to a large room to her left. Although it was dark, sunlight peeked in and revealed several large bookcases, all dark wood; *this must be the library or archive room.* In front of her, a hall led to the back of the house. To the right of the hallway, a staircase went upstairs. She glanced at the walls going up the stairs and could see lots of old black and white and sepia toned photographs. She wanted to examine them more closely but went outside, rather than take the chance of looking rude or nosey.

Casey relaxed on a comfortable faded red wooden porch swing. The cushions on it wrapped around her like a hug. She imagined that many a nap had overcome those who sat here in silence. The air smelled of fresh pine with only a hint of brackishness that reminded her the marsh wasn't far away. She nestled in as the swing hypnotically swayed back and forth.

"I see you are getting acquainted with Mr. Sleepy," Dorothy said, startling Casey as she had closed her eyes, enjoying the moment.

"Oh yes," Casey said, fumbling to sit up straight. "What an appropriate name."

Dorothy held a small metallic tray. On it, two delicate floral patterned white cups with steam swirling from them danced up into the air. Casey then noticed several little bowls filled with milk, sugar and honey accompanying the cups.

"The tea smells wonderful," Casey said. A mere whiff of its aroma tickled her senses and helped shake the sleepiness away.

"Thanks dear, it's an old family recipe," Dorothy said as she settled the tray on a small table between her chair and the swing. "I've been making tea since I was a little girl."

Casey smiled. "I had an aunt who made tea."

"How nice," Dorothy said as she fixed her own cup, "Help yourself dear, I hope I've covered all the essentials? You may want to try it with a dash of honey first. It complements the flavor better," Dorothy said as she noticed Casey reach for the cubes of sugar.

Casey's hands changed course and she used the small spoon in the honey dish to add some to her tea. With just a spin of the spoon, she could smell the difference in the pleasant fragrance.

"See, I can tell you are going to like this," Dorothy said watching her guest with great satisfaction.

Casey took a sip and reclined into the swing's cushions.

"It is comforting, I have to say." She felt the warm liquid caress her throat. She instantly felt her muscles relax.

"This tea will help with that bump," Dorothy said with a soothing voice. She enjoyed seeing her guests take delight in her tea. "Just let it flow through you. Soon you'll feel refreshed and invigorated." Dorothy danced her hand to illustrate the feeling.

Casey smiled wide, relaxing her head against a nice soft cushion. "Thank you," she said nearly forgetting why she had come all this way.

The two of them sat enjoying the subtle sounds of the woods. Birds darted back and forth from the variety of feeders that spotted the grounds. Chipmunks rustled the brush, chasing each other. In the distance, the faint sounds of the surf were just audible enough to act as soft white noise. She couldn't remember the last time she sat on a porch and just enjoyed the sounds of nature around her. Her eyes grew heavy.

"Comfortable dear?" Dorothy asked.

"Oh my goodness yes," Casey responded in a murmur. She realized how much she was drifting and worked to bring herself out of her trance. She rubbed her eyes and tried to conceal a yawn. "Sorry about that. That was rude, almost falling asleep on you."

Dorothy chuckled. "That is quite alright. In fact it's a compliment."

"Well your hospitality is exceptional," Casey returned.

Dorothy smiled and took a sip of her tea. "I'm just glad this little nook in the world still has its magic."

Casey glanced around the front yard and even though it had a non-distinct look to it, she had to agree. "I can see how one could want to grow old here."

Dorothy nodded in agreement. "It has been a long and wonderful life."

Casey smiled. It was refreshing to hear the sentiment expressed with such sincerity. She could only hope to have such contentment. Just then, Hunter crossed her mind. It was a passing thought but it shifted her demeanor.

"Are you alright dear?" Dorothy asked, noticing the change.

"Oh I'm fine, just an odd thought," Casey answered, not realizing she revealed anything.

Dorothy gave a light laugh. "I get them all the time."

Casey took another sip of her tea then stared off into the woods. Her concentration deepened as she tried to see through the thick budding underbrush ready to bloom.

"So my dear," Dorothy broke in, interrupting Casey's gaze. "You've come a long way to seek out my place. How is that I can help you?"

"Sorry again," Casey said, putting down her cup and taking one last glance at the woods before finally making eye contact with Dorothy. "Yes, um, I am doing an in depth investigation into the folklore of the Jersey Devil. As you know, myth and folklore are an important part of many cultures, whether exotic or local and I'm, in a sense, trying to get in touch with the fabric of this phenomenon in our area." Casey felt confident in the way she addressed her query. An invigorated feeling came over her as she continued. "Leeds Point has long been the birthplace associated with the Jersey Devil and with all the legends that are in circulation about it, I thought I would come here and experience the area for myself. I've learned that at least two locations nearby are the supposed birthplace of the legendary creature."

Dorothy smiled but the smile was more cynical than joyful. "I've heard that too," she said with a slightly slower rhythm to her voice. "But what do you think you'll find in these places if you were to see them?"

The question caught Casey off guard. She hadn't actually thought about what she was looking for or hoped to find. She had just wanted to see it. "Well, to be quite honest, I guess there is nothing that could be verified either way as to whether it was a birthplace or not."

"No, you couldn't and that's why the folks who own those properties don't take kindly to strangers walking about and snooping. The locations were once well known but years of silence have kept away a lot of curiosity seekers," Dorothy said, her tone protective.

"I don't mean to come off as some curiosity seeker, I'm trying to put together a definitive exposition of the folklore as thorough and in depth as possible," Casey said.

"I'm sure you mean well dear, but I have lots of pictures of the old places that would be far more satisfying than seeing them now," Dorothy said.

"I would love to see those pictures, but why wouldn't I want to see the actual locations?" Casey asked.

"Well dear because they are so dilapidated that they're dangerous to walk around and there is little, if anything, left to see." Dorothy paused. "And people round here can be very guarded; especially with the Jersey Devil."

"And you? Are you as guarded?" Casey asked noticing how Dorothy's tone had shifted without losing her sense of charm.

Dorothy grinned. "I protect my friends with a great deal of passion, as anyone who knows me will testify. My house and library here are an open book to all the lore that dwells within the Pine Barrens. Enjoy them, seek and as the ol saying goes, you shall find. I have so many books, essays, diaries and newspaper clippings on the Jersey Devil that I'm sure you can fill the pages of a very large book if you so choose."

"I look forward to having the opportunity to sift through all your information if you don't mind," Casey responded.

"Whatever you need dear, I will do my best to accommodate," Dorothy said.

"Thank you for your generosity," Casey returned. "Can I ask you another question?"

Dorothy nodded, "Of course."

"Do you believe in the Jersey Devil?"

"Why of course dear," Dorothy responded without a moment's hesitation.

This caught Casey off guard.

"Are you shocked that I answered that way?"

"I guess a little," Casey said with some amazement. "It's just that most people say no."

"Well that is a generally correct assumption, but not here. I know some people think I'm off my rocker, and maybe with some things I am but not on this," Dorothy said, then took another sip of her tea.

"And why's that?" Casey asked continuing her probe.

"Well dear, it's because I've seen it," Dorothy said without batting an eye.

Casey sat up. "You've seen it?" An adrenaline rush soared through her. "Where? If you don't mind me asking?"

"Right out here on this lawn," Dorothy said pointing to the center of the yard.

Casey looked out to the yard. She knew Dorothy wasn't lying, she could feel it. Her gaze drifted into the woods, she could picture it.

"It was a sight I'll never forget," Dorothy continued, her eyelids lowering just a touch. "At first I thought it was a leopard or bear or something but once I realized... I knew it was nothing like that."

Casey snapped out of her gaze right after Dorothy spoke. "My God, you must have been terrified."

"I was more shocked than anything," Dorothy said with a half laugh. "But yes, once my senses brought me back to reality, the fright was paralyzing."

"What did it do? What did you do?"

"It did nothing. It wandered about as I stood frozen in place," Dorothy said with some intensity. "I was over there," pointing near the corner of the porch that faced away from the road. "I can honestly say it was both terrifying and beautiful," she said with a degree of delight.

"You didn't scream, shoo it away or anything?" Casey asked. She was puzzled by Dorothy's response yet captivated at the same time.

"No dear. I thought I should, but either I couldn't or didn't want to. Either way, I didn't make a sound."

"Did it see you?" Casey asked.

Dorothy shook her head. "Not at first. It just roamed around. At times, it was still, so still that it looked as if it faded into the scenery, like a chameleon. I can remember blinking my eyes, wanting to rub them but I couldn't raise my arms, so I just blinked wildly until I was able to once again spot it… My, how there's never been a thing like it."

"You weren't scared?" Casey asked thinking how odd her last statement was.

"I was scared, I was exhilarated, I was frozen," Dorothy said with enthusiasm.

Casey sat back in her seat. "I was dumbstruck," she gasped, hardly believing she had just revealed her truth.

Dorothy turned to her. "I'm sorry dear, are you saying you've seen it?"

Casey wanted to back-peddle but knew she couldn't. Any lie would be obvious and lying wasn't a strong suit of hers. "I've had two experiences. One major and one, what I believe, was a minor one." She could feel herself turn flush as she spoke, but also refreshed to get the burden off her chest.

Dorothy nodded. "Do you want to tell me about it?"

Casey shrugged and couldn't really answer. "I, I don't know, it's all a bit fuzzy."

"Ease your mind dear. Breathe deep and let the memory form itself again. It will come," Dorothy said with a hypnotic tone.

"I don't know. I'm not that comfortable with it yet. I appreciate the help, but not now, maybe some other time."

Dorothy smiled.

Casey noticed something different. The charming grin had a hint of crazy to it or so she thought.

"I'm not going anywhere," Dorothy offered.

Casey tried to hide her nervousness as she took another sip of tea, which oddly enough still remained quite warm. "It's amazing how this keeps," she said noticing a trace of steam swirling up from the cup.

"Yes, that's what you get with homemade. Not like the processed stuff they sell in stores," Dorothy replied, her voice coming back to the sweet old woman that Casey first met.

Casey put the cup down on the table as she squared herself up on the seat. "May I see your library?" she asked, wanting to skip the entire encounter episode.

"Of course dear," Dorothy replied. She took one last sip of her tea, placed the cup on the little table and stood up to show her in.

Even with the lights on and the curtains open, the library room looked dimly lit with all the dark wood on the walls and dark shelves and dark covered books. Casey gazed with amazement at the old books, many of them appearing to be first editions. As she slowly walked through one of the aisles, a musky scent filled her senses. As they made their way to the back of the room, she noticed filing cabinets with lots of thin drawers and walked over to them.

"That's my archives of newspapers," Dorothy said moving past Casey and closer to a window where the light was better. "This is where you'll find most of the articles dealing with the Jersey Devil. Of particular interest are the sightings of 1909 from the Philadelphia papers and from some of the local Jersey papers."

"The actual newspapers?" Casey asked.

"Yes dear," Dorothy responded. "I just ask that you take great care handling them. Many are in protective wraps for better preservation from the elements."

"Of course," Casey replied running her hand along the cool edge of the light gray metal cabinet.

"I'm going to clean up a little," Dorothy said. "Just call me if you need anything."

"Thank you," Casey said looking at the many drawers. She went to ask Dorothy where exactly the Philadelphia paper articles were, but when she turned, Dorothy was gone.

Casey slid open a few of the drawers. Each drawer contained many newspapers. They were neatly stacked but as she fingered through them, she noticed the dates weren't in chronological order. She also saw that the filing of the different newspapers had no purpose as Philadelphia and New Jersey papers intermingled in each drawer without any rhyme or reason.

She was careful in how she handled the pages and every now and then would pause to look over interesting headlines. The papers weren't set up to feature the Jersey Devil, rather they were simply old newspapers and clippings stored away. Flipping through them randomly became an exercise in inefficiency with few results. Dorothy had told her to look in these drawers but she didn't realize she would have to dig through so meticulously.

By the time, she opened the seventh drawer, better than an hour had passed. Casey flipped through a few more sheets before she came across a headline in the Philadelphia Enquirer – Creature Haunts Region, The Jersey Devil Rises. She knew about the strange week in 1909 where the Jersey Devil had made appearances in that region but the stories all felt distant. Now, with an actual article in hand, her heart raced as she read about an encounter from that time.

Yet, as she read, the description of this beast was not the same as the thing she believed she witnessed. The creature described in the article was smaller, had a distinctive horse like head and small wings. What she saw was far larger, more muscular, with a snout but not all together horse like, more dragon-esque or even catlike. Its wings melded into its body until they unfurled, and they were large, black and menacing. She paused for a moment realizing this was the most detail she could recall from that day.

She soon found several more articles reporting incidents. It was all fascinating to her and she knew she had to make copies of as much of the material as possible. Looking at her watch, Casey couldn't believe three hours had passed. She needed to look over this information in more depth. She rustled through her bag to locate her phone. She needed to take pictures. It would have to do for documentation purposes.

She spent the next half hour photographing all the articles she could find. She set the papers as close to the window as possible for the best light. Some images came out blurry but hoped were legible enough to decipher.

When she finished, she put the papers back into their proper places. Just as she closed the last drawer, Dorothy walked in. "Have you found what you wanted?"

"Yes thank you," Casey replied a little startled. "There's so much more to look at, so I hope you don't mind if I come back."

"Of course, please. I enjoy the company and I love that the archives can be of use."

Casey was grateful. "Do you have other materials on the Jersey Devil besides newspapers?"

"Why, I have a whole section on it," Dorothy said as she walked down one of the aisles of books. Casey turned and followed. Dorothy didn't walk far when she turned to Casey and pointed at several rows of shelves. "There are many books, and essays in here; much of which you won't find anywhere else. I have some mainstream source material but you probably know all that stuff. These wonderful treasures are truly rare," she said as she continued to point them out proudly.

Casey reacted with surprise by the revelation. "Why haven't other people found this out?"

Dorothy shrugged, still looking at the books on the shelves. "I don't know… maybe because most don't know about this cozy little nook in the woods." She turned to Casey. "But you've found it dear. That shows you care and now you will have more information than anyone else. I hope you use it well."

"Thank you, I plan to," Casey said looking at the rows of books.

"Before you leave, I have something for you," Dorothy said leading Casey back out to the foyer. "Stay here, I'll be right back," she said stopping and making sure Casey came to a halt.

Casey found it strange the old woman seemed to protect that portion of the house. *It must be a privacy thing.*

Dorothy reappeared a few seconds later holding a small bag with handles. "Here you go dear, its tea bags of my homemade recipe. I thought you might like some."

"Thank you very much, that is quite generous," Casey said, genuinely touched at the gesture.

"Just remember to add honey, not sugar if you don't have too. It soothes the senses when mixed with honey."

Casey thanked Dorothy again for the tea and all her help. She said she would call before coming back, which would probably be in a few days. Dorothy said she looked forward to her return. Casey took another sweeping glance at the old house. She wondered how Dorothy was able to keep the place looking so nice despite some obvious needs. As she walked to her car, she looked at the tea, smiled and whispered, "I better pick up some honey."

CHAPTER 19

"What's going on over there Bill?" Hunter asked.

It had been a week since his suspension. The captain discouraged any contact with police personnel while the department investigated his case but Hunter wanted information. It wasn't in his nature to be out of the loop. He enjoyed work and didn't like being away from it for more than a few days. He even once cut a vacation short to go back to work because he missed it.

"It's a real cluster fuck here, I can tell you that," Bill Tanner answered. Bill was one of Hunter's closer associates in the department. A short stocky man, Bill didn't get along well with others, much like Hunter. The two of them didn't particularly care to work with each other but when working independently, they swapped ideas just fine. Hunter liked Bill's drive and his gruff, rough around the edges attitude. Hunter realized Bill mirrored him in many respects. He knew how the guys and top brass talked about Bill and figured that was how they probably talked about him. Hunter wanted to change and that was precisely why he listened to so many self-help CDs – for what that was worth.

"Any word on anything?" Hunter asked, desperate for news.

"What little I've heard is that they can't find enough evidence to get rid of you. If they did, it appears you have grounds to sue them for unlawful termination," Bill said. "But they have another quandary."

"Really," Hunter said, his curiosity peaking. "Is it my story?"

Bill laughed his full belly chuckle. "Your story…you bet your story."

"What about it?"

"Because they can't discredit it as easily as they thought and that in itself has their knickers in a knot."

"What are they trying to do then?"

"I believe they are going to call you in for further questioning. If I heard right, the autopsy on Staffen can't explain what the hell happened to him," Bill said. "And DNA hasn't helped at all. In fact, I heard they've administered several DNA tests. All of them are clean except for Staffen's and the chicken he was carrying."

"That doesn't surprise me," Hunter said knowing his earlier DNA submission revealed more questions than answers.

"And another thing… they can't find the shots you fired. In addition, there is no trace of a discharge from your weapon. It's as if your magazine wasn't at capacity. I heard one of the guys say you wanted to cover something up."

"Cover what up?" Hunter said on the verge of yelling.

"I don't know," Bill said. "You know how popular I am with the guys, and some of them have come up to me and said they thought your story was a bunch of junk."

"What would be my motive?"

"I don't know. I don't think anyone has a clue on that," Bill said. "You know they are scraping for anything."

"Who, Morgan? I know the captain and I don't always see eye to eye but I can't see him throwing me under the bus like this." Hunter said.

"I did hear the captain say the wounds on Staffen weren't like anything that he's ever seen." Bill said, then added, "I think they've mentioned mountain lion a few times."

"Mountain lion?" Hunter barked. "What I saw was no mountain lion. What killed that dog was no mountain lion. What killed Staffen was no mountain lion. And what I shot at, sure as hell, was no mountain lion."

"You're preaching to the choir on this one," Bill responded. "Listen. You know the drill. Come in. Tell the truth. Tell your story. That is all you can do at this point."

Hunter shook his head in amazement. "Bill. There is no drill for this one. This is X-File shit. This isn't some accidental shooting. I don't know what it is I witnessed but it isn't anything they can match on file somewhere."

"Whoa, whoa, whoa," Bill interrupted. "Don't let them know that. You can't give them any opening to question your mindset. Your shit will be toast in a hurry. You have to be in complete control on this issue. You get wishy-washy with them and start mentioning paranormal stuff and all that and they'll have a shrink showing you ink blots in a happy room painted with unicorns and rainbows…and you'll get fired."

"You're right, you're right," Hunter said. "All I have is my story and no matter how outlandish, I just have to stick to the facts as I know them."

"That's your greatest ally at this moment," Bill said. "That and you have eye witnesses."

"My story has to stand on its own merit," Hunter replied. "You know how reliable eye witnesses are. They bring Troy and Casey into separate rooms again and I can guarantee they will not produce the same story."

"From what I've heard, their stories aren't the same but they aren't that far off from each other either. In addition, they haven't said a bad word about you or blamed you for anything. In fact, they credit you with protecting them from whatever it was that attacked Staffen."

"That's all nice, but if it was that cut and dry I'd be back on duty by now."

"Just stay the course, keep your nose clean and it will be fine," Bill said. "Listen I have to go. I'll touch base soon."

"Thanks man, talk to ya," Hunter said as he heard the line disconnect. Hunter looked at his phone. He fumbled with it in his hand. Then Casey came to mind. It made him smile and put his troubles into the background. *I should just ask this girl out on a proper date.* Looking at his phone again, he punched in her number.

Hunter opened the door to his favorite Italian restaurant, Antonio's, letting Casey enter first.

"So, this Dorothy woman… a pretty interesting lady?"

"Thank you," said Casey as she walked into the soft-lit foyer. Hunter couldn't help but look over the dark blue dress that hugged her figure in an elegant, shapely way. It was the first time he saw her not wearing slacks or jeans. She looked far better this way…classy.

The restaurant's soft lighting set a pleasant mood. As Casey glanced around, she saw intimate table settings scattered along the edges, while larger ones occupied the center of the room. "Yes, Dorothy is a very interesting woman. So full of passion for her local history; it was refreshing."

The maître de greeted them and gracefully glided them past tables full of people, to a secluded spot by a window overlooking the quiet street.

"This place is nice," Casey said as Hunter held her chair out for her to sit.

"It's a favorite. I don't come as often as I'd like, but when I do, it never disappoints."

An impeccably dressed waiter wearing a finely ironed white shirt, black tie and black pants asked for their drink order. Hunter ordered a bottle of chardonnay he favored. Another waiter appeared with a basket of fresh warm bread and a small plate of oil and seasonings for dipping. The aroma of the bread brought a smile to both their faces.

"I haven't been to a nice restaurant like this in a while," Casey said as she glanced at the bread and then Hunter.

"I'm glad you like it," Hunter returned.

"You should see this old house she lives in," Casey beamed. "It has a Victorian layout to it but isn't quite that. There's a hint of southern plantation to it, if you know what I mean?"

Hunter nodded as if he did but that kind of visualizing was not a strong suite. "So the inside is nice too?"

"From what I saw it was immaculate. Her library is very tidy. It isn't what I would call organized but I think that's because I don't know her system, if she even has one," Casey said, then grabbed a small piece of bread and dipped it in the oil.

Hunter watched, seeing that she enjoyed the taste. He followed doing the same.

"She did seem a little odd in that it felt like she wanted to keep me from a certain part of the house."

"What's odd about that? Maybe she likes privacy," Hunter said.

"I guess. She just seemed guarded about it, that's all. She was so hospitable about everything else that it just felt strange… like she was hiding something."

"Maybe that knot on your head from smacking it in your car was clouding your judgement," Hunter said with a sarcastic grin.

"Yes, it reacts to selective suspicions," Casey countered.

"But all in all it was a successful venture?" Hunter asked while dipping another piece of bread.

"Oh yes…very helpful. I plan to go back next week. She said she has loads of stuff that people don't even know about."

"How's that?" Hunter questioned.

"I don't really know but given that she said she's witnessed the creature, I'm not going to doubt it until proven otherwise."

Hunter half choked his bread when he heard that Dorothy was a witness to the creature. "Wait, wait. You said she saw it.

What did she say, did she elaborate?"

"I thought you'd like that," Casey said, a playfully sly grin stretching across her face. "It was strange. As she shared her story, I could almost see it. It was as if I fell into a trance with her words."

"What did it look like to her?"

Casey had to think for a second. She couldn't recall. The more she thought about it, the more she realized that Dorothy never mentioned what it looked like; just that it was an experience. Then Casey's mind wandered back to Arthur's eyes and she began to feel the terror that he had witnessed.

"Hey!" Hunter said snapping his fingers, noticing Casey space out. "Are you okay? Is that bump having a delayed reaction or something?"

Casey shook her head and brought herself back to the table. "Sorry about that. I drifted." She lied. She didn't want to share that moment just yet. Instead, she smiled, grabbed another piece of bread and dipped it.

"You sure you didn't rap your head harder than you thought?" Hunter asked with concern.

"No, I'm fine," she said hoping to steer the conversation onto something else. "I drove home without a problem and everything has been fine since. I haven't been dizzy or having headaches. I wouldn't worry about it."

Hunter didn't want to press the matter. That wasn't his intention for the evening. "So, enough about the Jersey Devil," he said. "I just realized that we've never engaged in any kind of happy chat informalities. So, where are you from?"

Casey grinned. "Happy chat informalities… I don't think I've ever heard that one before."

"Hey, I'm an original," Hunter countered.

She laughed. "I grew up with my aunt in Freehold."

"Really," Hunter said. "That's too bad."

"No it wasn't, my aunt was pretty cool."

"No, I meant that you grew up in Freehold."

Casey laughed, "Shut up. It's a great town."

"Then I guess you didn't get out much," Hunter chided.

"Alright smart guy," Casey said with a smirk but liked the playfulness of the conversation.

"I'm just busting. Freehold is a fine town. Where in Freehold?" he asked.

"Just off Vine Street near the downtown area."

"Oh my. I can't believe I'm still sitting here," he said teasing as he pulled the napkin from his lap tossed it on the table.

"Stop," she said. "You don't even know the area."

"Unfortunately I do know the area. An old partner was from that section of Freehold."

"Really. What was his name?"

"Jimmy Vizco."

Casey's eyes opened. Sadness overcame her. Hunter immediately noticed.

"You knew him?" he said whispering.

"I knew his younger brother Bobby. It was a tragedy."

"Yeah, it was," Hunter said nodding.

Bobby Vizco had died trying to ride a cargo train as it passed through town. He and his friends would wait in an area where the trains would slow down. They would run and jump up to grab onto handles and ride the train for a mile to a spot where they could easily jump off. It was something lots of kids did but on that day, Bobby lost his grip and got caught under the train.

They sat silent for a moment.

"So where are you from?" Casey asked wanting to move on. "Please, let it not be some place with a tragic memory."

"I grew up in New Egypt," Hunter said.

"And you bust my chops about Freehold?" Casey said with a sarcastic stun in her voice. "How close do the blood lines run there?"

"Fair enough," Hunter said with a laugh. "I'm a Piney by some standards."

"Born and inbred," Casey added.

Hunter waved his hands. "No mas, no mas."

"Not a fan of that medicine are you?" Casey laughed.

"Not when you can't get past that stereotype."

The food came. She had a simple chicken franchisee and he ordered pasta and calamari with white sauce. He wanted the Zuppa de Pesce but knew he'd get the red sauce on him.

The conversation stayed light. They discussed their schooling and early jobs. Casey talked about going away to Boston and studying journalism and her first jobs reporting on local town meetings. She decided to come back to New Jersey when a friend of hers had a connection at the Asbury Park Press. She was at the job just over three years when layoffs started and she eventually became a victim of downsizing. She started doing freelance work and then came across The Evening Door. It was respectable pay and it covered her expenses. She also occasionally did some freelance reporting for area newspapers and some writing for News12 New Jersey, the television station.

Hunter listened with amused rapture. It was relaxing and even comforting to listen to Casey talk about her life. She did it with a bounce and vitality that he didn't have. He was more serious. His humor was more sarcastic than witty. Casey made him feel at ease. She seemed to flitter along with the conversation; hopping back and forth between stories without going into overly long tangents. Hunter interjected from time to time with details of his own life or to ask a question but for the most part, he let her talk.

For Casey, it had been a while since she had been on a 'date.' It wasn't for the lack of suitors; she just hadn't connected with anyone. The few dates she had over the last two years never drew enough interest for a third date. There were plenty of nice guys but no one ever swept her away.

Sitting with Hunter, watching him smile, listening, never dominating with his own stories, she actually felt a connection and she liked it.

When the check came, they were both surprised they had been chatting for over two hours. As Hunter guided Casey out of the restaurant, his arm slid down her side and lightly cupped her waist. Casey responded in kind by sliding in next to him. They both enjoyed the fit.

With the first date jitters mostly gone, they were relaxed on the ride back to her place. Pulling into her apartment complex, they both wondered what would occur next. Hunter's plan was to walk her to her door, maybe get a goodnight kiss and go home. Casey wasn't sure what she wanted but she didn't want the night to end like a high school date.

"Would you like some tea?" she asked as Hunter pulled into a parking spot.

"Tea…" Hunter thought tea was odd but certainly welcoming. "Sure, I'd like some tea."

"Great," Casey replied. "Dorothy gave me some of this homemade stuff that I had while I was there. It is very soothing."

Hunter smiled. "Oh, magic tea. This should be good."

Once inside, Casey immediately stepped into the kitchen and set up the teapot to boil. She asked if there was anything else she could offer. He said no. She took out two tea bags, which did not have the traditional string attached. She put her nose to the cup and inhaled the aroma, then passed the cup by Hunter's nose.

"Nice, isn't it?" she asked.

"It is," he said with genuine approval. "I'm not generally a tea guy but I have to say that does have a nice smell to it."

"Good, I think you'll really enjoy this."

Hunter wanted to hold her and give her a kiss but he hesitated and missed his opportunity. Didn't matter, he thought, if it's to be, then it'll happen. He turned and went into the living room. It wasn't long before he heard the teakettle whistle. Casey came out from the kitchen holding the two cups. She put them down on her coffee table and then settled in next to him on the couch.

"Smell's good huh," she said as she sat back.

"It does," Hunter, said making eye contact. He leaned in towards her. She didn't resist, he cupped her face and gave her a kiss.

Casey arched her back with nervous excitement. She had wondered what this moment would be like. As they continued to kiss, she relaxed into the couch bringing him with her. She placed her hand on the back of his head drawing him in to kiss her more deeply. Neither of them had been intimate in quite a while and they both relished the excitement of new romance.

When they finally broke their embrace, Casey fell limp into the couch with a satisfied smile. "You think the tea has steeped?" she asked.

"Well if it hasn't, we can give it a few more minutes."

Casey smiled and patted his cheek as she got up to go to the kitchen. "How do you like it?"

Hunter groaned softly. He wasn't thinking about tea. She caught the look in his eye and smiled.

"Honey it is," she said before he had a chance to respond.

When she came back, she brought honey, a little container of milk, some napkins and two spoons. "Here we go," she said and proceeded to fix both cups of tea. Hunter didn't care. Tea was tea. He had it from time to time, mostly when he had a cold.

Both of them sipped at the same time. Hunter was surprised at how smooth it went down. As it worked its way through his system, he felt a warm tingle come over him. He never had tea like this before and was beginning to understand why Casey enjoyed it so much.

"You like it, don't you?" Casey asked, seeing the relaxed expression on his face.

"I have to say, this is quite tasty. Far better than I would have imagined," he said. He took another sip. His usual intensity eased. The feeling was weird but at the same time nice. He wondered for a moment if the tea had something illegal in it but quickly shook off the thought. "This stuff is great."

"It is, isn't it," Casey said. She took a sip then another and began to feel herself fall into a trance but instead of fighting it, she let herself slide into the sleepy feeling. Her living room began to stretch away from her, almost becoming separate from it. She heard Hunter say something. She responded but didn't know what she said. It must have made sense because out of the corner of her eye, she noticed him take another sip then sit back into the couch.

As Casey continued to look straight ahead, a vision overcame her. She saw herself as a little girl playing in the woods alongside a creek. She could hear her mother call out. She turned and saw her mom. A rush of sensations overcame Casey as tears filled her eyes. She didn't remember much about her mother. Her mom had passed away before she entered kindergarten. Mostly, Casey had what she called shadow memories of her mom; nice thoughts she framed in her mind from stories her aunt had told her. But now, in this moment, she could see her mother clearly, lean, pretty, brown hair that cascaded easily over her shoulders, a fair face, roundish like her own and smooth complexion.

Her mother walked up next to her and kissed the top of her head. Casey felt a teardrop stream down her face. She saw herself point to a creature with a protruding snout and large teeth on the other side of the creek. Her mom turned toward the animal. She grabbed Casey with force and hurried her into the house.

From behind a screened in porch, she watched her mother pointing at the creature, which had now grown much larger. Its face was fierce and it looked to howl at her mother. Casey heard her mother yell something and then watched as the creature turned and disappeared into the woods. When her mother saw that Casey had witnessed the scene, she became angry. Her mother was about to say something when suddenly Casey felt a tug and then another.

"Are you okay?" asked Hunter, his voice pulling her back to reality. "You alright?" he asked again. "Are you crying?"

Casey wiped the tear from her face. She could see the genuine concern on his face. "I saw my mother," she blurted out.

Hunter said nothing.

"I don't remember my mother," she said softly. "She died when I was four. But just now, I had such a clear vision of her." Casey began to sob.

Hunter wrapped his arms around her. "It's okay, it's okay." he said trying to soothe her.

She felt comfortable in his embrace. She wrapped her arms around him, clinging to him like a life preserver. She said thank you a few times but wasn't sure for what. He simply held her and stroked her hair.

"Boy, that's some tea huh?" Hunter said trying to lighten the mood. He looked at the tea, wanting to take it for testing.

Casey laughed a soft laugh as she pulled away to wipe her eyes. "I'm sorry about that. I can't even think why that would have happened."

"I'm going to say that it was the ass kicking tea."

"Did you feel anything?"

"I felt relaxed and at ease, with a hint of numbness I think," he returned. "I'd like to think it was the company that made it so relaxing." He placed his hand on her back and gave it a soft rub.

She turned to him, "I was expecting relaxation and peace." She looked off again. "I can't believe what happened. I have never had such a vivid vision of my mom." She paused. "Oh my, you must be thinking what kind of whacko did I get involved with here?"

"Stop it," he said. Yes, he thought it was odd but not enough to scare him off.

She wanted to describe the vision but decided against it.

"Are you going to drink anymore?" Hunter asked.

A look of worry crossed her face. "I don't know. Do you think I should?"

"Well, it is one way to see if there is some kind of mild hallucinogenic in it. It's either that or the taste or the smell triggered something in your subconscious to set your imagination in motion," Hunter said.

"You think?" Casey asked.

"Well if it's psychological, all kinds of triggers can set off different kinds of reactions and responses. An awareness that the tea could do something like that now gives you the power to render it moot. If it's a mild hallucinogen that caused your episode, powers of observation most likely will do nothing," he said.

She rolled her eyes. "That's reassuring."

"It's a theory," he said with a shrug.

"So now you're Einstein and Carl Jung?" she said with a grin. "Tell you what… the heck with the tea. Where were we before?" She leaned into him for a kiss.

They embraced and eased themselves into the couch, molding their bodies to the contours. Their kisses became more passionate; hands moved with emphasis, muscles tightened and loosened with excitement. Thoughts of what had just occurred vanished. Now they simply concentrated on enjoying each other. Hunter reached under her blouse and gently slid his hand along the soft skin of her abdomen until he came to cup her breast. She let out a moaning sigh, stopped him.

"Come with me," she whispered. Casey took his hand and led him towards her bedroom.

CHAPTER 20

The night was unusually humid for spring. The air was so thick it took energy just to breathe. To make matters worse, the air was dead still, no breeze for comfort. It felt more like an August night than an April one.

The flames on the candles outlining the small clearing within the woods stood perfectly straight. People dressed in dark robes with hoods draped over their faces rotated around a glowing fire. Five candles burned along the end points of a roughly fashioned star at the edges of the fire pit.

Dressed in similar garb, others stood in a semi-circle outside the inner one in total silence. In the dim light of the fire, beads of sweat shimmered and fell from the faces underneath the hoods, landing in the rough sandy soil.

The inner group rotated counter clockwise, stopping at each candle to chant, then moving on to the next one in unison. When the cycle completed, a low hum began to emanate from the whole group. At the top tip of the star, the lead figure, wearing a thick red belt around his robe, raised his arms. Slowly, he raised his head and in a deep voice, spoke in a tranquil rhythm.

"Oh majestic one whose darkness rules our heart, hear our praise."

The others responded in a low murmur, "May your name be praised."

The leader continued. "Hear our wishes and grant us your power to do your will."

Again a response, "To do your will."

The leader: "Give us strength to continue your deeds and have faith in you."

Response: "Deeds and Faith."

The leader: "Grant us wisdom that we may not falter in knowing your power."

Response: "Your Wisdom and Power."

The leader: "Give us understanding, so that we may know your lust and that we may bathe our souls in your spirit."

Response: "To Know Your Lust."

Silence followed except for the crackle of the fire. No one moved and all heads remained bowed.

The leader, raising his arms, spoke again. "This night we give blood to you our most sacred savior of darkness. We honor your power and enlist a new crusader to do your work, so that you may return to rule and enslave those who reject you, try to destroy you and dismiss you."

A college-aged girl appeared, flanked on either side by two hooded members who led her to the leader. She wore a robe like the others but her hood did not cover her head. She was slender and pretty with long dark hair that fell over her shoulders to her mid torso. The leader nodded to the presenters and they released her.

The leader extended his hand and she touched his palm with her fingertips.

"You have passed the deeds of initiation. Are you now ready to sacrifice blood in honor of the one we praise?"

"Yes," she answered.

"Do you take in your heart the lust of darkness?"

"Yes."

"Do you reject the ideals of God, his prophets and all his teachings?"

"Yes."

"Will you serve with honor and dedication, the deeds he pronounces?"

"Yes."

"And will you serve him loyally, preserve his name, and give your soul to him so that he may use the power of your spirit to conquer this world once and for all?"

"I will."

"Now, are you ready to complete your submission with blood?"

She responded, "I am."

The leader reached into his robe and pulled out a sheathed dagger. He placed the shimmering blade in the palm of his hand in plain view for her to see.

"With this act you give your soul, your life to the one who will one day raise his fiery kingdom so that all may bask in his power. And in that kingdom, you will have a special room where you will serve and know his loyalty because of this sacrifice. By giving your blood, you open your soul for him to draw strength; for him to break the shackles by which his jailer keeps him but cannot hold him forever."

She nodded. "I gladly give my blood, my soul and my lust to him. That he may conquer the world and all may tremble before him. That he will look favorably upon me as his loyal subject and in the coming end, see fit to do with me as he will."

The hooded leader raised the blade. He passed it slowly before her face. Her chest began to heave with deeper breaths but in all, she remained calm. The rest of the group began to voice a low, steady hum. The leader ran the flat side of the knife gently across her neck. She panted in excitement. The hum grew louder. The leader's hand touched the front of her neck and a rush of anticipation shot through her. Her breathing became more intense. She raised her hands to her shoulder, arched her head towards the sky then pushed the robe off her shoulders so it dropped to the ground, revealing her naked body. She trembled in excitement. The leader traced the blade of the knife over her entire body. The hum rose.

A sharp wisp broke the dead air. Members on the periphery of the formation felt the rush of air sweep by them. The girl became even more excited when she heard another sharp wisp cut the air as the brief sound encircled her. The hum of the group grew louder.

The leader spoke, "Show me your palms."

She turned them to him; they were moist with her perspiration.

"Know him as your keeper," he said as he took the tip of the dagger and pierced the skin in the middle of her palm. She moaned as the dagger dug in. Blood stained the tip as he withdrew it. He took her other palm and again he pierced the skin and she moaned even louder.

"Do you submit to his will?" he asked.

With her eyes closed, her knees buckling, she whispered, "Yes."

"Will you march for him as his soldier of darkness?" he asked.

She nodded. He then knelt to her feet. He took the dagger and again pierced the skin in the middle of her one foot. She curled her toes into the sand and moaned with ecstasy.

A sharp, quick screech broke through the hum. A few in the group raised their heads to see if the devil himself would actually appear. Others remained hypnotized, entranced in the ritual, humming louder.

The leader brought the dagger to her other foot. "Do you choose to walk in the darkness and reject the light?"

"Yes," she shouted as she gasped in excitement, her heart pounding.

This time the dagger dug deeper and with more force. She moaned in pleasure. The leader then ran the bloody blade up her leg and massaged her thigh with it.

She moaned again and then another screech broke through the darkness. The hum of the group grew even louder and more frenzied. Bodies swayed, hypnotized by the rhythm.

The leader gently placed the blade between her legs, pressing it on her vagina.

"With this last sacrifice, do you reject the blessing that was given to you as a child?"

"Yes."

The leader then turned the blade and quickly flicked it across her clitoris, cutting it and letting the blood pour onto the blade. She stood remarkably still and continued to breathe hard. He brought the bloody blade to her mouth.

"Now take and drink, for this is your blood that you give to him."

She stuck her tongue out and he lightly laid the blade onto it gently wiping both sides in her mouth. She swirled the taste of her own blood around on her tongue.

He withdrew the blade and sheathed it.

"Welcome sister of darkness, you are now a soldier of the one true essence." He pulled back his hood and the humming came to a low din. The leader was sweating heavy as he kneeled down to grab her robe and put it back on her. Another screech ripped through the night air, far louder than before. Many in the group now began to look around. A low gurgle hissed in the thickets, then shifted to another part of the dark woods. The sounds moved in waves. Hissing, gurgling, sniffing, panting, the sounds surrounded them. The leader turned in all directions until something caught his eye. An adrenaline rush surged through his body. His breathing became heavy. He saw flashes of little red dots moving about in the scrub.

"He has come to us!" he said, excited.

Others became unsteady as they twisted their bodies trying to locate the source of the constantly moving sounds.

"Reveal yourself master!" the leader shouted.

The girl then cried out, "Take me."

A great force rushed through the middle of the ceremonial area. A loud curdling screech followed. Several of the members fell to their knees, some in reverence, some in blind fear. The girl stood, arms out stretched, her robe open, willing to sacrifice herself. The creature aimed for her, smelling her, wanting to taste her blood and flesh. With a sudden thud, the creature knocked her to the ground and sank its fangs into her neck and shoulder, tearing deep into her flesh. She made only the slightest sound as the last breath of her life escaped into the thick night air.

Hardly anyone moved. Some didn't even know what had occurred. The creature turned to the leader. Their eyes met. The pulsing evil of the creatures red eyes captured him. He couldn't move. The creature hissed, showing its jagged razor teeth, and then pounced on him, digging into the leader's abdomen, shredding the skin into tiny pieces.

One of the members finally realized what was happening and screamed. The creature's head shot up from the bloody mess and zeroed in on the screamer. It could taste the person's breath and shot straight for him. Several others realized the immediate danger but froze with fright. The screaming man fell silent as the creature severed his head in one swift movement then feasted on the blood pulsing from his neck. A woman, standing right next to the latest victim shook, with terror. She wanted to run but could not move. The creature stopped his gorging, sniffed, and looked at her.

"Forgive me Lord," she whispered.

The creature screeched and tackled her. In seconds, it ripped her limbs from her body. Other members had now come to their senses and started to run. Like a flash of lightning, the creature pursued each one, tackling them, and disabling them by ripping off a leg or tearing deep into their skin rendering them powerless to move.

Other members, still frozen with fear began to cry, while others prayed for forgiveness. The creature showed no mercy, it just wailed in delight at its great bounty and continued its rounds, ripping limbs, and feasting on all of the blood and flesh. It circled the area one last time, sniffing, and hissing. It shook, screeched and writhed in pleasure as it looked over its kill.

Several beams of light then broke through the night. The creature turned towards them. The illumination of flashlights created swirling points of light about fifty yards away. The creature looked again at its hunt. It was full and satisfied. It stretched itself to it tallest height, belted one last horrific screech and disappeared into the shadows of the forest.

Hunter heard his phone buzzing because of the racket it made vibrating against his pocketful of change and keys. He found his pants on the floor and grabbed his phone. He didn't want to answer it but he needed to see who was calling.

He looked at the number. "Shit," he whispered seeing it was his captain.

"Yes sir," he answered. Hunter just nodded and answered 'Yes sir' or 'I understand' the entire time. When the conversation ended, he said thank you and hung up.

Hunter looked back at Casey sleeping, her bare back exposed and thought *things are starting to turn my way*. Getting back into the bed, he ran his finger lightly along her shoulder and arm. She stirred.

"Is everything okay?" she mumbled, her eyes still half closed.

"Everything is fine," he said still running his fingers gently over her soft skin. It felt nice and he didn't want to stop. "But my captain just called. Believe it or not I've been personally requested to assist in a case out of the county and he wants me on it immediately."

She gathered herself and sat up. "That's good," she said rubbing her eyes.

"I hope so. But it means I have to go."

Casey nodded. "Okay. Let me know how it goes," she said as she slithered back into the sheets.

"I'll call you later." He leaned over and kissed her.

The crisp chill of the morning invigorated Hunter. He felt fortunate for the chance to redeem himself, though he still didn't know any details about the case. The captain said he would fill him in once he reported to the station. As he took another breath, he wondered why someone from another county would need his assistance.

He wasn't driving five minutes when his phone buzzed again.

"Detective Matthews," the captain said. "Change of plans... I'm forwarding you details, contact info and location."

"Yes sir," Hunter replied, surprised at how all this was unfolding.

"It's a big murder case," Captain Morgan said. "A bizarre one; there was a request for you. How this has come about is beyond me but this captain, Captain Rackers has heard about some of your recent murder investigations and thinks you might be of some help."

"I understand sir," Hunter answered.

"Don't screw it up. Update me later today."

"Yes sir."

Over the next hour of driving, Hunter studied the information sent to him, mostly a profile of the area, population, demographics, crime, size of the police department and some notes on Captain Rackers, his contact. On several occasions, he found himself drifting on the road, making hard swerves to center his vehicle. At one point, he even had to pull over to read the information properly. Details about the crime scene were minimal; multiple murders out in the woods, bizarre wounds, not much else. But... he had a feeling.

As he continued down another long stretch of road, thick woods on both sides, his new GPS device told him he was on the correct street. Hunter wanted to see some sign of police activity to let him know he was close.

No sooner had he completed his thought than he saw a patrol car blocking an entrance to a small cut out in the woods. He slowed down and pulled onto the shoulder near the vehicle.

A giant of a man stepped out. Hunter could only guess he must have been the hometown football hero or its fabled protector. The very large and muscular police officer took purposeful steps towards Hunter who had rolled down his window to greet the giant man.

"Can I help you?" the officer asked in a deep stoic voice.

"Maybe," Hunter answered friendlier than he normally would. "My name is Detective Hunter Matthews. I'm here at the request of Captain Rackers. I was informed he is somewhere in this region. Is he beyond your blockade?"

"May I see some identification?" the officer asked, not changing his tone.

Hunter could see there was no amusing this man. He revealed his badge as well as his driver's license just to play nice. The hulk like man took the materials and told him to stay put.

The officer wasn't in his car long before he re-emerged and headed back towards Hunter. He handed back the items. "You can pass. Follow this road until it comes to a fork then take it to the right. You'll see the activity."

"How do I know you aren't setting up a trap and bunch of giants like yourself aren't going to ambush me then throw me around like a small toy?" Hunter said with a playful mocking.

The officer smiled but it wasn't friendly. "You look too easy to break. It wouldn't be much fun tossing around a skin bag of bones."

"Thank you officer… good to know," Hunter said while giving a casual salute.

The narrow sand road was barely wide enough for one average size car to get through. He hoped he wouldn't have to figure out how to deal with an oncoming vehicle. Thankfully, he saw the split appear quickly and noticed the road widened as he stayed to the right. Within a mile, he began to see vehicles parked to the sides of the road. As he slowly drove by, people began to appear. He spotted two EMT vehicles. Soon enough, a police officer stepped out in front of him and signaled for him to stop.

"Can I help you?" the officer said as he approached Hunter's car.

He was nowhere near as large as the officer guarding the entrance. Hunter poked his head out of the window, showed his badge and told him he was there to see Captain Rackers. The officer pointed to a spot for him to park.

Hunter noticed a surprising amount of people on the scene. His information said the police department was small but the activity going on before him was anything but that. There were no less than twenty people moving about that he could count. As he made his way into the melee, he asked a sergeant where he could find Captain Rackers. The sergeant pointed out a man who resembled what Hunter could only describe as a modern day Ichabod Crane: a tall man of at least six and a half feet and rail thin. He had a noticeable Adams Apple, a long distinguishable nose and a posture that bent slightly forward.

A swarm of people surrounded Captain Rackers. He directed the flow of activity, and controlled the scene with competence. Hunter was impressed as he began his approach.

"Captain Rackers sir," Hunter said.

Captain Rackers turned to Hunter the moment he heard his name called.

"Detective Matthews," Rackers said acknowledging him without having met him before.

Hunter reached out his hand to greet the tall lanky man and Rackers' firm grip confirmed that he was the man in charge.

"I wish I had more time for pleasantries detective but as you can see, there is nothing pleasant about the current situation," Rackers said.

"I understand," Hunter replied.

"Yes," Rackers acknowledged. "Anyway, Detective Matthews, I understand you have had an encounter with…" Captain Rackers pursed his lips wanting to be delicate but then tossed the notion out of his head. "The Jersey Devil or what could possibly be the Jersey Devil."

Hunter didn't know how to react. He didn't expect such a forward response. "I had an experience sir… that is correct. Now whether it was in fact the Jersey Devil or not, I'm not certain."

"Very well," Rackers replied. "Regardless of semantics, let's call it that until some zoologist can confirm otherwise because from what I have gathered, even with DNA, the identity of your suspect is still unknown. So right now, I need whatever expertise you may have gleamed from your puzzling cases, to help shed light on our most bizarre one. From what I've been able to gather, there are many similar traits to the ones you've experienced." The tall captain leaned over Hunter, making him feel more uncomfortable than intimidated.

"Why don't you fill me in on what you've discovered and I will see what I can offer," Hunter said.

A big smile crossed Rackers long thin face. "That is an excellent idea detective. I like a man of careful thinking and reason." He placed his long bony fingers on Hunter's shoulder and pointed with his other hand as he led him towards where a campfire had been.

It wasn't much of a fire pit but Hunter noticed that medium sized rocks of similar shape had been precisely stacked to form a tight circle. Even in the remnants of the embers, he could see that it was a carefully made fire.

"Ceremonial, ritual," Hunter said.

Rackers nodded. "It has been hypothesized."

Hunter looked around more closely and spotted shredded fabric randomly tossed around the grounds. "I'll venture it was some devil worshipping ritual."

Rackers grinned. "I knew my hunch to call upon you was correct."

"Were your men not able to make that deduction?" Hunter said continuing to examine the area.

Rackers tilted his head. "They were able to make it but it took them over an hour to draw that conclusion. And, they had many more pieces of evidence to go on. You made the same conclusions on far less and haven't even seen the victims or other evidence we have collected."

"I appreciate the kind words sir but the scene your men came upon, the initial shock of the find and the general chaos of the scene, anyone would take a while to put the pieces together."

"A humble man at that," Rackers said with amusement. "Humility and detectives don't often go hand in hand."

Hunter snickered to himself. *If he only knew.*

"Sergeant Harrison," Captain Rackers called out. The sergeant, who was talking to some other officers, turned and came towards them. "Sergeant, you have a preliminary timeline of what has happened and a complete inventory of all the victims and materials?"

"We have a good bead on it sir. Still a few odds and ends to go over. We also have a few officers combing the perimeter for any other evidence, or victims," Sergeant Harrison replied. "Still it's going to be a while to organize everything in a proper order sir."

"Yet it sounds like you have the situation in hand," Rackers said, standing at near attention with his arms held behind his back, his long chin jutting out. "I'd like you to escort Detective Matthews here and show him the scene. Brief him on as much as you can."

"Yes sir," the sergeant said, then turned to Hunter and asked him to follow.

Hunter looked back towards Rackers. The captain raised an eyebrow as he gave a nod.

"Over here detective," Sergeant Harrison gestured. He pointed to a small cut out in the woods. At first glance, it looked like a small camping spot until he noticed a covered body. "This was the first body found," the sergeant informed him.

"Who found it?" Hunter asked as he kneeled down closer to the victim.

"Hunters," Sergeant Harrison replied.

"Hunters?" Hunter blurted out, surprised by the response. "So we have witnesses?"

"We have three people who came onto the scene."

"Where are these people?"

"Back at the station. They were quite shaken up. Two of them threw up all over the place. When they calmed down, we were able to get some information. None of them saw or heard anything."

"Can we hold them until I have a chance to see what they have to say?" Hunter asked, not sure what his authority was in this case.

"I'll find out for you," the sergeant said. "But after this body was found, the second one was found over here," and he walked around to the other side of a tree only a few feet away to another covered body. "It's gruesome under there. You can take a look if you like. We've photographed nearly the entire site. The EMT's want to start removing bodies but Rackers had them hold off until you got here."

Hunter nodded as he listened. He went back to the first victim. He pulled back the sheet to reveal a head. Nothing looked out of the ordinary. It wasn't until he pulled the sheet down further that he saw a shredded open torso. Hundreds of tiny shards of skin just barely hanging onto the body while chunks of organ appeared to resemble a thick brew of dark stew. Hunter felt his stomach twinge and he quickly pulled the sheet back over the body.

"Terrible sight huh…," the sergeant said. "I blew chow the first time I saw it. A lot of guys did."

"I can understand that," Hunter said, choking back vomit that had run up his throat. "Tell me what you know. Does anyone have a theory about the order of the kill? Who was first?"

"I do not believe we have anything like that detective but I can find out."

"Fine," Hunter said. He stood up and composed himself. "How many bodies are there?"

"Sixteen that we have found."

"Sixteen?"

"Currently… we are continuing to look."

"Okay. Show me."

The sergeant pointed to three other bodies. Bracing himself this time, Hunter leaned over one of the bodies and pulled back the sheet. The wounds looked remarkably similar to the first victim. Something with extraordinary precision had sliced these people to shreds yet left only a neat pool of blood.

"This certainly wasn't done by one person or even a group," Hunter mumbled.

"I'm sorry," Sergeant Harrison said, not hearing him.

"Nothing," Hunter replied. "Just thinking out loud."

"Any idea how many people you think did this?" the sergeant asked.

"No, not yet," Hunter answered, surmising Captain Rackers hadn't shared his alternative viewpoint with some of his staff. "Has anyone found any defensive wounds or signs of restraint?"

"Not that I've heard," the sergeant answered. "But I've been overseeing the operation rather than doing any kind of investigative work."

Hunter walked over to the next body and the next. The wounds were all similar. The damage to the bodies was vicious. *Whatever these people set out to do, something went incredibly wrong.* It was hard to fathom exactly what occurred until he remembered how that creature tore Staffen into pieces within seconds. With that vision in mind, his gaze took him to the fire pit. He stood up and walked to it.

"Sergeant?" Hunter called. He cocked his head. "Do you see anything odd about this fire pit?"

Sergeant Harrison took a minute to look it over. "Not really."

"I think I see something….a pentagram," Hunter said.

"A pentagram?"

"Yes. It's a bit messy, but I see five points along the ring of the pit," he said while pointing out the tips of the star. "Someone tried to fashion a pentagram in the pit." He looked further and noticed a candle partially buried in the loose packed sand around the pit. "Sergeant, check around the pit and see if you can find any candles."

"We've found several candles scattered about the place earlier. We photographed them and bagged them" he responded.

"Good," Hunter replied. "But let's see if we can find any either in or just outside the pit," Hunter said. In minutes, the two of them located the other candles that marked the outline of the pentagram.

"That's freaky stuff," Sergeant Harrison said.

"It is," Hunter exhaled. "I think we can move on from speculation to certainty that this was some sort of Devil Worshipping ceremony gone wrong." Hunter then asked. "Has the hospital been notified about what's coming its way?"

"I believe so. The degree of how much they know is another matter," the sergeant answered.

"I need to know now and I need for hospital personnel to keep this as quiet as humanly possible. If news of this gets out, there will be a massive panic and TV trucks running every which way through the area," Hunter said.

"You can't keep something like this quiet for long," the sergeant responded.

"You're right about that but if we can get a day.... even a half day." Hunter's voice trailed off as he looked into the woods. "We just need a day."

# CHAPTER 21

"I need to stay down here sir," Hunter said to Captain Morgan from his cell phone while sitting at a desk back at the police station. He filled him in about the devil worshipping ritual and the brutality of the crime. Hunter informed him they found the vehicles a mile away in a parking area that hunters and fishermen often used. They surmised four cars transported all the victims. The cars contained the identity of six victims. The rest still had Jane and John Doe classifications.

"I understand," Captain Morgan, answered. "Just how long do you think this is going to take? I'm sure they have a lot of paper work to file, the bodies have to be processed and the evidence organized." Morgan paused knowing Hunter would not like what he was about to say. "Besides, Captain Rackers has to call this into the State Troopers. A murder like this is too big for his taskforce."

"I understand but you know when that happens, this will become big news and send the area into an unnecessary panic," Hunter pleaded. "And you know the state police will never pursue the angle I was called in for"

"What are you saying?"

"Those people weren't killed by some mass murderers or wild ritual suicide," Hunter said. "From what I've seen, there's only one answer."

"And that is?" Morgan asked closing his eyes, already knowing the answer.

Hunter took a deep breath. "The same thing that killed Staffen, Joe West, those two hunters and would have most likely killed me."

"The Jersey Devil?" the captain said as if baiting him.

"Yeah, for lack of anything else, let's call it that." Hunter answered.

"And you are basing this on what evidence?" Morgan asked.

"On the lack of evidence that it can be anything else," Hunter answered. "The site shows no evidence of a struggle, no weapons, no signs of anyone having been restrained, no signs of an ambush and with the apparent level of destruction, no defensive wounds. Nothing points to a murder that we can rationally explain."

Morgan paused. The idea still sounded ludicrous.

Just then, Captain Rackers walked into the room. He half heard the conversation. "My boy, I like your keen perception and passion." He waved for Hunter to hand him the phone. Rackers took it and promptly got to the point, "I would like to borrow your man for a short spell if it is alright with you captain."

Captain Morgan rolled his eyes at hearing the request. "He can stay as long as you need him."

"Thank you sir," Rackers said bowing a little as he answered. "You are most gracious." Rackers paused a moment as he pursed his lips and looked skyward, squinting his eyes.

Hunter watched with mild amusement. Rackers had the characterization of a 19th century detective with his demeanor, language, and posture.

Rackers handed the phone back to Hunter. "I believe I'll try and hold off until tomorrow about informing the state. But as you know, it must be done. There is simply no way of getting around this sticky wicket."

Hunter was relieved to hear he had more time. "Thank you sir." He turned his attention back to his captain. "Sir, thank you for this opportunity; I'll keep you up to date."

"Good," Captain Morgan said, and hung up.

"Where to start?" Hunter muttered.

"Yes," Captain Rackers said his ears ever so sensitive to the softest of murmurs. "I'm assembling a team for you. I will have them report to you within the hour." Captain Rackers bowed, turned to leave the room then paused to offer another piece of advice. "Don't hesitate to use whatever resources you feel you may need."

"Thank you sir," Hunter said. *Resources....Casey.*

Casey sped down the Garden State Parkway. She was excited. Dorothy had called and wanted to share something important. Hunter called almost immediately after, wanting her to join his investigation. She decided to visit Dorothy first. Hunter was going to be busy outlining his hypothesis to a new team and setting up an investigation plan. Casey figured if Dorothy offered any useful insight that it might serve Hunter better when she finally arrived.

As she drove through the center of town for the second time, she slowed to look at Arthur's antique shop. He was a sweet old man but his haunted expression sent a shiver through her. She wondered what he was doing. She wondered if he knew she had returned.

The drive to Dorothy's didn't feel as long the second time but it wasn't any less intimidating. The trees still leaned over the road as if peering into her car. As she made her way past the first bend, she could feel a twinge of goose bumps shoot up the back of her neck. She peered into the woods wondering if the beast was there.

The small entrance to the road came up quick and she nearly passed it again. Casey pulled into the driveway and parked in the same spot as her last visit. She walked up the porch stairs, knocked on the door and waited. There was no response. She tried the doorbell. Nothing. Even though Dorothy had made her feel welcome and told her to treat the house as a friendly place, she still didn't feel right about just opening the door and walking in. Instead, she walked the length of the porch, trying to peer in the windows. She first looked along the library but couldn't make out much except for the shapes of the bookshelves. She walked past the front door again, stopped to listen, but still heard nothing. She walked towards the kitchen end of the porch. Casey felt apprehensive. Dorothy seemed so guarded about this part of the house. Casey sensed it was off limits. Slowly she went to look into the kitchen through the outside window when she heard a voice. Casey screamed, knocking her head on a hanging planter. She turned to see Dorothy standing a few feet behind her holding a tray of tea.

"Sorry dear, I didn't mean to startle you. Are you alright?" Dorothy said with a concerned tone. "Oh my, you've banged your ahead again."

Casey thought she heard a hint of a chuckle minced in Dorothy's words.

Casey put one hand on her chest and the other on her head. "I think I'll be okay in a minute. You really scared me." She looked back up at the planter. "And what's with banging my head when we meet?"

"I see that. I'm truly sorry, that was not my intention. I heard you knock and ring the doorbell but I was preparing some tea for us. I'm sorry I couldn't get to the door sooner. I just can't move from place to place as quickly as I used to."

Casey understood. "No I'm sorry for my impatience. I hope you don't think I'm rude for trying to look into your house. I wasn't sure what to do. I thought something might have happened."

Dorothy smiled. "I understand dear. I'm an old woman. You knock and ring the doorbell and no one answers, it's understandable that you would want to see if I had fallen."

Casey nodded.

"Sit dear" Dorothy said motioning to the swing. "This tea is nice and fresh."

"Thank you," Casey said as she sat back into the swing.

"I take it your drive here was fine?" Dorothy asked handing her a cup.

"It was fine, and thank you," Casey said. She wanted to say something about the way she felt the last time she had sipped her tea but she couldn't bring herself to it. "So you had something you wanted to share with me."

"Yes dear. I do have some news. Compelling news."

Casey sat up in her seat and leaned closer.

"Last night I could not sleep, which is not uncommon but this was different. I found myself wandering this big ol house. Something was not right. I decided I would make some tea. The same kind I gave you. It can help with sleep."

Casey wondered if the tea had something in it, she might be allergic to. She once had a bad reaction when taking a sleeping pill. It made her jittery and lightheaded rather than sleepy.

"Anyway, while boiling the water, I kept getting the feeling I was being watched. I even called out, 'who's there?' But of course, no one was. I poured my water in to the cup and let the tea steep." Dorothy paused and then looked pensively into her cup.

Casey could see fear in her expression. She watched the old woman's face drain and her body seemingly become frail.

"Then I looked out into the yard and slowly, very slowly I could see it; the figure of the beast," Dorothy said, her voice quivering.

Casey gasped. "It came back?"

Dorothy looked at her with big empty eyes. "It stepped out of the shadows of the darkness and revealed itself to me. Our eyes met. I became paralyzed. I couldn't move."

Casey put her cup down. She reached over and lightly touched Dorothy's arm. "Are you okay? Did it do anything to you?"

Dorothy smiled, grateful for her concern. "No dear, it didn't do anything and I'm fine. I just wanted to share it with you. It had been so long since I'd last seen it that I had nearly forgotten how truly frightening it is. The fear was far greater than I ever remembered."

"But you are okay. That's what matters most," Casey said.

"Yes. But I fear something terrible happened," Dorothy said, her eyes going empty and dark again.

"Why do you say that?"

"Because whenever it shows itself something terrible always happens or has happened," Dorothy whispered, her bony fingers clutching the cup and bringing it up to her mouth for another sip.

"So you've seen it more than twice?"

Dorothy sighed. "Yes."

Hunter looked at the team Captain Rackers had promised to provide. He imagined more than just the three men who sat before him. It was going to dwindle to two, since one of them, Jack Reilly from the county K-9 unit, was only his for the next four hours.

"Welcome gentlemen," Hunter said with steely confidence. "As you are aware, we have a gruesome and puzzling tragedy on our hands. Your captain has guaranteed me your utmost confidence and discretion as we work this case over the next twenty four hours – give or take."

Hunter briefly explained why Rackers asked him to help investigate the crime. The faces, skeptical at first, turned to intrigue, transfixed by the oddity of the circumstances. Hunter expressed how they would most likely never experience anything like this again and that they should use extreme discretion in how they talked about this case. He said the first order of business was to go back to the scene of the crime.

When they arrived at the location, Hunter approached the officer who was protecting the scene and identified himself. The officer was expecting him, which Hunter found odd because he had not told anyone his plans. The officer explained that Captain Rackers notified him with instructions to give Hunter complete access to the crime scene. Hunter wasted no time. He immediately directed his two officers, Ken Berkman and Eric Muskov to split up and work their way outward about ten yards and then back, looking for anything odd, including hairs or fibers. He had told them a fiber from a prior scene contained unidentifiable DNA and explained that if they could produce another sample, then they could cross check for a connection. Hunter was able to secure some pieces of clothing from the victims and had Jack Reilly from K-9 use it hoping a singular distinct scent might emerge. If so, maybe there would be a distinguishable trail aside from the victims. He didn't think the dog would find anything because past dogs didn't come up with anything. Still, he had to see if this time might be different.

Hunter went to work around the fire pit. He examined the circuitous route the worshippers walked. Looking at the pattern, he worked to recall his tracking knowledge. As a youth he found it fascinating that people could simply study terrain and detect the slightest imperfections to reveal who or what had passed through an area, how long ago and the rate of speed. At one time, he was a pretty good tracker but now, looking over the trampled terrain, he wished he hadn't let those skills go to waste.

The best he could determine was that the participants had dragged or shuffled their feet through the sand as they circled. He determined this by the little pilings of sand that were interspersed in the circle. He hoped for a solid footprint but found nothing. Besides, with all the earlier activity, nearly all signs of discernible tracks and footprints had disappeared.

Taking out his small notebook, he drew a rough outline of the clearing, placing the fire pit in the center. Starting closest to the fire pit, he drew little dots in his notebook representing the bodies of the victims. He kept walking and jotting based on the little flags in the ground, placed there by other officers, to show where each victim lay. At first, the dots resembled a jumble. He continued jotting down the locations of the bodies, while examining the terrain, when a pattern emerged. He took his pencil and connected some of the dots. A smile creased his face. Three sets of five disjointed circles. *What was the purpose of 16 when three rings of five made more sense for a ritual?*

Hunter heard one of his men coming. It was Officer Berkman. "Did you find anything?" Hunter asked.

Berkman shook his head. "I went way out. I looked for odd tracks, broken tree branches, hair samples. I couldn't find anything, not on this pass anyway. Do you want me to go out and comeback from another angle?"

Hunter said no. "Let's keep it to this section now and see if we can find anything."

It wasn't long before the other two officers returned. Both came up empty. Hunter told them not to be discouraged. The angle they were working was so unusual that the likelihood of finding physical evidence was slim. He shared that the other scenes lacked evidence as well.

"Have you found anything interesting sir?" asked Muskov.

"I have," Hunter, answered. "But I have yet to solidify its meaning." Hunter told them about the circles and the three layers of five. He was certain of a ceremony but he couldn't figure out why there were sixteen people rather than fifteen.

Muskov asked to have a look at the drawing. Hunter handed it to him when he noticed Muskov's watch.

"Today's the 6th…," Hunter said, half asking.

"Yes," Muskov answered.

In a whisper, Hunter said, "6, 1, 6," then shook his head. "Not quite 666," he said louder.

"No," Muskov said with a gleeful surprise. "Better."

Hunter looked at him quizzically. "How better?"

"The original ancient Greek number for the devil is 616 not 666," Muskov said. "666 was a misinterpretation that stuck. Besides 666 always sounded more ominous. 616 is what some experts believe was meant to be the true number of the beast."

"Today's the 6th, there were sixteen people, 616," Hunter said. "It's always the simplest explanation no matter how hidden." Silence ensued as they all looked at the fire pit. Hunter's phone rang. "Matthews... Really? That is interesting... Oh my..."

# CHAPTER 22

Dorothy brought Casey into the library. They walked past the bookshelves and over to the filing cabinets where Casey had examined the newspaper clippings. Dorothy walked to and pointed at a drawer that Casey had yet to look in.

"Here dear," Dorothy said. "In here you'll find stories that have a certain oddness to them."

"Are these Jersey Devil related?" Casey asked. A shiver shot through her as she looked at the handle of the drawer. Her hand trembled as she reached to open it. At first, she saw only newspapers. There were no glaring headlines or gruesome pictures. She felt her nerves ease. She fingered through the clippings but didn't see anything of note.

"Go beyond the divider I placed in there. Take some of those out and I'll show you," Dorothy said. She hovered over Casey like a mother hen introducing her new chic to the world.

Casey took out a few clippings. The papers were yellowed and fragile. She took great care as she placed them on the top of the cabinet and fanned them out. She traced her fingers lightly across each clipping. She read the headlines: *Three Missing Hikers Found Dead, Hunters Can't Explain Attack on their Dogs, Woman Cleared of Gruesome Murder, Farm Mutilations Go Unexplained.* Then at the bottom of the series she read, *Man Blames Jersey Devil for Killing of Three.* Casey became lightheaded. She reached out to the cabinet to keep her balance.

"Are you alright dear?" Dorothy asked placing a comforting hand on her arm.

"I think I'm just a little overwhelmed." She took a minute to get her equilibrium back. "Are the rest of the clippings similar to these?"

"Some, yes, but mostly farm animal stories," Dorothy replied.

Casey couldn't believe the good fortune of information unfolding before her. "Thank you for all this," she said but was confused. "Why me? You hardly know me."

Dorothy beamed. "Because I trust you. I knew you were trustworthy from the moment we met. I have great instincts when it comes to people my dear."

Casey smiled cautiously. She was grateful for the access yet felt a twinge of uneasiness about it. "This is awfully kind of you."

Dorothy laughed. "Oh my dear, it's my pleasure to share this history with you." She paused. "Would you like something to drink? I was going to make myself some more tea. I can bring you some if you wish?"

Casey was thirsty but not for tea. "I'd love some water," she said.

"Water it is," Dorothy said and exited the room.

Casey turned her attention back to the newspapers. She took out her phone and began to take pictures of the different clippings. As she examined the articles, she noticed the dates covered a wide span of time from the nineties going back to the early sixties. She focused on one about a man, David Hastleton, who claimed the Jersey Devil killed his family. The crime took place nearly twenty-five years ago.

Dorothy returned with the water and a piping hot cup of tea. Casey could smell the fragrance. It seemed more pungent but appealing none-the-less. Casey placed the papers down and took the glass of water.

"Oh thank you,"

"The tea is for you too if you like," Dorothy said.

Casey looked at the cup sitting on the tray. There was something intoxicating about it. "Thank you," she said still looking at the cup on the tray.

The house phone began to ring. It surprised them both. "Just give me a shout if you need me," Dorothy said as she turned and walked away. Casey watched the old woman move with grace and hoped when she reached Dorothy's age she would have that much vitality and grace.

Casey wasted no time getting back to photographing the newspaper articles. She tried not to get involved with reading them. Her time was limited and she knew Hunter was waiting on her. Yet certain articles stood out and she couldn't resist giving them a glance. Having learned to speed-read a bit it was easy to capture the gist of an article. The farm animal mutilation stories resembled the case Hunter had initially investigated. Most of the articles never mentioned the Jersey Devil, yet Dorothy lumped them in with other Jersey Devil stories.

She also came across stories pertaining to David Hastleton's trial. This time she didn't have to open the paper to find the story, it was the headline: *Hastleton Found Guilty on All Counts.* Another article reported he received life in prison with no chance for parole. As she continued to search through the different newspapers, a pattern appeared. All the stories happened within approximately fifty miles from her current location.

She reached for another sip of water, when the cup of tea grabbed her attention. She reached for it and stopped. Something didn't feel right. Casey broke free of the pull and pushed the tray away. She continued to work. She couldn't believe all the stories before her that had gone untold over the years. She had read Jersey Devil material but had never encountered the stories she was now seeing.

"Did you not like the tea?" Dorothy said, her soft voice floating through the air.

Casey was getting used to Dorothy appearing out of nowhere but it still startled her. "I... I haven't tried it. I've been busy with all this great material."

"I could warm it up for you."

Casey felt a chill. Part of her wanted to sip it and another side said to beware. The anxiety of the moment caused her to feel flush.

"It's something new I created. I think you will find it quite intoxicating," Dorothy said with a salesperson's ease.

Casey stared at the cup. Inside her mind, she felt two battles competing for her attention. One said to reject the tea and the other, the more comforting voice said to take it and enjoy.

Dorothy picked up the cup and ever so slightly brought it towards Casey. "Would you like me to refresh it?" she said, her words penetrating into Casey's consciousness.

Casey didn't know why but she said yes. Dorothy smiled and took the cup back to her kitchen. Casey stood watching Dorothy move as if she were floating. When the doorbell rang, the sound of the chimes broke the spell and Casey shook off the trance. Dorothy put the cup down and answered the door. It was a deliveryman with a package. Casey quickly shook her head, turned, looked at the newspapers and decided that she had gathered enough information for one day. She needed to leave and catch up with Hunter.

Hunter's temporary office was a small steel gray interrogation room. Captain Rackers provided extra chairs, pads, pens, a landline phone and two small desks to make it a functional workspace. It was more than suitable for a twenty-four hour investigation. Hunter looked at his watch. It was just after 2pm – half the day gone. They now had positive ID on eight of the bodies. In front of him lay a folder with the most recent photos of the crime scene accompanied by a brief, unofficial summary, pertaining to some of the mortal wounds the victims had suffered. He sat down to look at it. He sent Muskov and Berkman to pick up food and discuss what they had all discovered. Jack Reilly left, having to report to his county office and assist in investigating a possible gang killing. Gangs existed in the region and reports of recent activity drew the spotlight towards them. Rackers ordered a roundup of some local members for questioning in both the devil worshipping case and other recent suspicious activity.

Hunter needed to organize his facts. If he could find a connection to the Jersey Devil via this devil cult, facts and intuition would lead him to an answer. All his training steered his mind towards traditional approaches. He had to shake that, otherwise he knew he would simply be wasting everyone's time. He had to open himself to alternative suggestions. Still, the foundation of the investigation had to lie in the facts at hand. That much he knew.

He decided to start with the known victims. He needed to know more about the people and the group. What was its purpose? What was the routine? What were they looking to achieve out in the woods? Even though there was no evidence of defensive wounds, he simply did not believe these people willfully succumbed to slaughter.

Hunter organized the various folders on his desk. He opened one that had summaries about the wounds of the victims. It was hand written and he had trouble reading it. The handwriting was awful, but the words *unknown origin*, were decipherable and written several times. There was no signature or contact information but he noticed a common denominator, hospital letterhead. He wanted to know who sent this information. As he stood to leave, Muskov and Berkman walked in.

"Great, you're back," Hunter said. "I have to find out something. You see that small pile of folders on the desk? Divide it up between yourselves and find out everything you can about the victims, I'll be right back."

Hunter asked around about who had delivered the information to his desk but no one knew. He went to Captain Rackers's office. The door was partially open. He knocked and poked his head in to see the captain busy with paperwork.

The captain greeted Hunter. "Detective, how goes your investigation? Have you anything to report?"

Hunter paused. "I have my guys doing some background checks on the victims. We worked the crime scene again. I found an interesting pattern and we're checking it out. I'm certain now, beyond any doubt, that this was a satanic cult."

"Oh," Captain Rackers replied as he tapped his long boney fingers against each other. "How did you come to that conclusion?"

Hunter went on to explain the numerology in the pattern. The captain informed him that rumors had circulated about such a group in the area but it was never confirmed. Hunter asked about the hand written notes pertaining to the victim's wounds on hospital letterhead. He said it was rather odd to receive information without a source in a police folder.

Rackers made a grin; a sly one. "You see detective, I have many dealings with all sorts of people. Many of them would rather stay in the shadows. I let them have their anonymity yet I also want my officers to know the origin of certain information in case they need to dig more… Understand?"

"Yes. Your own version of cat and mouse," Hunter answered. "But hospital letterhead?"

"Discretion is vitally important detective, especially in these odd circumstances." Captain Rackers said. "I'll just add that you asked for time. I can grant a little. Others however have duties and protocol they must adhere too. In instances where I've asked them to bend the rules a little, well…they must have no connection to it. I will assume you get my meaning?"

Hunter said he understood.

"Oh, by the way, did you say earlier you had some kind of expert coming to assist you."

"I did." Hunter answered. He did not recall saying anything to the captain but he had come to realize this was no ordinary police captain.

"Good, I look forward to meeting this person and hearing their insight." Rackers went back to his paperwork without saying another word.

"How's it going guys?" Hunter asked as he walked into the cramped investigation room.

"We haven't made much of a dent. We're reading over these reports to see where we can go from here," Officer Berkman said.

"We've also made some calls to see what we can find out about our victims," Muskov added.

Hunter nodded in agreement. "So what do we have so far?"

Both took turns explaining what they knew. It didn't look as if any of the victims had a sordid past. The ages varied. The oldest victim was a senior who had not been identified and the youngest looked to be a college age woman but she wasn't identified either. However, Berkman noted, she did have several wounds that looked like knife punctures but nothing official. Hunter thought it was an interesting observation and asked to have it followed up. Overall, it was a diverse group of people. Emily Harding, a homemaker with three kids, 38, married for fifteen years. She was a semi active member in her church, at one point involved with girl scouts, and participated in school activities, otherwise quite ordinary. *Why the hell was she involved with these people?* Hunter thought. James McClaren, 50, cable installer, divorced, two kids. Not much else of note. *Bored or desperate to meet people* was Hunter's initial assumption. Jack Bennett, 43, single, IT at a casino in Atlantic City.

He was involved with his church as well. His credit report was good. He had several accounts with internet dating services – *follow up on this to see where it might lead.* The other identified victims all had rather ordinary histories. *Something binds them together.* Hunter needed to find that thread. *And where's Casey?*

Casey looked at her phone. "Do they have any cell towers around here?" she said as she moved her phone from place to place in her car while trying to drive. It frustrated her to see two bars then no bars, then one bar and on and on. She wanted to tell Hunter she was on her way. She sent several texts but Hunter had not answered any of them.

It dawned on her that she forgot the name of the town she had to report to. She pulled over and took out her map, then tried to get her map app working so she could use that as well. She rustled through her purse for the name of the town Hunter gave her…Jenkins Neck. When she found it and located her position on the map, she hit the pedal. "Off to the middle of nowhere."

Once she passed Smithville and the entrance to the parkway, her surroundings became desolate. Soon, thick walls of trees adorned both sides of the road, similar to the environment around Dorothy's but more dense.

Checking her phone's map app, she saw that Jenkins Neck was on the southeastern edge of Wharton State Forest. If she took Rt. 561 out of Leeds, she would need to hop on 563 North and follow it. Hunter had said the area had a *Deliverance* feel to it. As she continued deeper into the region, she wondered why anyone would want to live out here.

The turn for route 563 caught her attention. The intersection gave the impression she was in a different era. A general store looked like something from the Great Depression; old brick structure on the verge of crumbling, a dirt driveway where she could see the breeze rustling up a dust dance. On the adjacent corner stood a burnt out gas station with boarded up windows, looking as if a stiff wind could knock it over. While waiting for the light to change she looked at her phone and noticed it had a strong cell signal. She pulled over to the shoulder to check in with Hunter.

Before she could dial, her phone rang.

"Where are you, you okay?" Hunter said, his voice hurried.

"I'm on my way, I just turned down 563. I feel like I've time warped into the wrong place."

"Good. I mean the part about being on your way. I have a lot on my plate. I've told some people I've got an expert coming to assist."

"What expert? What are you talking about?"

"I'll explain when you get here. A lot has taken place in a short time." Then he changed his tone into a whisper. "Meet me at the Hideaway Diner. You can't miss it. It stands by itself on your left as you come into town. You'll see it. You should be here in about twenty minutes. We'll talk more there."

Casey pulled into the diner. It didn't look encouraging. The metallic shine of the building's trim was long gone now pocked by large sections of rust. The parking lot resembled an exploded minefield, with crater like potholes dotting the entire expanse. Maneuvering her car in an effort not to ruin her front end, she noticed many of the windows of the diner had a thick coat of grime. She tried not to pay any more attention to its faults. What she already witnessed chased away her appetite.

As she climbed the cracked cement stairs, she knew what was coming. As expected, when she opened the door a heavy musk smell assaulted her senses. She looked at the worn 'welcome' rug that had clearly outlived its use and wondered why it hadn't been put to rest. *Does anyone else smell that?*

She spotted Hunter as he casually gave her a wave. He looked tired. For a second she wondered whether she should kiss him or if he would kiss her but the moment faded when he sat back down and settled in.

"Lovely ride?" he said with a smirk.

Casey sat. At least she didn't stick to anything. A quick glance at the tile floor and she guessed it was replaced within the last decade, maybe two. "Yeah, very lovely... if I was fascinated by pine trees I'd be in heaven."

"You know the pine is a particularly lovely tree. A proud tree one might say," he cracked.

"Yes," she said with a sneer. "So you had me come all this way to discuss the positive attributes of pine trees?"

Hunter leaned back against his bench. "Well yes. I thought it would be best if we conversed about the distinctive traits of the Pinus rigida here, in the heartland of the said species."

Casey pursed her mouth and tried to hide her surprise that he could spout off the scientific name of south jersey's most prestigious tree. "Nice... how long did it take you to memorize that little tidbit?"

Hunter grabbed his coffee. "Not long at all really. I studied a bit of ecology at one point. I toyed with the idea of being a forest ranger. It turned out there was no money it."

"And police work has proven to be a lucrative career choice?" she returned.

"Better money anyway," Hunter said before changing the topic to more serious matters. "There's been a terrible tragedy here." His expression went blank. "Sixteen people brutally murdered."

Casey gasped. "My god, how, where, what happened?" she blurted trying to keep her voice low. "How does this involve you?" she asked, but as the words came out, she knew the answer.

Hunter looked at her with a vacant stare. "Why do you think I asked you to join me? You've been researching this. You've been over at that library with what's her name..."

"Dorothy."

"Yes. Have you found anything interesting? We're up against time and, quite frankly I have nothing to go on except my hunch about the Jersey Devil and hunches without clues are worthless in my business."

Casey shook her head in disbelief. "How did this come about? How'd they come to you?"

"The captain here, Rackers, heard about our incident and the cases I'd been investigating. He tagged the Jersey Devil angle… I don't know how, but he's a peculiar guy. He's open to alternative solutions. He's not suggesting it is the Jersey Devil but he isn't ruling it out. Now I have until the morning, at most, to see if I can come up with anything."

"This is too bizarre," Casey said.

"No kidding," Hunter added. "I'm trying to keep this from the press, at least for today. We don't need a panic on our hands. Lord knows no one is going to believe what I'm investigating and God forbid my investigation gets out. This place will become a circus and a joke at the same time."

Hunter continued filling Casey in on the case. With her mouth agape listening to the details, her head swam in confusion. Then a thought came to her. *Dorothy said whenever the beast appears something bad has happened.*

# CHAPTER 23

"That's interesting," Hunter said at hearing about the resources of information Dorothy had provided for Casey. "This Hastleton fellow… I'd like to find out more about that. The other stuff is haunted house stories. I can't do anything with it except keep it on file. But a murder case connected to the Jersey Devil… well that offers insight we might be able to utilize."

"We should talk to him and quickly, if it's at all possible," Casey said.

"I can find out, but procuring an interview is a delicate matter, let alone on a tight timeframe," Hunter said.

"Can't hurt to try," Casey said.

"No it cannot. Let's get back to the station and I'll see what I can do."

The drive over to the police station took less than five minutes. However, along the way Casey noticed several dilapidated homes just off the road. They all fit the Piney stereotype: cluttered yards with rusted cars, old tires, lawn mowers, outdated appliances, broken playground sets and more dogs than the owners could reasonably afford.

Pulling into the police headquarters, Casey laughed to herself seeing that taxpayer's money went into providing a brand new police station complete with shiny new cars. It was the only building she had seen resembling recent construction; a ranch style structure with a stone façade, the color of faded red brick. The large radio tower that rose up resembled something NASA might design.

Hunter escorted Casey into the building. Hunter didn't say much as Casey followed him through a small maze of cubicles. He finally opened the door that led into his temporary office.

"Very homey," she said looking around at the Spartan conditions. "Is this where they bring people who break double secret probation?" she teased.

"It'll do," Hunter answered as he sat down and grabbed a folder he didn't recognize. He missed her attempt to ease the tension.

"Can I pull a chair up?" she asked, standing near his desk.

"Yes please," he said. "Where did my guys go?" He pointed to the folders on the other table without looking at them. "Go through those, I'll be right back."

Casey stared at the folders. She knew she was about to witness some terrible images. With a deep breath, she opened up the folder. To her surprise, it was just paperwork. With another deep breath, she flipped the page. There it was in 8X10 glossy gory glory, one of the victims, abdomen torn to pieces and clumps of dark things she couldn't identify. Her stomach churned. She fought back the urge to vomit.

Hunter walked backed into the room with a tall glass of cold water and put it in front of her. "It can be rough if you're not used to it," he said. "Some people never get used to it. It's tough stuff to stomach... literally."

She smiled meekly and reached for the glass. The cool water soothed the acidic trail in her throat as she swallowed. "Thank you."

He sat down. "Turns out my guys are looking into a few things about some of our victims. Let's hope they can get us closer to an answer of some kind."

"At least they're being proactive," she said after taking another sip of water.

"Good to see they got some detective in them," he answered. "Tell you what, while you look through those files how about you give me that phone of yours so I can download those articles and go through them. Who knows what I may find."

Casey handed over her phone. Hunter took it, pulled the proper USB cord out of a small bag and plugged it into the laptop. "How many pictures did you take?" he asked.

"It felt like hundreds," she replied as she continued to glance at the different pictures in the folder. They seemed to all meld together. One ripped apart torso looked just like the next. Pictures of victims with missing limbs followed and once again, she felt her stomach turn. She willed herself to look through them all.

Once the download completed, Hunter went looking for the David Hastleton case. Casey took pictures of them in chronological order making for easier organization. Reading, he learned the murders took place in Leektown. Hunter had seen that name before, located its whereabouts in relation to their current station, and estimated it was roughly twenty minutes away. Hunter read on learning that Hastelton's lawyer wanted to plead temporary insanity but Hastleton didn't. There were snippets about the families' reactions but little detail on the finer points of the case.

After reading the articles, he called Captain Rackers and asked about the jurisdiction of Leektown and if he knew anything about the Hastleton case. Rackers said the state police often patrolled that area but other communities chipped in as part of a shared services program. The captain said he'd find out about his second question and would call him right back.

Hunter didn't have to wait long for an answer. In less than ten minutes, Captain Rackers informed him that a local cop from a nearby town answered a domestic dispute call that turned out to be the Hastleton case.

"His name is Al Commrant, he's retired now," Rackers said. "The good news is that he is still in the area."

"Thank you sir," Hunter said.

"Are we going on a field trip?" Casey asked with some whimsy after Hunter hung up the phone.

"We may my dear, we may," he answered in the same tone.

Wisps of a light fog floated across the windshield as Hunter drove down the empty county road. The dank weather made the thick two-toned green and brown woods look that much more menacing. Noticing a chill had set in he turned on the heater.

"Creepy at times isn't it?" Hunter asked, breaking the silence that had gone on for a couple of minutes.

"Hypnotic," Casey replied keeping her eyes trained on the woods.

"It's an odd place but it has a unique beauty," Hunter said.

"It's both frightening and beautiful. It has a pull. One part of me can't see why you would want to isolate yourself out here. Yet at the same time, there is something marvelously serene about it. Hauntingly peaceful; it's a dichotomy I know but that's what it says to me."

"That's quite an expression," Hunter noted. "You should jot it down. It's very descriptive."

"I've already written something similar to it," Casey said finally taking her eyes off the woods to make contact with his.

Hunter smiled. "I'm glad you're here."

Casey agreed but now that Hunter expressed himself personally, not professionally, they didn't know exactly how to broach the subject of their relationship. The uncomfortable silence grew heavy, neither sure what to say.

Hunter began to laugh. "I can't believe I feel like an awkward teenager. I thought I had gotten beyond that."

Casey laughed too. She agreed. Feeling more relaxed, she said she had thought about their night and told him how nice it was. She was glad they crossed the line.

Hunter nodded with approval. He reached for her hand and she shifted hers to meet his. He squeezed and held it for a moment, then let go to make a turn.

"I just want to let you know, that I'm all about keeping this part professional," she said taking her hand back and putting it in her lap.

"Of course, as I would expect," he said completing the turn. "But afterwards…" he said, his voice trailing off with a tease.

She returned a sly grin. "Afterwards sounds fun."

After driving through miles and miles of woods, they both expressed relief at the sight of a neighborhood. After a few turns Hunter pulled into the driveway of a finely manicured property. The edging along the walk and driveway displayed precisely cut lines. Potted plants, evenly spaced, adorned the walkway leading to the front door. Meticulously shaped hedges bordered the front of the bluish gray single-storied house. As they walked up to the front door, a light rain began to fall. They hurried their steps to get onto the covered porch. Hunter rang the doorbell. A few seconds later a short plump white haired old woman with a hint of a slouch answered with a delightful smile on her face.

"Hello!" she said with zest. "You must be the police officers who have come to see Al. He's been waiting with great anticipation for your arrival. Please come in." She swung the door open wide. "He's in his study. He likes greeting first time guests there," she said. Then she whispered, "He likes to show off his achievements. It's so cute, I just love it." She put her hand to her mouth as if she had said too much. "It's this way," she said taking the lead.

Casey and Hunter tried to keep themselves from chuckling. When the old woman turned away, Casey mouthed to Hunter, *she's so cute.*

The old woman knocked on a door and lightly sang "you-who, your guests are here."

"Send them in, send them in Edna," came a big baritone voice. Hunter could tell he was a cop, commanding and intimidating with that voice. They walked in and a tall, well-kept man with thinning gray hair who did not look seventy years old stood up from behind a large wooden desk. He walked up to both of them, shook their hands, and introduced his wife Edna Commrant and himself Al Commrant. He pointed to some chairs and asked them to sit. Al asked Edna to bring in some cold glasses of water and some crackers and cheese for the guests. Edna smiled and quipped that she had already cut up some and that she would be right back with everything.

They entered what was a small bedroom converted into an office. Photographs, citations, and medals neatly encased in box frames adorned the walls along with two large stuffed pike and a deer head. A large dark wooden desk took up a good portion of the room. Behind it, a finely custom-made bookcase stretched across the wall, loaded with a large collection of dark colored leather bound books.

Casey found the room charming. Hunter marveled at the volume of police pictures. In just a glance, he could see the yellowed photos of Al's early years on the force and the progression of pictures leading up to his retirement. It was a well-documented representation of his life on the force.

"So I understand you kids have some questions for me," Al said, sitting up close to the desk, attentive and ready to commence with the questioning.

"Ah yes sir," Hunter said not sure how to proceed. "Well, I'm working... we're working a special case." Hunter looked at Casey almost hoping she would telepathically help him out. "And we are stumped, so to speak, and your name came up as someone who might be able to assist us."

"Always glad to help where I can. I received a call from your captain, Rackers. He said your case had abnormalities but he didn't give me details. He said you would explain." Al said.

"Yes." Hunter replied, took a moment, and then dove straight into it. "We want to inquire about the Hastleton case."

Al's optimistic expression faded. They could see his body language shift as his wide shoulders caved in around his sinking neck. "Yes, the Hastleton case. Not one of the triumphs of my career."

"Why would you say that?" Casey said jumping into the fray.

"Well, for one, I took some ribbing on that case while it was going on and then for a while afterwards," Al said looking away. "I was never someone who got ribbed. But after that case, I was fair game for a while. I was still respected but there were whispers here and there."

"What happened? What did the guys think?" Hunter asked, probing softly.

"You've read the case?" Al asked assuming they had.

"The newspapers… Casey found some archival stuff but it's not complete," Hunter said. "I haven't had time to find out more. We're up against a deadline…"

"The state…" Al said with a touch of disdain. "The state likes to tidy up messes and put a bow on them. Don't get me wrong, the troopers are great cops and most are upstanding guys but the state bureaucracy sometimes…" he left it at that.

"Can you tell us what you remember about the case?" Casey asked. "We're interested in what you saw and experienced at the crime scene."

Al sat silent for a moment. "I think Hastleton was either robbed of his life or was the most insane and efficient killer that ever walked the earth."

"What makes you say that?" Hunter asked, leaning in towards the desk.

Al softened his tone. "I got a call about some unusual screaming going on by the Hastleton place. They had a history of domestic disturbances. It was never serious. One of them gets drunk and someone says something stupid and it sets off a whole lot of yelling." Al recalled. "When I came to the house, everything appeared normal. I knocked on the door. All I could hear was a man crying." Al paused. "The door was unlocked. I put my hand on my weapon. I couldn't remember the last time I had to do that. I announced that I was coming in. Slowly I made my way towards the crying. Soon enough, I saw Hastleton at the kitchen table sobbing like a baby with his head buried in his hands."

Al paused for a second not looking at anything in particular. "I startled him. He cried, saying that he couldn't believe what happened. I asked what happened and he cried that they were all gone. Who was all gone, I asked? He stood up, walked to the back door and pointed out towards the woods. He said they were picking blueberries when it happened. He said he was close to the house bringing back a huge basket of berries when he heard the screams. At first, he thought they were playing with him. But the screams… he said… you can't make those kinds of screams when you're just playing around. Hastleton said he dropped the basket and ran to them. When he arrived at the small clearing where his wife and kids had been picking, he looked and saw that their bodies had been mutilated, ripped open. He didn't know what to do. Then he said that out from the bushes came this beast…this terrible beast with wings and the head of something like a horse and a cougar, with red eyes. It looked at him and hissed.
He could see blood and flesh around its mouth. Then in a flash, the beast flew past him, screamed and disappeared into the trees. He said it was the Jersey Devil."

Al stopped to collect himself. Hunter and Casey sat enraptured waiting for him to continue.

"I ran out the back door and down the path and came onto a scene that I could never have imagined," Al said. "There was so much blood. All three bodies ripped completely open, almost all the skin was gone and several organs exposed. It took all I could muster to get back to the car and radio for help. I could still hear Hastleton wailing away inside the house. I went back to him. He was a shivering mess. I couldn't believe that a man could do that to his family."

Al fell silent for another moment before looking up to meet their gaze. "I believed him," he said gently. "I can't say it was logical but that hollow, lost look in his eyes, told he was not guilty. They say the eyes are the windows to the soul... when your life is breached like his was, my eyes saw that this man was not guilty." He paused, choking back a tear. "And that was my ticket to ridicule. After the state came in and took over they sent him off to a facility for evaluation and he's never breathed fresh air since."

Hunter reached into his bag and pulled out a folder. He grabbed a couple of the glossy photos from the crime scene. "Did they look anything like this?"

Al took the photos and his expression was his answer. Al bit his lower lip and they could see he was trying to stave off tears. Al placed the pictures on his desk and pushed them back to Hunter. "It was exactly like that," he said. "Are you saying this has occurred again?"

Hunter nodded. "But this time it's sixteen people."

Al's head dropped. "I knew no man could do that kind of damage. When the state troopers came to do the initial investigation, they asked me all sorts of questions about the scene... what I saw, what he said, if I contaminated the scene. I told them the facts as I knew them and started to offer my two cents, but they dismissed me. I wanted to help Hastleton as much as I could because I just didn't think he could do that to his family. Don't get me wrong... Hastleton was no choirboy but he wasn't a violent man like that. Still, the state wasn't buying the Jersey Devil thing." Al stared out the window. "Can you blame them?" Al fingered at his desk like there was a small hole he needed to dig at. "They never established motive and they never found any weapon, but that didn't keep the courts from sending him away for the rest of his life." He paused again, still digging away at his desk with his fingernail. "I don't know what else I can offer you but I will help anyway I can."

"No, you've been a great help," Hunter added. He didn't know what else to say or ask, though he felt their visit wasn't complete.

"Have you ever witnessed it?" Casey asked breaking the silence.

Al sat up. "No," he said rather bluntly. "I'd heard stories throughout the years. You don't live in these parts and not hear stories. I even investigated some weird farm animal killings but could never conclusively report that the Jersey Devil did it... But when I saw Hastleton's eyes, I knew he experienced something more terrible than anything I ever wanted to know."

"Did his family have any say in the matter? What did they think? What were their thoughts on the trial?" asked Hunter.

"His family was small, quiet. I don't recall any of them believing he was guilty. Like I said, he was no choirboy. He got into his scrapes at local bars. He could run his mouth. He and his wife would argue, but I don't ever recall them laying hands on each other or the kids. No complaints like that ever came from them or the neighbors. They liked to scream at each other... that's all."

"Can you tell us anything more about his family connections?" Casey asked.

"A little; his parents are gone. His sister, I think moved to Florida and he had some eccentric cousin who lives near the shore. A quirky lady; nice, from what I can remember," Al said, a smile coming back. "He did have a good friend who lived not too far from here. I can't recall his name. I think he owns an antique shop in Leeds. Quiet guy… they were big drinking buddies. I know because I hauled them in a few times and let them dry it out in the tank. Real characters those two."

Casey felt her stomach sink as she thought of Dorothy and Arthur. *Could they be connected to this case?*

"Knock, knock," said Edna as she walked in with the crackers and cheese. She scurried over to a small table by a window looking out to their yard. "I heard you guys being so serious, I figured I'd wait. I didn't want to disturb you. Then I heard my Al lighten up and knew it was a good time to come in."

Hunter and Casey thanked her. Edna happily made them plates with equal pieces of Swiss and cheddar with two types of crackers. They felt like children getting snacks during a recess break in school. Edna made a plate for Al as well and placed it right in front of him, giving him a soft kiss on his head.

Edna straightened herself up and cleared her voice making it known she was going to add her two cents. "I won't keep you from your important work but I remember his friends name was Arthur, Arthur Leeds and he did move to Leeds and he does, or at least did, own some kind of antique shop. As for his connection to the town's name I am not sure of that history." She paused as if to catch a breath before continuing. "He was a quirky guy, kind of shy, except when he was drinking, then he was all balls and fire." She stopped and looked out the window as if more information was coming to her from that direction. "And the woman's name was Dorothy. I can't recall the last name though. It was kind of strange."

Al laughed. "Thank you dear," he said in a way that meant she could leave.

Casey felt a rush of adrenaline pulsate through her body. "Dorothy? Does she live in Leeds as well?"

Edna thought for a moment. "I believe she does but I can't be certain."

Casey slumped in her seat. Hunter asked if she was okay just as Edna spoke again.

"But I believe she passed away a few years ago, if I recall correctly."

Hunter noticed Casey's demeanor shift and wanted to move the questioning forward. "So Al, the state had nothing to convict Hastleton with?"

"Nothing," Al said. His face turned bitter. "Like I said, no murder weapon and a flimsy motive. They brought up the domestic issues over the years and then created innuendos that he may have had relations with one of his daughters. That he was unstable. Essentially, they came up with enough smoke and mirror crap to convict him. And, the lawyer he had didn't help; some newbie who didn't know the difference between Mens Rea and the Men's Room. He did nothing. It was a sham. Half-truths are enough truth to most people when it comes to Piney's."

"Was Hastleton a Piney?" asked Casey.

"He came from that," Al said. "But unless you really make it or leave here, that kind of stereotype never leaves you."

"You're very sympathetic to the man. Did you ever follow up and see how he was doing?" Casey continued.

Al hesitated. "It doesn't leave here." He looked them both directly in the eyes. "Yes I did. I visited him twice." Al fell back into his chair as if a great weight had suddenly lifted. "He swore to me that he had nothing to do with their deaths and that he loved his family deeply. It hurt to listen to him. Not only could I hear the pain but I felt it as well. He'll rot in jail and he knows it. He came to grips with it rather quickly. I felt bad because in all my years of contributing to this community and helping people, there was nothing I could do for him."

Hunter shimmied to the end of his chair and leaned onto Al's desk. "I know this might be hard, and I apologize for bringing all this back up, but maybe you can help us out just a little more. If we can prove that these murders we are investigating aren't murders of the conventional sort, it could help him and maybe even get him exonerated." Hunter looked at Casey before turning back to Al. "We believe, in fact, that the Jersey Devil did kill these people."

Al looked at them with skeptical surprise. "I'll help you but you've got a tough hill to climb if you think you're getting anyone with clout to buy into your theory. I know a little about your Captain Rackers. He's considered peculiar," Al said before changing gears. "You want me to look at those pictures again and see if I can identify anybody?" He motioned for Hunter to hand him back the folder. "You want to know why your captain is peculiar?"

They both looked at him, curious to hear his explanation. "He was a ghost chaser in Philadelphia... a good cop, highly decorated but he was considered... eccentric. As he moved up the chain, his eccentricity got him clobbered politically by those who found him too odd for prominent positions in the department. He sometimes called on psychics and other mediums to investigate crimes. It was a bit too unorthodox for those in powerful places. He had some great success but not enough to warrant the constant pursuit of their assistance. He caught quite a bit of flack and when the pressure became too much he transferred out of state. The city of Philadelphia gave him glowing reviews; much of it deserved. People in the area welcomed him. He is an honorable man and in a region where eccentricity is common, it didn't matter to folks what quirks he had. Still, it's hard to leave your past behind." Al turned his attention to the pictures, examining them as if he was still on the job.

Hunter stood up, recognizing an opportunity to grease the wheel. "You mind if I look at your pictures?"

"Not at all," Al answered with pride.

Hunter marveled at the old police cars and the uniforms, noting how the styles had changed over the years. Al looked serious in all the pictures but carried a passion for the job where the others looked stoic and lifeless. Hunter's eyes moved from picture to picture, examining them with a certain degree of reverence. He stopped when he got to an old black and white of a police car that had a single light on the top. Looking more closely he saw Al or at least he thought he did.

"That's my dad," Al said proudly, seeing Hunter had focused on the one image. "Pretty neat the way the cars were then."

"Yes, amazing how things change," Hunter said.

"Time is a funny thing," Al said. "Don't waste it. It goes by far quicker than you know. Too bad it takes some folks too long to realize it." He looked down at the pictures once again, examining them. "As for these, I don't recognize anyone. If you want, make me a copy, I'll have some of my contacts see if they can help you out." He put the photos back in the folder and slid it to the front of his desk. "But those wounds look identical to what I witnessed, if that helps at all."

"I'll have copies made and sent over. Thank you for your time," Hunter said. "Just one more thing before we leave…have you dealt with any kind of satanic cults?"

Al looked surprised by the question. "Cults? No. Kids doing stupid things in the woods, yes, but nothing like you're suggesting."

A light drizzle fell as they drove out of town. Casey couldn't shake images of Arthur from her mind. "I know you think this wasn't the most productive meeting but Arthur Leeds, the guy Edna mentioned, that was the name of the antique shop owner I ran into and had that creepy experience with."

Hunter wanted to hit the brakes and pull over. "What?"

"Yeah, the old man I told you about when I was at that diner," she said.

"I didn't connect it. You never mentioned his last name," Hunter said.

Casey thought about it and realized he was right. "We didn't need to make it a big thing in front of Al, did we?"

"No of course not," he answered. "What about Dorothy? Do you think it could be the same woman? I know Edna said she heard she was dead but hearing and knowing are two different things."

Casey nodded. She could sense things might be adding up. "I think I may need to pay them both another visit."

"And I'll be joining you," Hunter added.

# CHAPTER 24

Captain Rackers sat behind his desk, hands crossed neat and proper to match his perfect posture. "I have spoken to the coroner and she is quite shaken by what she witnessed with those bodies."

"What about time? Will she abide by our time request?" Hunter asked.

"She didn't like it the first time I asked," Rackers said. "She is not about to risk her career or even remotely have her motives questioned, if you get my meaning. She did say she will delay calling the state. Her excuse is the extensiveness of brutality and trying to examine and process all the bodies. However, that only gives a few additional hours."

"That's at least something," Hunter replied, then shifted his gaze to Casey, who hadn't said much since their return from Al and Edna's house.

"It is something," Rackers added. "And as much as I wish I could adhere to my initial estimate of a twenty-four hour window," he looked at his watch, "I feel that number is dwindling rapidly. I cannot appear like I'm hiding something."

Hunter looked at his watch, 7:50pm. He understood. He had the feeling his extension request wouldn't be honored. The case was too big. "So, essentially my investigation is going to wind down," Hunter replied more as a statement than a question.

Rackers raised his brow followed by a nod. "I'm sorry but you know as well as I that the State Police will not lend any validity to your investigation. I'd rather terminate it than have you fall under scrutiny. My reputation precedes me, yours does not…at least not yet."

"I'll gather my things then," Hunter offered.

"Not so quickly," Rackers said. "I will determine the hour of that."

"But sir, I have nothing. I have no concrete evidence or even a possible whereabouts of this creature to make any further efforts worth your while," Hunter said.

"Nonsense," Rackers said standing slowly from behind his desk. "Your team confirmed the why, for the victims being out in the woods. You've helped identify some of them. You've correlated that these types of wounds have a history to them, that in fact, as brutal as they are, they are not unique to this case."

"You can thank Casey for that sir," Hunter added.

"And I shall. Thank you Ms. Windall for your services in this case," Rackers said with a touch of a bow. "Now Detective Matthews… you should concentrate your efforts on continuing your investigation until otherwise notified. One never knows what can reveal itself at any given moment. As I'm sure Officer Commrant explained I have no qualms seeking alternative solutions to strange or difficult cases."

Casey and Hunter's body language gave away their knowledge of the captain's past.

"I know good cops, thorough ones, when I meet them or hear about them," Rackers said. "Officer Commrant, from all accounts was an exceptional officer eclipsed by a freakish incident. My history is no secret, especially to those in the region who were already on the force when I entered the picture."

"That explains the ESP." Casey said.

"No Ms. Windall," Rackers answered on the heels of her words. "It's knowing your job." He stopped and smiled. "Just like I know the two of you have forged a bond beyond the bounds of this arrangement."

They both looked at him with stumped expressions.

"I have no issue with it because I see that you currently have boundaries that work for the two of you and that is what I call professionalism. I hope you can maintain it," Rackers said rather pleased with his deduction.

"Sir," Casey said in a defensive tone.

"No need for an explanation," Rackers interjected as a knock sounded on his office door.

Officer Berkman popped his head in. "There's been a sighting."

What?" Hunter said. A sudden feeling of 'this is my chance' overcame him.

"Yeah, over at old lady Falanner's place. She says some big flying thing has killed one of her dogs," Berkman said.

All three looked at Captain Rackers as if waiting for his blessing.

Rackers slowly smoothed the front of his uniform, looked at the three of them and said with complete nonchalance, "I believe time has decided to grant you a big reveal."

Hunter turned to Officer Berkman and Casey. "Let's go."

Hunter followed Ken. They sped quickly through the dark unlit roads. The patrol car's flashing lights made it easy to keep up and not worry about getting lost. Hunter radioed Berkman to turn off the lights before getting to the house. He didn't want to startle the creature or the woman. Within a minute, the flashing lights stopped as the car made a left turn.

The surface of the road went from paved tar to hard gravel and the shoulder disappeared from view. Hunter made a quick right turn that threw Casey into his lap. She straightened herself and held on as they began to hit potholes with a thunderous charge.

Hunter cringed, unable to see the large depressions in the road but felt he wasn't missing any of them. His frustration abated when Berkman hit his brakes and slowed down to a stop. With no streetlights, it was hard to see anything except for what was directly in front of them. Hunter rolled his window down to get a better look. He saw Berkman flash the spotlight out into the woods to their left. As the beam panned, it revealed a small house about a hundred feet off the road. With the spotlight trained on the house, they watched Officer Berkman get out of his car. Hunter followed. Casey found herself stuck to her seat. Her heart raced and her breathing became rapid.

*Enough!* She shouted to herself and got out of the car.

"This is the right house?" Hunter whispered as he came up to Ken, who now stood directing the spotlight.

"There are only three houses on this road. She's the first and the others are another thousand or so feet down the road," Ken said.

"Why are the lights off?" Casey asked whispering.

Hunter answered. "She could be watching whatever it is out there. Lights on in the house can diminish your visibility looking out."

"Maybe," said Ken with warning in his voice. "Mrs. Falanner is a bit of an eccentric... something of a gun nut."

"Oh great," Hunter said. "So you're saying she might be hunting this thing from in her house?"

"It's quite possible," he said. "We need to proceed with caution."

"What about turning on the lights and running the siren to let her know we're here?" Casey asked.

"Number of reasons: One, we could startle her and two we could scare off the thing we want to find," Hunter answered.

"Still... her knowing we're here is better than possibly getting our butts shot off by Annie Oakley. Imagine you guys having to fill out a report saying you didn't want to scare off the Jersey Devil," Casey said.

Hunter and Ken looked at each other. "That wouldn't make for pleasant paperwork," Hunter said. Ken agreed.

"But don't you think the spotlight signals that we've arrived?" Ken asked. "As you can see, it's quite bright."

"That's a good point too," Hunter said. "But let's pan the spotlight across her house again a few times and see if we can get any kind of acknowledgement from her."

Ken nodded and began to move the beam of light across the area like a prison search light. No reaction came. The house looked lifeless. The spotlight exposed the disrepair and neglect that had taken its toll on the place as well as all the assorted items strewn about the makeshift porch and lawn.

Just then, they heard a gunshot pierce the night's silence, followed by a scream. Ken moved the spotlight in the direction of the shot. The beam of light briefly caught a dark shape flying in the air. A terrible hissing and screeching sound wailed for a few seconds before stopping.

Both Hunter and Ken drew their weapons.

"Keep the light trained on that area and call backup. I'm going in for a closer look," Hunter said. He took a couple steps when he felt a tug.

"What the hell are you doing?" Casey said.

"I'm doing what I'm supposed to be doing. Finding out what the hell is going on," Hunter said with force. He was sweating and she could tell he was nervous.

"Then I'm coming with you," she said.

"The hell you are," he said, pushing her hand off him. "Just stay right here for a minute." Without pause, he turned and headed towards the house, keeping his body low. Hunter had just crossed the road and taken a few steps into the driveway when he heard another blast, followed by another piercing screech. The spotlight moved further away and cast no light on his path. He stopped, waiting for his eyes to adjust to the darkness. Once he could see well enough, he picked up his pace moving down the uneven driveway. When he reached the house, everything fell quiet except for the pounding of his heart. He pulled out a flashlight and brought it up to his drawn pistol but did not turn it on.

"Where's he going?" Casey whispered to Ken, having caught a glimpse of Hunter's movement.

"He's checking out the scene."

"Shouldn't he knock on the door and let her know the police are here?"

"I think she knows we're here. I mean we spotlighted the damn thing. If she didn't notice that, I'm not sure what we can do. She's armed. We have to be careful." Ken answered.

It made sense to Casey. "How about if I sweep the spotlight and you go back Hunter up?"

"You sure?"

"It's a light. I think I can manage it."

"If you need to tighten or loosen the drag, turn this handle, and if you need to turn it off for whatever reason, this is the switch right here," he pointed to a dark spot that Casey could barely see.

She nodded and took over. She couldn't help but notice how fast Ken moved down the driveway as his figure disappeared into the dark. She looked behind her, nothing but a wall of black.

Hunter turned the corner from the front of the house and worked his way along the side until he reached the edge of the backyard. He couldn't see much. He took a few deep breaths. As his eyes adjusted even more to his surroundings, he began to notice what appeared to be automobile parts and old chicken coops littered throughout the backyard. He also identified the tree line that bordered the woods from the backyard.

Glancing around the back of the house, Hunter noticed a screened in porch. He tried to spot someone, anyone. He hoped he might hear the old woman stumble around but heard nothing. He needed to know if she was still keeping watch and more importantly, her location. Looking down, Hunter noticed some sizable rocks by his feet. He decided to pick one up and toss it towards the woods, hoping the noise would elicit a reaction and reveal her position. Slowly he kneeled down and gripped a stone. It was cold in his sweaty palm. Taking a step away from the wall, he spotted an old door leaning against a tree. He threw the rock as hard as he could. He missed but heard the stone rustle into the woods. He thought he heard movement from the porch but still couldn't see anyone. He bent down to pick up another stone. He squared up again to throw it when he felt a tap on his shoulder.

Startled, he dropped the stone and it clanged off an old hubcap lying by his feet. A shot rang out. He fell back against the side of the house. "What the hell are you doing?" he whispered angrily as he realized it was Ken.

"I came to back you up," Ken said keeping his voice and body low.

"You left Casey?

"It was her idea," Ken returned.

"Of course it was," Hunter, said noticing the slow pan of the spotlight along the treetops. "I'm going to throw a stone and hopefully hit that door over there. With any luck she'll shoot and we'll be able to locate her." Hunter picked up another rock. Again, he took on a pitchers stance before throwing it. This time the rock struck the door with a magnificent bang. Another shot rang out. Hunter and Ken could make out a figure repositioning itself but not from the porch. They saw someone duck behind what looked like a chord of wood.

"Alright, now that we know where she is…what's next?" Ken asked.

"What's the woman's name again?"

"Jane Falanner," Ken answered.

Hunter turned towards her position. "Mrs. Falanner, this is the police! Please do not shoot. We are at the side of your house. Are you okay?"

There was silence for a moment. "I hear you. Did you see it?" she asked, her voice cracking.

"Yes, we saw it. Now I need you to put your gun down, so that we can come over," Hunter answered.

"You can come over but I'm not putting this gun down," she yelled. "That damn thing just killed my two dogs and now I'm going to kill it."

"I understand your anger ma'am but do you understand that you are also endangering us and yourself," Hunter returned.

"We're all in danger," she yelled. "I can see it just beyond the trees. It hears you. It's watching us."

Hunter and Ken looked into the woods but couldn't identify anything except the shapes of the trees intermixing with the black of night. "Where, Mrs. Falanner?" Hunter asked. "Where do you see it?"

"You see that big fat tree towards the center of the yard that sits on the edge of the woods?" she asked.

Ken tapped Hunter on the shoulder and pointed it out to him. They both looked but could not see anything unusual near the tree. "Ma'am. I cannot see what you are talking about but we are going to come out from the side of the house and walk over to you."

"You do that. I got my eye on that S.O.B. I'll cover ya."

Hunter turned to Ken with a sarcastic grin, "She'll cover us."

"Don't laugh. She's better with a gun than some of the guys on the force," Ken said. With guns drawn, the two of them turned from the side of the house into the backyard and quickly moved along the cement pathway that led to the porch.

"We're just about to you," Hunter said.

Mrs. Falanner had positioned herself behind an old wood bench and a stack of firewood. It was a good spot to take cover and within seconds, they joined her.

"If you boys came to disarm me, you're going to have to yank this rifle out of my cold dead hands," she said, never taking her eyes off the woods.

"Ma'am, you called us remember?" said Ken.

"Yeah and that means exactly what?" she said coldly. "Of course I called. What was I supposed to do? Shit boy, what kind of brains you got in that head of yours?"

Hunter waved Ken off. "What exactly happened that you called this in?" Hunter asked still trying to spot the creature.

"I heard some banging in the backyard. Thought it might be some raccoons but it sounded a little loud for them. I grabbed my gun here and flicked on the back porch light to get a better look, when holy shit, did I see this thing hopping around the back yard. I had no clue what it was, but my boys started to bark all in a tizzy. I let them out after it. I followed. In an instant, that damn thing gutted my babies. I managed to get off a shot. It dived for me and I fell to the ground. It missed. I ducked into this spot, saw it in the trees and I fired another shot. That's when it started to toy with me."

"When were you able to call us?" Ken asked.

"My cell phone. Boy, what kind of cop are you?"

Hunter looked at Ken and this time gave him the cutoff sign. "You said you saw it in the trees?" Hunter asked.

"Yeah, its right beyond that big tree I was telling you about," she said, her eyes constantly fixed on the spot.

Hunter tried to locate it but couldn't make anything out. He looked at Ken to see if he could spot anything but he signaled that he saw nothing. "Ma'am. I'm going to shine a light on it because I can't see what you're seeing."

"Good. It'll give me a better crack at it," she said. "Maybe we can flush it out and nab the damn thing."

"Well let's not be too trigger happy, let's see if we can locate it first," Hunter said. He trained the flashlight at the tree and flicked it on. His aim was good and it illuminated the tree. Slowly he panned the light but could not make out anything unusual. "I don't see anything. Do either of you?"

Both of them answered no. He moved the light all around the yard. Ken soon joined in with his flashlight. Neither one of them could locate the creature.

"Mrs. Falanner, do you see anything?" Hunter asked.

"I swore it went right in there by that tree," she said, getting a little upset with herself.

Neither one doubted her. Looking out into the yard Hunter asked about the location of the dogs.

"Just by that old cart," she said pointing to the far corner of the yard to their right. Hunter and Ken pointed their lights in that direction. Almost immediately, they saw one of the dogs, lying motionless by an old wooden two-wheeled cart.

"Alright ma'am. I need you to lower your weapon and please, put it in the house," Hunter said. "Ken you can call off that backup."

Ken thought for a moment then whispered 'shit'. He looked at Hunter. "I never called in for backup."

Hunter dropped his head. "Really? What if something had happened?"

"I told you. Ass for brains," she said. "And who are you, the new chief?"

"No ma'am. Detective Hunter Matthews."

"Good for you," she said with less attitude. "And I'm not putting this gun away."

Hunter didn't want to make an issue out of it. "Fine ma'am, but could you aim the weapon towards the ground while we investigate the scene?"

"I can do that. I'll be your cover."

"Please," Hunter said putting his hands up in a pleading manner. "I beg you to use extreme caution."

"Listen sonny, I've been handling rifles and pistols longer than you've been able to shit on your own accord. I think I can manage."

Hunter shook his head. "Fine." He looked at Ken. "Go get Casey and bring her over here. She doesn't need to be by herself." Ken nodded and left. "Ma'am, could you at least go inside and put on a few lights. Do you have any floodlights for the backyard?"

"I have one up on the house there. I'll put that on," she said.

Hunter came around from the pile of firewood with the flashlight pointing on the dead dogs. He moved slowly, always glancing about to see if the creature was somewhere on the edge of the woods. As he got closer to the dogs, he could see the large pool of blood that had stained the ground. The dogs were about five feet apart. At first, he couldn't see any wounds but as he walked closer, he noticed one of the animal's undersides cut open. A closer look revealed a long clean gash from the front legs all the way to the genitalia. Closing in even more, he could see organs protruding from the gash. He feared how Mrs. Falanner might react if she saw this scene.

Just as the floodlight for the backyard went on, he heard Casey's voice. As she walked towards him, he blocked her from getting a closer look.

"You don't want to see this," he said. "It's two dogs."

"Two dogs?"

"Yep, basically they have the same style of wounds as the human victims," he said.

Mrs. Falanner came down the porch stairs with her rifle in hand, pointing it at the ground. They watched as she semi-waddled her way towards them.

"My boys, they're really dead ain't they?" she asked.

"Yes ma'am," Hunter said. "It's not a pretty sight. I don't know if that's something you want to see at this time."

She blew off his advice. "Well what's the difference if I see them now or later? I've got to bury them."

A rustle in the woods caught their attention. Mrs. Falanner cocked her rifle. None of them could tell exactly where the sound came from, so Hunter and Ken used their flashlights and panned into the recesses of the woods where the floodlight didn't reach. Hunter detected what looked like an opening to a trail. He asked where it led and she told him it went to a pond and creek, about five hundred feet away, that she used for fishing and hunting.

Hunter looked at them. "I think we should check it out."

Ken nodded in agreement but it didn't come off enthusiastic. Mrs. Falanner grinned as if it was her pleasure to go hunting. Hunter thought about protesting her involvement but he knew she wasn't going to stay behind unless he had her restrained.

"You up for it?" he said to Casey.

"After you detective," she answered.

"Who's the chippy?" Mrs. Falanner asked.

Casey went to say something but Hunter cut her off. "A consultant for the state," he answered.

Hunter led them onto the narrow trail. They had to walk single file. Mrs. Falanner walked behind Hunter, followed by Casey with Ken covering the rear. They tried to walk quietly but it was futile. With every other step, they snapped a stick or crunched leaves, which sounded like a marching band in the silence of the night.

Hunter kept his flashlight fixed on the trail ahead. The light from the house that had helped illuminate the entrance to the trail soon faded. Peripheral vision became useless. Hunter slowed the pace to a crawl as he maneuvered along the twisting path. Ken used his flashlight to scan the woods on either side as they walked.

The five hundred foot walk took far longer than anyone expected. When the four of them finally arrived at the end, the scene before them began to brighten. Looking up, Casey noticed the cloud cover overhead began to break up allowing a bright half-moon to cast some light onto the scene. The reflecting light shimmered on the water's surface just ahead of them. The edges of the treetops separated from the evening's dark. Ken and Hunter panned their flashlights to get a better lay of the land.

Hunter was the first to step out into the open sandy area, which was dotted with a few small clumps of scrub. Panning his flashlight along the shoreline, less than fifty feet from where he stood, he noticed a set of eyes staring at him. They all saw it and froze before realizing it was only a raccoon. As they ventured further out, they put more distance between themselves. Casey made sure she wasn't more than an arms-length or two from Hunter.

"Isn't this fun?" he said to Casey.

"The perfect second date," she answered.

The three of them didn't know exactly what to look for or how long they should continue to search. Mrs. Falanner, on the other hand, was on a mission and her rifle remained at the ready. Ken occasionally checked behind them to make sure nothing had followed.

"It's here," Mrs. Falanner said as she turned herself around.

"How do you know?" Casey asked.

"Because of the silence," Hunter said.

"He's right," Mrs. Falanner, said adjusting the rifle in her hand. "The night woods are never this quiet. There's always something scurrying about or crickets and such making noise."

Hunter aimed his flashlight at where they had seen the raccoon but it was gone.

"So what do we do?" Casey asked as she gripped the back of Hunter's shirt. She wished she had a gun.

"It's hunting us," Mrs. Falanner said. "It's watching and waiting. It's a smart S-O-B."

"I wish you would stop saying things like that," Casey shot back trying not to sound too frantic.

"You're out of your league girlie. I guess you're more like a desk consultant rather than a field one. This is his world and you're just going to have to deal with it," Mrs. Falanner sneered back. "Any of you guys don't have the ball sacks to hunt this thing, you can leave. I'll be damned if some shit ass beast is going to get the best of me without a fight."

"I think we should all just cool down," Hunter said more as an order than a suggestion. Then he looked at Mrs. Falanner. "I've let you have way more free reign with this than I should. You can still find yourself in jail with a list of charges that you don't want to deal with."

"Yeah, like anyone is going to do anything to an old lady," she snickered.

"As a matter of fact, yes…especially when it comes to guns around cops and resisting arrest or any kind of assault." Hunter said spot-on serious as he continued to keep an eye out. "You just keep on believing that myth that old folks can get away with anything they want."

Mrs. Falanner got the point. Hunter was the only one of the group she currently respected. She breathed a frustrated sigh and loosened her grip on the rifle.

Hunter could sense her compliance. "Are we okay?" he asked her.

"I'm fine," she said, clearly unhappy by the shift of power.

"Good," he said more relaxed. "Alright then, let's try this. We'll give it about fifteen minutes. We'll fan out from a small circle. Keep your eyes fixed into your zone, this way we don't have to worry about what's behind us or movement from the sides." Everyone agreed and immediately began to shape into a circle. Casey's zone veered towards Hunter, as she was the only one without a weapon.

The silence made time crawl as they each took slow methodical steps away from each other. Twice Casey looked at her watch to see less than two minutes had passed. Her eyes adapted well enough to see some details in front of her but the wall of trees before them loomed dark and ominous.

"Screeeeeeeeeeeeyaaaaaa," a loud screech roared from a point no one could discern at first. They all lowered themselves to the ground except Mrs. Falanner who raised her rifle and scanned her zone. Casey moved closer to Hunter.

"I can tell you that was no owl," Ken blurted as he crouched down with his pistol aimed out into his zone.

"You're right about that," Mrs. Falanner said, her eye trained through the sight of her rifle. "That was the beast."

"Yes it was," Hunter said. The scream made him flashback to his moment with the creature. Vague and blurry images briefly filled his mind. He tightened the grip on his pistol.

"It's over there," Casey said pointing to the other side of the lake.

"Where?" Hunter asked trying to see where she was pointing.

"Where?" followed Mrs. Falanner with eagerness.

"On the other side of the lake, in the middle portion" Casey said.

"How do you know that?" Mrs. Falanner asked.

"I don't know," she said.

"A hunch is as good as anything," Mrs. Falanner said training her aim in that direction.

Another loud shriek shredded the silence of the woods. This time it sounded like it came from behind them. They all turned to their rear except for Casey. They saw nothing.

"What the fuck," muttered Hunter as he darted his eyes all over the scene. He felt a tug on his shirt. He turned and looked at Casey, "What's up?"

She said nothing but pointed across the lake. Hunter turned to look and immediately adrenaline flooded his body. Floating on the other side of the lake, a dark creature with a long wing expanse appeared to hover. It flapped its long wings slowly, making no sound. It began to head towards them in slow motion. It appeared as a dark shape swallowing what little light illuminated the area. Then it revealed its eyes and its blood red glare penetrated the night like a beam of light.

"Guys," Hunter said with a fright in his voice.

The other two swung around. Ken stumbled trying to steady himself. Mrs. Falanner readied her rifle and grumbled, "Die you bastard." She pulled the trigger but all they heard was a click. It misfired.

With a rush, the beast screeched and was on them before they could react. Mrs. Falanner fell to ground, knocked down by its passing force. Her rifle dropped from her hands. Hunter did his best to keep an eye on the creature but the thing moved so fast it was nothing but a dark blur, undefinable.

Ken fired his weapon. The beast swatted him with its wing, knocking him over as if tossed out of a moving car door. The creature appeared to stop for just a moment before attacking Ken. Hunter fired at the beast. It stopped and turned towards him. Hunter watched as its piercing red eyes began to pulsate and glow. Hunter trained his pistol on the beast. Aiming straight at it, he began to go numb. The eyes of the beast locked into his gaze. The whole world began to blur around him yet he could now see the beast more clearly. It had a dark thick tough coat of skin, almost fur like but not. Its head, a long snout, similar to a horse, yet it also reminded him of a bastardized dragon. Its long dark wings resembled that of a bat but with a thicker texture. Unfurled fully they were nearly twice the size of the beast. Then with a rush, it came straight at him. He couldn't move. This was it. Time froze as he waited for the impact. Then from a distance, he heard a muted scream, "NO!" Suddenly something blocked the path between him and the beast. He fell over as he watched the creature soar by and disappear into the woods.

"Hey," Hunter heard a voice say as he felt someone slapping his face. When he opened his eyes, Casey was kneeling over him. "You okay?"

Hunter shook off the trance. He couldn't quite wrap his thoughts around what had just happened. "You're okay?" he said to Casey.

"I'm fine. I think it's gone," she said.

Hunter slowly sat up. They spotted Ken trying to stand up. Hunter looked over to where Mrs. Falanner lay. She was motionless. "What happened? I froze didn't I?" he said still stunned. "It paralyzed me with its stare. I couldn't break its hold," he stammered.

"It's okay," Casey said as she rubbed his back.

"What happened? I should be dead."

"I don't know," she said. "I dove in front of you but I don't know how I did it. I just reacted I guess."

"You saved me?" Hunter said drawing her closer. "Thank you," he whispered into her ear. Hunter worked his way up to a standing position. It was then he noticed his gun missing. He turned around, located it a couple feet away, holstered it, and began to move towards Mrs. Falanner. Ken also began making his way over to them.

"She's unconscious but alive," Hunter said with his hand on her neck, feeling a strong pulse. "How are you?" he said to Ken.

"What the hell...I saw that thing on the lake, and then the next second I'm knocked over and feeling like I just got body punched."

Mrs. Falanner groaned. She turned her head to one side and mumbled. None of them could make out what she said.

Hunter placed his hand behind her head and cradled it.

"Can you hear me Mrs. Falanner?"

She groaned some more before finally opening her eyes. Ken and Hunter both helped her sit up. Mrs. Falanner raised a hand to rub her face and eyes.

"Did someone kill that bastard thing?" she grumbled. She opened her eyes and saw them all hovering around her. "I'll be fine. You can stop your worrying."

"Just stay seated for a minute," Hunter said.

She placed both hands on the ground for support. "So can anyone tell me what happened?"

"We were attacked," Ken said.

Mrs. Falanner just shook her head in disgust and let out a deep sigh. "You just ain't all there, are you? I know we were attacked genius."

Casey spoke. "It happened all so quick. Ken shot at it but it knocked him over. Hunter got off a shot too. Then it screamed and flew away."

"That seems odd," she said.

"Why?" Casey asked.

"Because I fired several shots at it in my backyard and all it did was tease me, but he fires one shot and it's gone. What do you have in there some kind of special bullets chief?" Mrs. Falanner said, returning to her old spitfire attitude.

"There's more to it than that," Hunter said.

"Not much more though," Casey said interrupting him. She didn't want him going on about her saving his life. "How bout if we get out of these woods and back to the house."

Mrs. Falanner agreed. "Sounds like a plan."


It was nearing ten o'clock. Casey, Hunter and Ken sat in their makeshift office exhausted. Neither of them knew how to report what they had experienced. The first of the state troopers had arrived, sequestered away in Captain Rackers' office. Hunter had yet to report in but was certain the captain knew of their return.

He tried to replay the scene in his head. He could visualize everyone out in the clearing. He could see the figure of the beast, even recalled firing off a round, but after that, his memory went blank. The next moment he could remember clearly was tending to Mrs. Falanner then returning to her house where she turned down any treatment and refused to file any kind of report. She just wanted to be home so she could bury her dogs.

Casey also tried to recreate the whirlwind of events. She too had a hard time piecing together exactly what had taken place, but felt empowered by how she handled herself under pressure. She never considered herself the heroic sort but her actions had spoken otherwise. Exhausted, she longed for a nice hot shower and a comfortable bed.

"Guys!" came a shout that jolted them all. "Captain wants to see you."

Hunter looked at Ken and Casey. "Here we go."

Captain Rackers greeted all three by name and asked them to sit down. He wanted a personal briefing before completely relinquishing control of the investigation over to the State Police. "So, you were gone far longer than I anticipated. Do you have any information that I should be aware of?"

Hunter explained in detail what occurred. Rackers listened with great interest. As the story unfolded, his body crept increasingly forward across his desk, mesmerized by what he was hearing. When Hunter finished, Rackers fell back in his chair.

"My goodness, that is quite a story," he said exhaling as if he was a witness.

Hunter appreciated the captain's willingness to listen but the briefing felt empty. "So what happens now?" he asked looking for guidance.

"Well. As you may have realized, the State Police are going to take over. I've given them everything we have gathered that is pertinent to this case," Rackers said.

"Anything about our investigation?" Hunter asked not sure what to expect.

"I mentioned something vague about it but they were quite confident about how they wanted to handle things," Rackers answered.

"How did they find out about the killings?" Casey asked.

"The hospital…A large accident occurred involving several people and once at the hospital they encountered some odd delays, and distractions. That didn't play well and they were alerted to the situation," the captain said. "They seemed more perplexed than angry upon hearing about it. I simply said we thought we had a solid initial lead but it didn't play out."

"But that still doesn't answer my question about our investigation?" Hunter asked.

"Well in a way I believe it does," the captain said smiling. "Officially the case has been transferred to the State Police. You do not work for me in an official capacity. I brought you in as an advisor with no specific ties. If the State Police see fit to pursue that particular angle of the investigation, it will be their prerogative to seek it out."

Casey and Hunter looked at him with baffled astonishment.

"So what I'm saying is that you're on your own to see it to a finish." He paused, absorbing their expressions. "Why don't you get some sleep? I'll call your captain and see what I can do to spare you an extra couple days but that's the best that I can offer you."

"Thank you captain, you've been most gracious," Casey said.

The captain stood and reached out his hand to her. "It has been delightful meeting you. I wish I had the opportunity to talk with you more, you seem to be a charming young lady."

Casey smiled. She nearly curtsied in response to his formal demeanor. Hunter reached out his hand and thanked the captain for all he had done. Hunter asked how they should handle the Falanner incident. The captain replied that he didn't think the state police investigators would consider it part of the case.

"Let's deem it a separate and unusual incident," Rackers said before bidding them farewell one last time.

As they walked out of his office, they could see the hustle of state trooper personnel working the room, manning computers and talking on the phone. No one seemed to pay any attention to Hunter and Casey as they made their way out of the station. Once outside Casey looked at him. "What now?"

"There's a hotel not far from here. I was thinking hot shower and sleep. We can plan our strategy in the morning. We know *what* we're dealing with. Now we just have to figure out exactly *how* we're going to deal with it."

"Sounds like a plan," she said, her voice tired and trailing off. "I'll follow you."

# CHAPTER 25

They both fell into a deep sleep. The showers had felt great. The hot cascading water soothed their bodies and minds. When they hit the bed, it only took seconds before slumber overcame them.

They hadn't been asleep for long when Casey's phone began to ring. The high-pitched tin of the ringtone banged into both their minds like a church bell. They both stirred under the covers.

"Why is it so loud?" Hunter mumbled.

Casey slapped around the edges of the bed trying to locate it. "Where are my pants? I think it was in my pocket last."

"I don't know," he said. "Why is it so loud? Did we rent an echo chamber?"

Casey slid off the bed towards the direction of the sound. With the shades drawn, it was near pitch black and her eyes hadn't adjusted. "I can't see anything," she blurted still half asleep.

"Oh good, I thought it was me," Hunter said half sitting with his back up against the wall. He clumsily reached over to the lamp and turned it on. The light created another shock to the system and they both reacted as if they had bad hangovers.

Casey found her pants and pulled the phone out of the pocket but not before it sounded one more terribly loud ring. "Hello," she murmured still not quite awake. There was a long pause. Hunter looked at her naked back as she sat on the floor. She nodded a lot and he could hear her say 'okay' a few times.

"Turn the volume down on that thing and come back to bed," Hunter stammered when she hung up the phone.

"I have to go," she said her eyes half closed with her chin on the edge of the bed.

"Have to go? Go where?"

Casey crawled onto the bed. Hunter smiled as her naked body came closer to him. With a sleepy grin, she cupped her body into his. "That was Dorothy. She said she fell, hurt her leg last night, and couldn't fall asleep. She was wondering if I could come over and help her."

"Is it bad? Shouldn't she call 911?"

"She said it's sore and she needs help moving a few things and was hoping not to have to deal with any stairs, at least not without some assistance."

"Does this woman have any family?" Hunter asked confused.

Casey half rolled her sleepy eyes. "I honestly don't know but I get the impression she has been alone for a long time. It's not a big deal."

"So you're going now?" Hunter asked. "What time is it?" He saw his watch on the nightstand by the lamp. He grabbed it. "It's twenty to four…, jeez, we've been asleep for like two hours."

"That explains the brick in my head," Casey said. "Yeah, I'm going to go. I'm going to take another shower, wake up a little more and head over." She put her hands in her hair and could still feel the dampness from her previous shower. She rolled over to the side of the bed, stood up and gave a long stretch.

"That is sweet," Hunter said admiring her body.

Casey turned and smiled. "I'm glad you think so," she said walking into the bathroom.

Hunter pictured her naked in the shower. The image woke him up faster. *Maybe she'd want company* he thought. He liked the idea. He heard the shower water turn on and decided to wait another minute before surprising her.

Counting down the seconds, he got up and stretched. Just as he decided to give a ten count, his phone rang. He looked over at the nightstand where it was. "Please. You've got be kidding," he mumbled. He looked at the number and sighed. He brought it up to his ear, "Hunter here."

He hung up the phone and listened to the shower. He leaned his head against the bathroom door and let out a long slow breath. He knocked on the door and walked in. "Hey" he said.

"You coming in?" Casey said half teasing. "I'm just about done."

He liked that they both had the same idea. Yet he knew it wasn't going to happen. "As much as I'd like that, I just got called in."

"That's not a positive tone of voice I'm hearing," Casey said as she turned the water off. She grabbed a towel off the rack and pulled it around her. "Are you alright?"

"Troopers want to talk to me about my story and what I was investigating."

"I thought Rackers was going to avoid that?"

"There's only so much he can do. Besides, what we were doing wasn't going to stay a secret in a small station. I just thought I'd get more than two hours sleep," he said as he turned on the faucet in the sink to wash his face.

"Are you in any kind of trouble?"

"Not unless they think we haven't been forthcoming with information."

"Are you bringing your folder of stuff?" she asked as she toweled off.

"I was thinking that you should take it with you," he said.

"Is that the smart thing to do?"

"Not really," he answered. "They have most of our stuff. The only thing I didn't copy for them were my notes and your notes." He splashed some hot water on his face and washed it quickly with one of the hotels plain white wash clothes. "Now if they have their own X-Files team, they may want an update with all our extra information."

Casey gave a half-hearted laugh as she went to get dressed. "I'll take the stuff with me."

Hunter turned and followed her. He really just wanted to catch another glance of her naked body before he left. He wasn't disappointed as Casey let her towel drop and started to get dressed.

"The towel must be sad now," he said as he walked by.

"It was time to let it go. It served its purpose," she teased and gave him a wink.

"You know that hurts," he said as he began to get dressed.

"How long do you think your meeting is going to take?" she asked.

"I have no idea. Depending on what they want out of me or how much of a prick they want to be, this could be as short as an hour or all day long."

"Do you want me to give you a call?" she asked not sure what to say next.

"I'll call you. It'll be better that way," he said. "You think you'll be out at Dorothy's for a while?"

"I'm sure I'll be there for a bit but who knows," Casey answered. "She's a very sweet old lady. Quirky as hell but I like her, plus she's been so helpful with everything I've asked about, helping her now is the least I can do."

"She does seem a bit of an odd duck. But hey… if she's willing to give you all sorts of information and insights into this whole thing, I say we try and get as much from her as we can."

Casey agreed. Part of her couldn't wait to mention what had happened just a few short hours ago. Then she felt a sudden cautiousness and wondered if that was wise. A strange uneasiness seeped into her. She didn't know why but all of a sudden, she felt protective of her experience.

"If this wraps up early I'll come out to you. I want to meet this Dorothy," Hunter said interrupting Casey's deepening train of thought.

"I think that would be great. You'll like her. She's quick with her mind," Casey said, thankful for the interruption. She finished buttoning up her blouse, walked back into the bathroom to brush her hair and put on a little makeup.

Hunter finished getting dressed and ran his fingers through his hair. He wasn't as concerned about his appearance. He breathed into his hand to sniff his breath. "You have any mints or gum?"

"I think I do," she said. After dabbing a little make up on, she walked out of the bathroom. Hunter was putting on his shoes just about ready to go. She grabbed her purse and fumbled around in it. "I've got some gum."

"Great, can I have a piece?" he asked.

"Sure," she said with a coo. "But kiss me first."

Hunter came up to her, took her in a tight embrace and gave her a nice long kiss. As they both pulled back, they smiled. Casey's grin was long and sly.

"What?" he said with half a laugh.

"Take two pieces."

Hunter watched Casey pull out of her parking spot and he followed. He couldn't believe they were up and out so early. He generally didn't get angry when it came to police procedural stuff. It was what he had chosen to do with his life and knew inconveniences came with the job. Yet this instance had him particularly annoyed. He wondered what the state police could possibly want from him. He hoped he could just answer a few questions and leave.

Pulling into the station, he saw the place packed with State Trooper vehicles. He walked into headquarters with a casual stride. He was tired and still agitated. He knew his current attitude was not going to benefit him or the officers he had to see. If they would have asked him to stay and answer questions earlier, fine, but to call him back less than four hours after he left was absurd. So now, he was cranky.

The station buzzed with activity. Phones rang constantly and people shuffled from one desk to another. He didn't recognize anyone in the sea of bodies. He walked around slowly looking for a familiar face. He was making his way towards the captain's office when he felt a tug on his shoulder.

"Can I help you?" said a voice in an unfriendly tone. Hunter turned and saw a hulking man who looked like he would split all the seams on his gray blue uniform if he breathed too deep.

"Why yes you can my good man," he said with a degree of smarminess. "I'm Detective Hunter Matthews. I was called in special to speak to the man, men, woman, women or whatever assortment of authority is in charge."

The officer didn't care for the tone but relaxed his posture. "Captain Rackers is the captain of this station but you must be looking for Captain James, he's the lead on the murder investigation."

Hunter nodded. "I know Captain Rackers. He sent me on my way a few hours back so your Captain James must be the one who ordered me to come back in. Who are you?"

"Sergeant Greentree," the trooper said taking a half step closer to Hunter as if to intimidate him. "Captain James is with Captain Rackers now."

"Then I'll show myself in. I know the way Sergeant. Carry on. Surely, you have local villagers to terrify. By the way, one of your kind also works for this department, I'm sure it will be a wonderful family reunion when you two see each other." Hunter flashed him a sarcastic grin then moved on.

Captain Rackers' door was closed. He didn't want to knock but knew he had to. After taking a couple deep breaths he rapped his knuckles on the door and heard the captain tell him to enter.

"Ahhhh, Detective Matthews," said Captain Rackers standing up. "Come in. I want you to meet Captain James of the Jersey State Police; he'll be leading the investigation."

Captain James pointed to a chair and Hunter sat. The captain, well-groomed, medium build, hair short, the uniform clean and newly pressed, looked the part of a state police captain. He was all business.

Captain Rackers sat back in his chair. "Sorry about bringing you back in so quickly, but the captain insisted. He wants all his bases covered before making his assessments and steering the investigation into a particular direction."

By all appearances, Rackers looked extremely well rested for a man who hadn't slept in a day. Hunter still felt like a sledgehammer walloped him in the head.

"Yes, I've been informed that you were investigating an unusual angle to this case," Captain James said with little emotion.

"Unusual in what regard?" Hunter asked. Captain James tugged at his uniform, not pleased with the response. "In regards that you are essentially chasing ghosts in the woods to put it bluntly," he said.

"Blunt is good. It's honest. Better than stinking up the room with a bunch of bullshit," Hunter said with a grin on his face. Out of the corner of his eye, he caught the look of surprise on Rackers' face.

"Let's just shoot straight then," Captain James said holding his composure. "I can understand you being upset about being called back so quickly. I know you're tired and would rather sleep a few hours before being bothered by me but guess what?" his tone turned grim. "I don't give two shits if you don't get another wink of sleep for the next week. If you want to play that coy, smartass detective shit, I'll have your ass pushing so much paperwork, you'll think twice about ever busting my balls.

Hunter kept his smile. "Listen captain. How you think you'd accomplish that is beyond me. I don't work for this station." He could see he caught the captain completely off guard. "I was called in as a specialist, a freelancer. I'll answer whatever questions you want me to answer but beyond that, save your threats for those you can actually scare."

Captain James contained his fury. Captain Rackers sat motionless, beyond shocked. Hunter could see his reaction had left Rackers speechless. He gave a subtle nod to Rackers acknowledging his surprise.

"Very good then detective," Captain James said in a controlled manner. "I would like to ask you a few questions about your case, and then I have a thing or two I would like to add before we wrap up this lovely get-together."

Hunter crossed his legs and slid back into the chair. "I'm fine with that but before we get into this, would it be possible for me to get a cup of coffee?"

Captain James looked over to Captain Rackers who immediately ordered a pot of coffee brought to his office. Meanwhile, James began to ask Hunter a series of questions regarding why he took his particular point of view, why he didn't believe a gang or psychopath was involved and if he had any tangible evidence that would lend credence to his theory.

Hunter briefed him on cases he was involved in that had similar wounds, no DNA and mysterious circumstances. He explained the formation of the pentagram in the fire pit; this was news to Captain James. Hunter informed him that he believed the victims were willing to sacrifice themselves in some kind of ritualistic offering to Satan. He also mentioned that he had uncovered other cases, paralleling this one, where the wounds of the victims had very similar traits.

Captain James listened with intent. He thought the premise too absurd to believe, let alone all the manpower and time spent wasted on such an absurd angle. However, he did appreciate the idea of thinking outside the box. Captain Rackers defended their actions, citing the unusualness of the circumstances and reiterated Detective Matthew's experience with similar cases.

"Do you really think the public is going to believe that story?" Captain James asked Hunter, before looking over at Captain Rackers. "Do you think the state can stand behind that as its official explanation?" James continued, "Do you understand the criticism and ridicule that we would take? Let alone empowering every ghost hunter with a gun to run amuck. It would be bedlam." Captain James looked away with disgust. "Even if this story of yours had a scant of truth to it, there is no way the state could support it. It would destroy credibility. I'm sorry."

Hunter understood. He had no issue with an official stand by the state. He expected it all along. "So what do you want of me?"

Captain James immediately had an answer. "I want you to keep your mouth shut about this. You are to keep this out of the papers. I don't want to see your name anywhere near this story." James looked at them both like a father scolding his children. Then he turned to Hunter. "I know about your friend. If she knows what's good for her she'll be very delicate in the manner she treats this topic, if you get my meaning?" Hunter did but didn't intend to keep Casey from writing whatever she wanted. Captain James continued. "My number one duty is to protect the people of this state. Are we understood?"

Hunter nodded and took a sip of his coffee. "So you want me to say nothing?"

Captain James nodded. "You think you can manage that?"

"Do you want me to stop looking into it?" Hunter asked.

Captain James stood still for a moment before answering. "What you do with your time is your business. Just don't interfere with us or say anything stupid to the press and I believe we'll be fine."

Hunter couldn't believe his ears. The captain had in fact just given him permission to pursue his own investigation. Hunter placed the cup of coffee on Captain Racker's desk. "Are we finished?"

Captain James extended his hand, "Are we understood?"

Hunter looked him in the eye. "Yes we are."

## CHAPTER 26

The road to Dorothy's continued to give Casey the creeps. It didn't matter whether it was day or night. The whole stretch of road smothered her with unease. As she pulled into Dorothy's driveway, she only saw two lights on in the house, the porch light and the ever-mysterious kitchen light. She turned off her car and sat there. She felt exhausted. So much had happened in the past twenty-four hours and here she was back where her whole day had begun.

Casey got out of her car and took a second to look over the front yard. The first light of morning had begun to take away the deep shadows of the woods. For a moment, she thought she might see the beast. She wondered if it was out there.

With one eye on her surroundings, she knocked on the door. She waited, expecting Dorothy to answer, but heard nothing. Everything seemed eerily quiet. Remembering Dorothy had said she hurt her leg, she put her hand on the knob and turned it. Slowly, she pushed the door open and stepped inside. Casey felt like she was breaking in. It felt wrong. She called out Dorothy's name. No response. She took a few steps and grimaced when the floorboards creaked. The hall light was on but dimmed. Standing there, she was uncertain of what to do. She looked around. All the rooms were dark except for the kitchen. It always intrigued her, the way Dorothy appeared to take refuge in there. She crept closer to it, trying to be as quiet as possible. She couldn't recall Dorothy ever making a noise walking across these floors, while her own steps creaked and moaned like a dark symphony. She just about made it to the entrance of the kitchen when she heard Dorothy call out.

"Casey, is that you?"

Casey turned her head to look back towards the foyer. Nobody was there. She paused to listen. Maybe she was hearing things. Then she heard her name again. She started back towards the front door. "Hello," Casey called. She heard her name repeated but couldn't locate the source.

"Dorothy," she shouted louder. She took a few steps towards the stairs near the foyer.

"Casey?" Dorothy called again, faint and distant.

"Yes, it's Casey. Where are you?"

"Down in the basement," came her muffled voice.

*Down in the basement – of course.* Casey walked over to the basement door. She turned the handle but it didn't open. "It's locked."

"It just sticks at times. Pull real hard, that should do it," Dorothy instructed.

Casey tightened her grip on the knob and yanked at it. The door flew open and she nearly fell over before hitting the wall.

"Are you alright?" came Dorothy's light voice sailing up the stairs.

"I'm fine. I just yanked too hard." She came to the doorway and instantly encountered the thick dampness of the basement. She carefully descended the creaky wooden steps. With each step, she feared she would fall through. When Casey came to the bottom of the stairs, she saw a sea of old furniture and boxes haphazardly strewn about. "Dorothy?" she called.

"Yes dear, over here," Dorothy said, though Casey couldn't see her.

The basement resembled a collection of garage sale rejects. Casey saw broken chairs, dinged up dining tables, coffee tables with gashes on them, dusty old oil lamps, chipped depression ware, an old typewriter with missing keys, piles of old newspapers and general clutter scattered about. Marked and unmarked boxes were stacked at various heights. A layer of dust covered everything. She finally squeezed past an old armoire and around a filing cabinet and saw Dorothy sitting in an old wooden rocking chair with a photo album on her lap.

"Are you okay?" Casey asked as she approached.

Dorothy looked at her with a big smile, "I'm fine now dear."

"What happened?" Casey asked.

"I came down to see if I could find some old cooking ware, then realized that I didn't prop open the door. When I turned to go back up the stairs, I stepped funny and turned my ankle. I fell and hurt myself. I thought I might've broken my hip or leg and you know what that can mean for an old person."

"Are you sure you're okay?" Casey asked with more concern as she kneeled down to take a look at Dorothy's ankle.

"I feel much better, thank you. I'm sorry I disturbed you but when I was finally able to get up, I was scared, so I used the phone down here to call you. I knew keeping that old rotary was the right thing to do," she said, looking towards the old black vintage candlestick phone propped on a small end table against the wall.

"As long as you're okay. Can you get up?"

Dorothy tried to stand with Casey's help but began to stumble. "I'm sorry dear it still hurts a little too much. I don't know if I can truly make it up those stairs."

Casey lightly ran her finger around the swollen ankle. "I think it could use some ice. Do you have ice in the freezer?"

"Yes. If you want to wrap it in a towel, they are in the tall narrow closet by the jelly cupboard, you'll see it, it's the only tall closet in the kitchen. Plastic baggies are in the middle drawer under the counter to the left as soon as you walk in," Dorothy said.

"Would you like some water or something?" Casey asked, as she made her way to the stairs.

"Tea, dear," Dorothy said with a smile. "You can have some if you'd like."

She never did get her coffee and tea sounded great, especially Dorothy's tea. "Where do you keep it?"

Dorothy told her it was in a blue glass container on the counter to the left of the sink. Casey nodded, went up the stairs and headed towards the kitchen, *the mysterious kitchen.*

As Casey came closer to the seemingly forbidden room, she slowed her pace. Rather than just walk in, she peeked in first. Casey laughed a touch seeing the dated looking room, with yellow tinted flowery wallpaper, light brown cabinets simply constructed with daisy handles, a faded Formica counter too, and stiff wooden kitchen chairs with embroidered cushions surrounding a round table covered by a white lace tablecloth. It reminded her of her aunt's grandmother's kitchen. She found the plastic baggies and filled one with ice before wrapping it in a towel. She filled the teapot with water and placed it on the stove to boil. She grabbed the towel and headed back downstairs.

Dorothy was sitting comfortably in her chair, flipping pages in an old photo album.

"Here's the ice for your ankle," Casey said. She looked around for something to elevate Dorothy's leg and found a sturdy looking box. She placed it by Dorothy and reached for her leg.

"Let's get this ice on your ankle," Casey said as she propped Dorothy's foot up and settled the ice in place. "Just try to keep it still and you should be fine. I have to check on the tea."

The water had yet to boil. She opened cupboards looking for cups to use. When she found them, she placed two on the counter by the stove. She grabbed the container Dorothy described and opened it. The strong aroma hit her. The smell had an instant calming effect. The water boiled and she prepared the tea.

Dorothy was delighted when Casey handed her the cup. She immediately took a big whiff and Casey watched her face relax. For a second, it looked to Casey that Dorothy actually got younger.

Casey smiled and inhaled the steam from her own cup. She felt her neck and shoulder muscles relax. When she took a sip, the warmth traveled through her as if the tea knew exactly where it needed to tend. She leaned against the table, and felt the weight of the day melt away.

"It's good isn't it?" Dorothy asked noticing how relaxed it made Casey.

"Mmmmmmmm," Casey answered with a sleepy smile.

"I think this might be one of my better ones," Dorothy said relaxing into her chair.

"They've all been good but this one may certainly take the cake."

"Thank you dear," Dorothy said as she opened up her photo album again.

Casey raised her cup and let the aroma envelop her. Her mind fluttered in a relaxed flighty way that was good. "I wish I could make this myself. Maybe one day you'll show me how."

"Of course dear, it will be my pleasure," Dorothy replied.

Casey glanced down to see a number of black and white and sepia toned pictures on the pages. She watched Dorothy glimpse at the images and then turn the page. Casey began to pay a little more attention to the pictures. The people all looked around the same age, early twenties. She thought the images were from the 50's or maybe the 60's. The style of clothes reminded her of her aunt's photo albums. The girls were in dresses buttoned up to the neck, the boys in slacks and white dress shirts or shorts and white t-shirts. She thought it both nice and sad to reminisce about the past. She wondered how many of those people were still alive. Casey watched Dorothy turn page after page, seeing similar faces appear at the same functions and parties. When Dorothy finished with the album, she asked Casey to place it on the table and hand her another one. Dorothy wasn't particular about which one. In fact, she told Casey to run her hand over the albums and pull the first one she thought felt good. Casey passed her hands over the many old bindings, some more dried and fragile than others. With no particular thought, she stopped at an album with frills along the sides. The leather cover didn't look as aged as the others but it was still quite old. She pulled it out and handed it to Dorothy. Dorothy beamed and told her it had been many years since she last looked at that one.

Casey paid more attention to the pictures. Dorothy began to narrate each page. Some of the photographs had faded badly. Dorothy pointed out relatives, aunts, sisters, nieces. Casey noticed there weren't many men in the pictures. Dorothy explained that there weren't many boys in the family. After several pages, Casey noticed one girl who had a familiar look. The features of the girl resembled her aunt. For a second, the thought frightened her but she didn't know why. Her aunt had grown up in the south jersey region but never talked much about it. Still, she kept her eye on the pictures as Dorothy continued to share memories while flipping through the pages. Then as she turned another page, Casey observed a series of pictures dominated by boys. Casey asked who they were. Dorothy hesitated and appeared to search her mind to recall their names.

"There just weren't a lot of boys in our family. That gene wasn't the dominant one I guess," Dorothy said with half a laugh.

With the turn of another page, the boys again appeared in most of the images. Dorothy still hadn't mentioned their names. Casey asked again who they were.

"Well dear," Dorothy said. "That one boy is Arthur Leeds and the other boy is David Hastleton. You read about him in the newspaper clippings," she said nonchalantly.

Casey felt a lump in her stomach. Dorothy didn't say anymore as she continued to flip through the pages. Casey couldn't shake the flush feeling that began pulsating through her body. Dorothy put her finger on the picture of a young girl, no more than about sixteen, the one who looked like Casey's aunt, and tapped it lightly. Then she flipped the page and tapped her finger on the picture of another little girl. Casey asked who they were.

With ease Dorothy answered, "Your aunt and your mom."

Casey thought she misheard, but her mouth began to quiver. "My mom? My Aunt Marie? You knew them?" Casey felt her heart pound against her sternum.

"Of course dear. We grew up together," Dorothy said without looking up from the album. "We were neighbors for years. I babysat them when they were kids."

"My aunt rarely talked about living down here and my mom..." Casey stammered. She used the table to steady herself. She was shaking. "My mom...no one talked about her much and I didn't ask. I mean, I wasn't interested. My aunt was my mom as far as I was concerned." Casey paused trying to absorb the news. "How come... how did you know anything about me?"

Dorothy looked up at her. "Dear, I knew the instant I touched your hand. Remember when we sat on the deck. I knew then that you were of my blood."

Casey pushed herself off the table and staggered backwards. "Your blood?"

"Yes dear. Your aunt, your mom, we are of the same family tree. Our grandmothers are the same. I just happen to be the eldest in the line but had no children to pass this gift onto."

"My aunt never said anything about relatives still being down here. I come from a very small family," Casey said half-confused. "I was told our family left the area."

"No dear. You come from a large family, a family with a great history."

Then why would they move north and leave this place?"

"They ran away dear," Dorothy said with insistence.

"Ran away? Away from what?"

"Their history. Their bloodline."

Casey felt panic, tension and anxiety take over. "Why would they run from that? Were they criminals or did someone shame them out of the area?"

Dorothy grinned and shook her head. "Don't you know dear?"

"Know what?" Casey half yelled as she clenched her fists. Tears began to well up. She could hardly speak.

Dorothy stood up. "It's you," she said. "Your aunt escaped with you but I told her there was no escaping from this."

"My mother?" Casey asked in quiet disbelief.

Dorothy was calm. "She was the one who bore the keeper."

"Keeper?" Casey shouted. Confusion riddled her consciousness yet deeper within an awakening began to stir. "Keeper of what?" she asked, afraid of the answer.

"Why the beast's keeper my dear. It's been you all along," Dorothy said as she reached out to touch her.

Casey recoiled and stumbled away. She turned a corner to escape and found herself further from the stairs. After falling over a box and going around another old armoire, she stopped cold in her tracks. Her eyes locked on an old crumbling fireplace built into the wall but it didn't look functional. The bricks outlining it barely clung together. She then noticed the wall around it was different from the rest of the basement. It began to dawn on her that Dorothy's house was built around this older foundation.

Dorothy stood up from her chair. She limped around the corner and saw Casey standing over the old fire pit. "That's right dear. It's the birthplace of our legacy. It's the birthplace of our own true blood brother."

Casey stood horrified. She couldn't take her eyes off it.

Dorothy came up beside her and lightly placed her hand on Casey's arm. She whispered to her, "You can still see the faint stain of blood on the floor from the birth."

Casey wanted to run from the hellish scene but she couldn't. She was both fascinated and horrified by the site. Her breathing became rapid. Dorothy ran her old hands down Casey's arm and locked fingers with her. "See my dear. I can now go to rest."

Casey felt the chill of Dorothy's grip. She turned and looked into the old woman's eyes. They shimmered with a deep darkness, the same hollow vacant look that Arthur's had. However, where Arthur's eyes revealed fear, Dorothy's expressed joy and power.

"See dear, it's your destiny. You can run all you want. Your aunt tried to runaway but she couldn't move far enough. Her history haunted her and it anchored her. You'll never be able to run from it either."

Casey began to realize now why the beast didn't kill them at Mrs. Falanner's place and why the beast didn't kill her when it killed Staffen. Her mind drifted to dreams from her youth. Were they dreams? Did she actually experience the beast when she was a little girl? Her aunt never really left the Pine Barrens, they had simply moved to the very northern edge of them.

"Is it a wonder why you became a ghost chaser, fascinated by the paranormal? You were reaching out, searching for your ultimate destiny," Dorothy whispered staring at the fireplace.

Casey began to fall into a trance. Slowly the boxes and clutter of the basement faded away, replaced by the brick, mortar and wood of the original house. A crackling fire appeared and she began to hear the sounds of a woman in pain. Soon, Casey could see the woman, a homely sort, sweating, grinding her teeth in pain, lying on the floor. There's a midwife with a bowl of hot water. Casey can hear other voices, children's voices in the background. The pregnant woman is writhing in pain. The midwife encourages her to push. Casey can hear thunder in the distance, rain beating against the house, and the wind howling, as if calling for evil to join them. The woman is pounding her fist into the wooden floor planks. She is cursing and screaming.

"Leave me be," the woman seethes. "Let this child be a beast of the devil. Let it be damned. It haunts me as its bastard father haunts me now." The woman grabs the young midwife and stares deep into her eyes. The midwife stares back and sees only two large deep black holes. The longer she stares at the woman, the more she can see and sense only hate.

The woman pants heavily, saliva flying from her mouth. Her attention shifts away from the midwife to a small girl who looks on, her daughter. The woman snarls, her eyes narrow as the pain of labor grows. "Listen to me child... Men be damned. Fools! They are all weak fools." She starts to curse again as the baby begins to exit her body. With one final agonizing scream, she pushes, and the child is born.

The midwife is trembling. She holds the deformed child in her hands. She is afraid to show it to the woman. The midwife begins to cry, the child is grotesque, hardly a child at all, its arms misshapen, its head elongated, bones protruding to fine points at the joints.

"Throw it in the fire," cries the mother. "Throw it, it's cursed."

The midwife can't move as she holds the twisted, disfigured child in her arms. She watches as the child mutates into something else. The child's face contorts and it begins to cry with a hiss and a squeal. Its legs bend backwards at the knee and its feet begin to produce sharp talons. One of the talons penetrates the midwife's skin and draws blood. In a panic, she tosses it into the fire. The mutated child squeals and squirms in the hot embers, but does not fully burn. They all watch in horror as it transforms. A tail forms, leathery wings sprout from its body and it screeches loudly, rattling the walls of the house. Then in an instant, it flies up and out of the chimney. They hear it wail into the night and fade away, lost in the sounds of thunder.

Casey stumbled as the vision faded. Dorothy grabbed her, steadied her.

"What does this mean?" Casey asked feeling exhausted.

"It means, dear, that you are the new Keeper. You just experienced what I saw when I first became aware of my destiny," Dorothy said, slowly releasing her grip.

"Keeper? I'm no Keeper. I don't want this…" Casey said pulling her arm away. "This isn't who I am."

Dorothy smiled but the smile wasn't sweet and her eyes were no longer those of a kind old woman. "It is you dear. It is you."

"I can't do this," Casey gasped, nearly stumbling again. "This is not me." She grew angry. "I am not that."

Dorothy tried to comfort her. "I know it's hard to fathom, but if you search deep… deep within you… you'll find it's true."

Casey began to cry. "Stay away." She turned and stumbled her way towards the stairs. She wasn't quite sure what to do. She wanted to leave but a strange force pulled at her. Casey slowly walked up the stairs.

Dorothy watched, smiled and whispered. "I know it's tough now dear, but you will learn to live with it, embrace it, love it."

A chill overwhelmed Casey. She halted before getting to the top of the staircase. Her world became a blur but she could see Dorothy staring, not only at her but also into her. *You will be empowered more than you can imagine.* She heard the words and could feel a physical change.

Casey managed to get to the top of the stairs. It was there that she felt her phone vibrate. She fumbled for it. It was a text from Hunter. "Almost there," it said. "Arthur Leeds was ID'd as one of the dead." Casey's hand flew up to her mouth in shock. She needed to breathe. She needed fresh air. Fumbling up the last step, she ran for the front door. When she came to it, she placed her hand on the doorknob. She sensed something. She turned and Dorothy stood right behind her. Casey shrieked.

"You are running right into your destiny dear. Embrace it. You'll feel more warmth and love than ever before," Dorothy said with a soothing coo in her voice.

"Arthur is dead. He died trying to exorcise that thing from all of us," Casey said shaking.

Dorothy's smile transformed into a dead stare. "Arthur was weak. As a boy, he was weak and so was his lunatic friend David. You remember David don't you?" she said. "David was weak too. He wanted out of the family but could not escape the bond of our blood. Both of them were nothing more than frightened little boys. They couldn't handle their lineage. You see dear, it's in the eyes. You saw Arthur's eyes. I can see in yours that you did. You saw that he was scared. He was weak. You look into my eyes and you do not see that."

"I did see him. He was haunted," Casey said with spite and pity.

"Haunted is a good word. He was full of fear and weakness. The men who enter our lives are rarely strong and the ones that are, never stay. They can't handle our strength, afraid it will reveal their weakness. We hold the power," Dorothy said with complete pride and confidence.

"Hunter is not weak," Casey said.

Dorothy giggled. "Your young man…the man you saved this past night. He is not as strong as you dear."

"How did you know that?" Casey stuttered.

"My sweet dear, I know everything about my beloved brother."

"Brother?"

"Yes dear. He was born male before the curse set in. There is a soul trapped in that body that you call a beast," Dorothy said quite seriously. "It is our duty to protect him. You see, the eldest child of Mother Leeds was a girl by the name of Patrice. After tending to her mother through that fateful night and most of the next day, she set out to find her brother. She didn't know what compelled her to do it, but she wanted to protect him. It was on these very grounds, not far from here by a small pond that she found him.

Though the poor thing had a curse upon it and its body transformed into a hideous creature, it was still a frightened young being. She went to him. She wanted to take care of him. He sniffed her and knew her scent was of the same bloodline. She went to hold him but he was scared and he bit her. She felt her whole body go warm. She found herself drawn into him, almost hypnotized. When their eyes locked, it sealed her fate that she was to be his Keeper. She took on and embraced the curse or as I see it, a blessing, forever bound. She lived over a hundred years and the responsibility of being the keeper was passed to my grandmother who lived nearly one hundred twenty years before passing it to me." Dorothy paused, setting her stare into Casey's eyes.

As much as Casey wanted to look away, she couldn't. Dorothy's gaze held her still. "You see, dear. Your mother gave birth to you first. You are the eldest of the line and a woman. You bear the blessing and I am now passing it to you."

Casey fell numb. She couldn't shift her eyes from Dorothy. Dorothy's soul seemed to meld with hers and pass a spirit into her. Casey tried to resist but could feel herself slowly losing the fight. She felt herself surrendering. She wept. She did not want this cup passed onto her.

"Dear, there is no use in fighting it," Dorothy said. "It is your birthright. You know it. When you first saw him all those nights ago, he would have killed you if you were anyone else. Instead, he ran away, at first confused. You think you saved your young man but it was your brother who spared him because of you. He knows now that it is you who will look after him."

Casey's mind drifted back to earlier that night. The scene of her saving Hunter played out in slow motion. She could see the creature at the wood's edge after it had thrown Ken. It was going to kill him but Hunter fired a shot and diverted its attention. The creature spotted Hunter and prepared to attack. Casey saw herself diving towards Hunter just as the creature moved to strike. She then saw herself slapping the pistol out of Hunter's hand. She wasn't protecting Hunter. She was trying to protect the beast, her brother. Casey gasped as the apparition faded.

"That's right dear," Dorothy said with a soothing tone. "The visions never lie."

Casey's hand still held the doorknob. She took a deep breath and released it. She felt her old self-slipping away, succumbing to her fate.

"Now dear, it's time for you to meet your destiny," Dorothy said reaching for her hand. "There is still so much for you to understand." Together they turned the doorknob and opened the door.

# CHAPTER 27

The sun's morning light felt warm and the air refreshing. Casey took a deep breath. Her shoulders relaxed as she walked across the porch. Dorothy guided her over to the swing. "Some tea dear?" she asked, making sure Casey sat comfortably on the cushions. Dorothy looked over the yard. "It is a lovely day isn't it." Casey nodded but said nothing. "I'll be right back."

Casey sat in a daze, numb. Her mind swirled with thoughts of the past, the events of the present and thoughts of the future. She searched her mind trying to reconcile the revelation. Thoughts about the beast flooded through her. She could see it. She could see herself by it, tending to it. Then other thoughts took over. She thought of Hunter. She thought about his embrace, the way he kissed her, the way he made love to her. She eased into the cushions of the swing as the thoughts began to bring her out of her daze. A battle was raging in her mind and she felt powerless as to which side would win.

Yet, a new voice began to grab hold, a voice unlocked from the depths of her sub consciousness. She tried to hold it back but the force would not relent and continued its slow push to take over. New thoughts began to permeate: *He is coming... Come and see... Embrace the new you. Love the new you.* Casey felt her old self begin to slowly peel away, falling like shards of scraped paint.

Her eyes grew heavy. Her head bobbed. She became drowsy. She felt herself drifting when her phone began to vibrate. She ignored it. It continued to vibrate. Her old self rose to the surface and it stirred her to answer it.

She pulled the phone out of her pocket and looked at it, a text from Hunter: *In town, have news - see you in a few minutes.* Her mind swirled. Would she reveal to him what had happened? Would he try to take her away? *No*, a voice whispered in her mind. Would he want to hurt her? Would he want to kill her brother? A strange sense of protectiveness overcame her. *No, he will not harm him.*

Dorothy came out with the tea. Casey reeled inside. She did not want to give up the life she knew. She had an interesting career, a new boyfriend. She concentrated on thoughts of their lovemaking as a way to stay present. She clung hard to the vision but they were slipping away.

"I love the smell of a new day," Dorothy said as she handed Casey a cup of tea.

She didn't want it but found herself taking it, like an addict not able to say no. Nearly forgetting all her previous feelings, she looked over at Dorothy and said, "This is a lovely day. I could get used to days like this." A distant voice screamed within her, *Noooo!*


Hunter made his way down the long desolate road towards Dorothy's house. He saw why the road creeped Casey out. Thin meandering street, no real shoulder, trees, and branches reaching out; he wondered what school kids imagined when they traveled to visit the library. The smell of marsh and pines made for an odd fragrance. The aura of the trip gave him the feeling he was traveling to a haunted house. He laughed at the thought but still felt anxious as he got closer.

The turn came up fast. He saw Casey's car in front of the large house. He was impressed and immediately understood why Casey wondered how an old woman could keep such a place in good shape.

As he pulled up next to Casey's car, he saw her and an old woman sitting on the porch. *Dorothy... must be.* He almost honked the horn but quickly realized the cheesiness of the gesture. He got out of the car and said hi. They both rose and although he glanced at Dorothy all of his attention went to Casey. He wanted to grab her and give her a deep kiss but knew it wasn't appropriate. Instead, he held out his hand, "So you must be Dorothy."

Dorothy greeted him with her big friendly smile, "and you must be Hunter, it is a pleasure to meet you."

Casey smiled. She was relieved to see him. A sense of normalcy overcame her. "So you found the place with no problem?"

"Yeah, no problem at all," he said as he looked around the yard. "You sure are out of the way out here, but it's very nice."

Dorothy looked him over. "Would you like to have a seat and can I get you something?"

Hunter walked to sit next to Casey, "I'm fine but thanks," he said.

"Surely you must be thirsty. Let me get you something so you two can catch up," Dorothy said with her sweetest voice. "Can I at least get you a glass of water?"

"A glass of water would be great, thank you." He watched Dorothy walk inside the house. "Nice women."

"She's very pleasant," Casey said, her earlier worries having waned, almost as if they never happened at all. "What's the news you said you had?"

"You're not going to believe this but they actually want us to continue with our investigation," he said with excitement.

Casey smiled wide with surprise. "That's terrific. How did that happen?"

"The state police have nothing to go on. I explained a few things we had uncovered and, though the state won't support our theory, they will look the other way while we continue our investigation. There's only one hang up," he said reaching for her hand. "I have to keep my mouth shut and they suggested you watch what you write." He shook his head no. "You write whatever you need to." Hunter looked around the yard and admired how the light fell perfectly across the landscape, warm tones saturating the budding greens of spring. "When this case wraps up, you are going to have one hell of a story to tell."

"How long do you have?" Casey asked.

"My captain is giving me a week to work on this. He'll reevaluate my situation when I return."

"That's great news."

"It's great news for both of us. It will make your work easier since we have access to this," he motioned to Dorothy's house, "and plenty of time to do some field work together."

Casey smiled but in the back of her mind, darker thoughts began to swirl again. She tried to keep them at bay. "So what's our first move?"

"I was thinking a big lunch… some sleep then start fresh tomorrow. We've both been up since yesterday and when this rush wears off, we'll be like the walking dead."

Casey looked at him with relief. "I'm exhausted. I could use a deep sleep," she said as she cozied up to him.

They sat quietly for a minute before Hunter spoke. "I forgot to ask, what exactly happened here?"

"She fell in the basement and couldn't get up the stairs," Casey said not telling the whole truth. "She turned her ankle pretty bad."

Hunter made an odd look. "Well she doesn't seem to be showing any ill effects from it now. I didn't notice a limp or anything."

"I don't know," Casey said more tired than worried. "I put some ice on it and we chatted and she showed me lots of pictures from her photo albums."

Hunter put his hand on her head and ran his fingers gently through her hair. "This is nice," he said.

"It is," Casey said feeling comfortable. "I think Dorothy wants me to have this place," she said with a whisper.

That struck Hunter as extremely odd. "What? Why?"

Casey felt caught. She wasn't sure what to say. "I'm not sure. She's really taken to me I guess."

"It sounds a little nutty," Hunter said with half a laugh. "You've met what... a couple times?"

"Many more than that," Dorothy chimed in as she handed him a glass of water

"What?" Hunter stood up, stunned at the news. "I don't understand."

"She's my niece. She gets all of this when I pass," Dorothy said. "Shocking dear?"

"Yes, quite," Hunter said still dumbfounded. "When did all this happen?"

Casey spoke softly. "I found out earlier this morning. She explained it all to me."

"Explained all what?" Hunter said addressing Casey then looking at Dorothy, "How do you know that you are family?"

Dorothy smiled. "I've always known dear. It was she who had to find out."

Hunter's instincts had him immediately suspicious. "This is too strange," he said. "I don't understand how this unfolded."

Dorothy looked over at Casey, then towards Hunter. "You see dear, after her mother died, her aunt was awarded custody and wanted to get away from this area and make a new life for herself. She felt she had the right to take Casey from her family roots."

"I can understand that, but how did you know it was her, that she's your niece, cousin, whatever and why would you just give her this place without really knowing her?" Hunter asked, still standing, suspicious of any answer.

"I've always known. I've never forgotten about her. Besides, her aunt would make the occasional trip down here and talk. She could never really escape. Casey can't either," Dorothy said.

"Escape? Escape what?" Hunter said. He could see that Dorothy's pleasant smile had faded. "Was she abused? Was there abuse in the family, physical violence, sexual misconduct? Was she escaping from that?" Hunter felt Casey's hand tighten around his arm as if to say 'back off'.

Dorothy straightened herself. She didn't like Hunter's tone or assumption. "No. Absolutely not! We had a very loving and nurturing environment. Nothing like you're suggesting."

"I apologize if you think I'm accusing," Hunter said backing off a touch. "I just found your word choice...peculiar."

"Her aunt felt the need to run away. I'm not exactly sure why. She was kind of the black sheep of the family. I'm sorry I can't tell you the details as to why she left but she took our little Casey with her," Dorothy said. "But now Casey's back... all of this is rightfully hers."

Hunter no longer bought the sweet old woman façade. His instincts told him there was more going on. "So there are no other heirs? Casey is it?"

"She's was chosen!" Dorothy said with great confidence.

"Chosen? Chosen for what?" Hunter asked. Again, he could feel Casey tug at him.

Dorothy placed her cup down and sat up straight as if ready to scold. "She was chosen to have all this. Her only choice is to accept it."

"This is crazy. She has to accept?" Hunter said with a mock laugh. "What... free will doesn't exist in the Pine Barrens?"

Dorothy's smile turned sinister. "Free will, my dear, does not exist in this situation. It's her destiny."

"What on God's good green earth are you talking about?

This is ridiculous." Hunter took Casey by the hand and urged her to stand up. "We need to get going. We have work to do."

"*You* are welcome to do all that but Casey needs to stay here now," Dorothy said, as if claiming property and territory.

Hunter shot her a menacing glare. "Yeah, I don't think so. We talked about it and she wants to go."

Casey sat silent, her head down. Hunter ignored her body language. When he took a step towards the stairs, he had to tug Casey to get up. She followed like a reluctant child. He looked back at her. "Are you okay?"

Casey shrugged her shoulders. "I want to go," she mumbled with hesitance.

"What have you done to her?" Hunter snapped.

"I've done nothing but reveal the truth to her," Dorothy answered.

"Truth? This is crazy," Hunter shot back. He looked at Casey again. "Are you sure you're okay?"

She nodded a forced yes.

"You'll be fine once we get you out of here, get you something to eat and get some rest. You're exhausted," he said walking with her towards the stairs and down them. He was just getting to her car when he heard a frightening howl come from the treetops. His head shot up as he searched for the source of the sound. A chill ran through him. He knew that sound. "Casey, did you hear that?"

"I did," she said with energy, looking around as well. "Over there," she said pointing to the far end of the yard into a shaded area about a hundred feet away.

"Where?" Hunter asked looking around frantically in the direction she pointed. "I don't see anything."

"It's in there, I know it is," she said with a hint of joy.

"Did you see it?" Hunter asked.

"No. I just know that's where it is," Casey said taking a few steps towards where she believed it was.

Hunter walked in front of her and pulled out his pistol. There was another howl but less menacing. "You're right." They walked slowly, taking cautious steps.

Dorothy stood on the porch. She felt invigorated. Her skin smoothed and she ran her hand up and down her arms as if embracing some spirit within her. "You can't kill it," she said proudly.

Hunter glimpsed back at her. "What is she talking about?" he said to Casey.

"You can't kill it," Casey said with a calm even tone. She then looked him in the eyes. "You can't kill it Hunter. Go. Leave me. I have to stay."

Hunter put his hands on her shoulders. "What did that lunatic do to you?"

Casey's stare went blank. Her eyes darkened and became hollow right in front of him as if some spirit entered her and took over.

He looked back up at Dorothy who leered with pleasure. "What have you done to her?"

"I revealed her destiny," Dorothy said half panting then pointed to the woods edge. "Behold!"

Hunter turned. Standing tall, the creature emerged from the woods. It appeared larger than he remembered it, displaying itself fully, stretching out its long dark wingspan. Its clawed feet curled into the grounds brittle soil. Turning its head towards them, it let out another screech.

Hunter instinctively knelt to the ground in a defensive position. The beast took a couple steps towards them. Casey stood before the creature as if welcoming it while Hunter aimed his weapon at it.

"Casey, get down," he yelled.

Dorothy stretched out her arms. "Look at its glory. Look at the beauty of our blood," she said beaming with pride. The beast then leaped into the air and flew towards the house landing short of it. "Look at it," she cried out.

Hunter repositioned. Casey turned. Hunter grabbed her and pulled her behind him. "Are you alright?"

Casey said nothing.

"Kill it, weak man. It stands before you. Why haven't you shot at it?" Dorothy said with command.

Hunter couldn't understand why he hadn't fired a shot either. He had his pistol trained on it. He also had a clean line of sight but he still couldn't pull the trigger.

"You are weak!" Dorothy hissed at him. "I can't believe she let you impregnate her."

"Pregnant?" Hunter said to Casey with his weapon still pointed at the creature.

Casey had no answer but now that Dorothy said it, she knew Dorothy was right.

Hunter looked at Dorothy. "Listen up crazy woman, step aside or I am going to shoot this thing." He remained steady but his finger could not pull the trigger as he watched the creature slowly make its way closer to Dorothy.

"You'll never shoot it. You are too weak, too feeble. You'll never be man enough to kill my sweet blood." Dorothy said with pleasure.

"Back away!" Hunter commanded.

"No Hunter, don't" Casey pleaded. "Just go. Go and don't come back. Leave it be."

"I'm not leaving. I'm not leaving you and I'm certainly not leaving without putting that nut job away and lastly… I'm not leaving until I kill that thing," Hunter said, sweat dripping off his brow.

"You can't kill it," Casey said as tears streamed down her face.

The beast took a step towards them. Hunter yelled for it to stop but the creature continued. He fired. The creature vanished in flight. They both heard Dorothy yell as she fell back against her house, blood seeping out of her abdomen. The creature howled and screeched, the noise echoing all around them. Hunter frantically looked but could not locate the beast.

Casey began to scream and ran towards the house. Hunter followed, staying close behind. Casey hurried onto the porch and could see Dorothy breathing fast, gasping for her last breaths of air. Casey stared at the old woman whose skin now appeared to shrink around her bones. Dorothy looked at her with a fading smile. "He's all yours dear. You possess the power now." Dorothy grinned one last time; closed her eyes, took another breath, then became still.

"No, no, no, oh my God," Casey cried as she wrapped her hands around Dorothy's head pleading for her to come back to life.

Hunter put his hand on her shoulder. "Let's get out of here while we can," he said.

The howling shriek sounded again. They searched the trees but couldn't see anything. Suddenly the creature flew onto the porch, its force vibrating the wooden structure. It was less than twenty feet from them.

"Get over here," Hunter, shouted to Casey.

The creature turned towards Dorothy's body and released a bloodcurdling scream.

"Casey, please get behind me," Hunter shouted.

Casey stood with her back to Hunter, watching the beast. She wasn't sure if she was afraid or curious as she watched the beast take a step closer.

"Casey," Hunter pleaded. "Let me kill it… move."

With her back still to him she declared, "You can't kill it."

"What are you talking about? What did that woman do to you?"

"She revealed my truth," Casey said turning towards him looking calm and confident. "I asked you to go. I can't control what may happen."

"I can kill it," Hunter said, then raised his gun and fired two quick shots at the beast. The creature howled as it jettisoned back into the trees.

"Stop it Hunter, I beg you," she said facing him. "Please. This is beyond you."

"This thing has to be stopped!" Hunter yelled. "It killed all those people."

"No," Casey said. "Those people sacrificed themselves. I can see it now. They were haunted and the only way for them to find peace was through sacrifice. I saw the terror in Arthur's eyes. He hadn't seen rest since he first bore witness. He was family. It was in his blood but he was weak. He couldn't handle the bond. They were all family of one sort or another. All bound by the same bloodline no matter how faint and they were all haunted. They knew exactly what they were doing, what they had to do. You would have figured this out in time."

Hunter couldn't believe her irrational state of mind. "Casey, I don't know what that woman drugged you with, but we have to get you out of here, now."

A wave of emotion washed over her, she saw the man she had made love to, whom she cherished, whose embrace she yearned for. Her body loosened, the glaze in her eyes lessened. She felt...released.

Hunter saw it to and smiled. "Okay," he said as she came closer to him. Both of them relaxed into each other's arms. "We need to get out of here," he whispered and guided her off the porch.

"Yes," she said holding him tight. "I don't know what overcame me."

They had only taken a few steps off the porch when the beast came screeching through the air and slammed onto the earth a few feet away from them. Hunter let go of Casey, stepped in front of her and pointed his gun at the creature.

With a swipe of its wing, the creature knocked the gun out of Hunter's hand. Casey picked it up and rose quickly.

"Stand back," she shouted but not sure who she was referring to. Casey darted the gun back and forth from the beast to Hunter. She then noticed something. It made her tremble. Looking closer at the beast's hideous head, she noticed, ever so slightly, hints of a young boy's face just beyond the disfiguration of the creature's exterior. Casey saw years, no…ages of pain and weariness. Her heart broke. Pity ran through her. She let out a silent sigh as she looked upon her brother, their eyes meeting for the first time. She lowered the weapon.

"Shoot it!" Hunter shouted.

Casey just stood looking at the beast. It roared again, spreading its menacing wings. Casey then watched Hunter reach into his jacket and pull out a small pistol which he aimed and fired two quick shots at the beast. Casey also fired and the gun recoiled right out of her hand. She watched the beast disappear into the trees. Turning, she spotted Hunter lying on the ground. Blood oozed from his chest. He gasped for air. She ran to him and cradled him in her arms. She began to cry.

"What happened?" he choked. "I don't understand."

"I'm sorry," she said, tears streaming down her face. "But you can't kill it. You can't kill my family."

Hunter looked at her confused. The blood rising up in his throat began to choke him. "I wanted to save you."

"I am saved my dear," she said. "You have saved me."

"The baby?" he sputtered.

"It's a girl. She will bear the next Keeper."

"What?" Hunter coughed; the words became more difficult to get out. "I don't understand."

Casey brushed her hand through his hair. "You can't understand. I'm sorry."

Hunter choked trying to take in one last breath of air… his jaw quivered, air ceased to enter or escape…his eyes widened…then stillness.

Casey closed his eyes and laid Hunter gently on the ground. Her tears disappeared. She looked around and called for the creature. A moment later, it landed gently in front of her. Their eyes met once again. She smiled as she saw more clearly a small boy's face emerge from within the creature's head. Casey felt the bond that her cousins and aunts had known before her. She reached out to touch her brother's face. She knew she was bound to protect him.

"Go," she said. "I will keep us safe."

The beast backed off a step and then like the wind, vanished into the woods.

She looked at Hunter's dead body. She wasn't sure what to do. She stood there for a few seconds when a thought came to her. *I'll have some tea. The answers have always been in the tea.* She walked up the stairs of the porch. She glanced at Dorothy's lifeless body and then went inside. She walked to the kitchen and immediately opened the pantry. She pulled out a container she had never seen before; it just felt like the right thing to do. As she pulled out a teabag, a small piece of paper fell to the floor. She picked it up and unfolded it. Dorothy had written a note addressed to her. *"If you are reading this then the line has survived and in this house you will find all that you will ever need. The teabag you are holding will help with your concerns. I never did teach you how to make the tea but it will all reveal itself to you in time. Enjoy this special brew. Love, Dorothy."*

Casey smiled. She went over to the cupboard and grabbed a cup. She started the stove, placed the teapot over the flame then put the teabag in the cup. She looked outside. *What a lovely day.*

Epilogue

Casey held her baby close against her chest. She swayed and bounced her body enough to keep the child comforted. The baby cooed. Casey ran a finger over the child's forehead and through her hair. She looked around her yard as the early spring buds began to take shape. Soon the scrub and undergrowth would create a wall of protection.

Casey looked at the ground. She stood on the spot where Hunter had died. Their child seemed connected to this small speck of land. Baby Grace always calmed down when Casey stood there. The spot felt, somehow, softer whenever she walked on it barefooted as if it contained Hunter's essence. She often thought of him. She tried only to think of how they made love. She missed his embrace.

Standing there, she heard the rumble of engines grow louder. Two yellow school buses turned the corner and pulled up to her house.

"Welcome," Casey said upon seeing a teacher emerge from beyond the buses folding doors.

"Hi," the woman responded. "You must be Casey."

"Yes I am," she replied. "Are you Maggie Jades?"

"Yes, it's so nice to meet you. I couldn't believe when you called and found out we are cousins," Maggie said. "My mom said we had a few family members that she had lost track of over the years."

"I was equally delighted to learn about you as well. I come from such a small family, that to find a relative, well… I had to reach out," Casey said.

"And your beautiful baby, my goodness, she's adorable. Do you have any other children?"

"No, just my little Grace," Casey said looking down at her child.

"I'm from a family of all girls myself. It's kind of funny how so many girls are born into this family."

"It is odd but I guess it's what keeps us unique. I think women tend to carry on traditions better than men."

Maggie laughed. "I'll say. My ex never liked traditions."

The children began to exit the bus and form two lines that the other teachers supervised. Their chatter revealed excitement at the new surroundings and the fact that they weren't in school.

"And thank you for having us. The kids are so looking forward to doing there reports on legends of the Pine Barrens and hearing some of the stories you have to tell," Maggie said.

Casey grinned. "I look forward to sharing its rich history. They should never forget their roots."

Maggie nodded. "That is so true. My folks thought majoring in History was a waste but I found it uplifting and I especially love our regional history."

The class of eleven and twelve year old children looked eager to get on with the day. Casey told them to all meet up on the porch. She then turned to Maggie. "When I'm done with my little presentation would you like some coffee or tea?"

"Oh tea sounds delightful," Maggie said. "My grandmother used to make homemade tea."

"See… we are family. My Aunt taught me how to make homemade tea," Casey said, enchanted by the news. "I believe you'll find my tea…enriching."

"I look forward to it," Maggie said.

"It's a special family brew. It has a rich history that goes back to pre-colonial times."

"How appropriate," Maggie said.

"Yes…it is."